A FRENCH ADVENTURE

JENNIFER BOHNET

Boldwood

First published in Great Britain in 2024 by Boldwood Books Ltd.

Copyright © Jennifer Bohnet, 2024

Cover Design by Debbie Clement Design

Cover Photography: Shutterstock

A CIP catalogue record for this book is available from the British Library.

Paperback ISBN 978-1-80162-294-3

Large Print ISBN 978-1-80162-293-6

Hardback ISBN 978-1-80162-292-9

Ebook ISBN 978-1-80162-296-7

Kindle ISBN 978-1-80162-295-0

Audio CD ISBN 978-1-80162-287-5

MP3 CD ISBN 978-1-80162-288-2

Digital audio download ISBN 978-1-80162-290-5

Boldwood Books Ltd
23 Bowerdean Street
London SW6 3TN
www.boldwoodbooks.com

For my daughter Emily, with love xxx

When your 'normal' life ceases to exist, it's time to build a new one.

1

Vivienne Wilson slipped into the passenger seat and placed her laptop bag safely on her lap before clicking her seatbelt into place while her husband Jeremy stowed her suitcase in the boot of his Mini.

'I could have taken a taxi to the airport, you know,' she said, as Jeremy got in the driver's seat and pulled his door closed. 'But it's lovely of you to take the time off. You've been so busy recently, it's nice to have time together.' She kept the thought 'and that's the understatement of the year' to herself. For the past few months she'd barely seen Jeremy, other than at breakfast before he dashed out of the door for a long day at the newspaper where he was editor and currently in charge of a mammoth revamp of the six local Devonshire papers that were under his remit. She'd given up waiting for him to arrive home in time to eat supper at their usual time of 7.30. After several evenings of meals drying out as she tried to keep them warm for him, she'd stopped cooking evening meals and Jeremy had been reduced to egg on toast or pasta he cooked for himself at whatever time he arrived home.

Vivienne had felt guilty at first, knowing that he was under a lot of pressure at work. She had hoped that Sundays, now that both Natalie and Tim had left home, would become a day when the two of them would enjoy their time together, like when they were first married. Sunday papers, tea and croissants in bed, a leisurely drive somewhere for Sunday lunch. Instead Vivienne had begun to dread the weekends. Jeremy had been increasingly short-tempered and moody with her even on those days, so much so that she took refuge in her own study, catching up with social media and networking with other authors to stay out of his way. Accepting a contract to write a new book involving the Jazz Age in the South of France, and telling him it would need a lot of on-site research, even though Google was her go-to friend, was all part of the avoidance plan.

By the time she returned after two months away on what was virtually her own writer's retreat in Antibes on the French Riviera, the revamp of the newspapers would be finished and she and Jeremy could settle back into their normal married life once again, ready to celebrate their thirtieth wedding anniversary at the end of the year. She'd suggested Jeremy took some leave and joined her in Antibes for the last week of the retreat for a holiday, but that idea had been rejected instantly, even though he had been the one to urge her to go to France.

He shrugged. 'The paper can manage without me for a couple of hours. Sami is here for a few days, so I'm sure they can cope. They can always call me if there's a problem in the next hour,' he said, concentrating on joining the stream of traffic on the main road. 'I need to talk to you and I figured that this would be a good time.'

Vivienne glanced across at him in surprise. 'What about? And why not talk to me at home? Why wait until I'm about to leave the country for two months?'

'I thought neutral ground would be better for what I have to say,' he replied, his voice clipped. 'I'll explain over a coffee when we get to the airport. Right now, I need to concentrate on driving.'

Vivienne felt herself subside into her seat as anxiety flooded her body. Something bad was clearly going on. Was Jeremy ill? He looked tired and was definitely stressed. Was he about to be made redundant? The news that Sami, the deputy big boss, was in the office was unusual. No, the newspaper group he worked for was expanding, not contracting. Maybe Jeremy was being promoted, asked to move to one of the other towns and run things from there? She wouldn't mind that so long as they could live on the outskirts, she wasn't a fan of suburban living; these days, she much preferred the quiet of the countryside. They'd lived in their detached four-bedroom house for twenty-six years now and she would enjoy having a new house to sort out. Yes, a house move could be good, bring their relationship back on track.

There was, of course, always the possibility that he was having an affair with one of the female journalists he worked with. Vivienne cast her mind over the women whom she'd met at Christmas office parties. There had been a couple of new faces last year, but only one had really registered with her: Helen. A vivacious charming woman who was new in town and recently married, so surely it couldn't be her? Besides, it was impossible to think of Jeremy being unfaithful. Had she missed any tell-tale signs of him having a mid-life crisis? Had he truly been working all those hours on the papers – or was that a cover-up for something else?

'Jeremy, this is driving me crazy. For goodness' sake tell me what's wrong. Whatever the problem is we can sort it together. Are you ill?'

'No. But I'm not discussing anything while I'm driving.'

Vivienne risked a quick glance at Jeremy's set face. He'd always had what she called a good face for poker, not that he played, but it made it hard to see or judge what he was thinking. Did they have financial problems? They each had their own bank account and a joint one they both paid a monthly sum into for general household expenses. Their mortgage was due to finish soon, in fact this summer. Being mortgage-free could open up all sorts of possibilities for the money they would be saving.

'Shall we move house this year?' she said, desperate to get him talking about anything that might give her a clue as to what was wrong. 'The house value has gone up and with the extra money we could find somewhere out in the country. Not too far for you to commute obviously, but it would be lovely to live in the countryside.'

'No, I don't think we'll be doing that,' Jeremy replied, indicating before he took the slip road into the airport and then following the short-stay car park signs.

Once they'd parked, Jeremy took her case out of the boot and together they walked to Departures. Vivienne had checked in online but had to hand her suitcase in at the desk and Jeremy said he'd wait for her in the cafe across the foyer.

Five minutes later, a worried Vivienne joined him at the table he'd chosen in a quiet corner and carefully placed her laptop bag down before picking up her coffee and taking a sip. Jeremy, she noticed, had already drunk half of his and was fiddling with the spoon.

'What's this all about, Jeremy?' she said as the silence between them lengthened. 'You are starting to worrying me.'

'Viv, I need to tell you something. Something that in one way I wish had never happened because of the hurt that it is going to cause you, the children and other people, but it has happened and I can't deny it. Or walk away from it. Not that I want to.' There was a pause as he took a deep breath before looking Vivienne straight in the eyes. 'I have fallen in love with someone else and I'm leaving you. I'm sorry.'

A lengthy silence developed between them as Vivienne stared at him, open-mouthed in shock.

'You're having an affair?' she said when she finally summoned the necessary strength to say the words.

'It's more than an affair. I want to be with her permanently.'

'How long has it been going on?'

'Six months or so. I'm sorry, I didn't mean to... I wasn't looking to... it just happened.' He shrugged helplessly.

Vivienne, aching from the shock and hurt his words had unleashed in her, gave him a scornful look. 'These things never just happen, Jeremy. A conscious decision always has to be made – the choice usually being between yes I will have an affair or no I won't. There is always, *always*, a choice to do the right thing.'

There was a painful silence before Jeremy said quietly, 'I'm doing the right thing for me. I'm telling you now so that while you are away on your own you'll have time to adjust to the situation. To the idea of... of things being different when you return.'

Vivienne stared at him. 'What things in particular?'

'Me moving out. Selling the house. Divorcing. Us telling the kids, telling my mother.'

'Stop right there. You are telling the kids and your mother. On. Your. Own. Your affair is yours to confess to. Alone. It's your decision to break up the family, hurt the children and your mother in the process.'

Vivienne closed her eyes and rubbed her face, trying to conceal how shaken she was by Jeremy's admission. She'd known this man for thirty-two years, lived with him for nearly thirty years, loved him, been faithful to him, born two children and never in all that time had she ever dreamed he could behave so cruelly, so selfishly, so impersonally towards her.

The Tannoy crackled as a disembodied voice announced the flight to Nice was boarding. Vivienne fought back the tears she refused to let fall in front of him and tried to control the thoughts that were reeling around in her head. Should she stay, go home and talk things through with Jeremy? Would there be any point? By bringing her here with little time for discussion before her flight, to tell her about his affair, he'd indicated that he had no intention of talking about it in any detail. It was a *fait accompli* as far as he was concerned. There was no point in her cancelling her plans, but if he thought she was just going to turn the other cheek, or whatever the saying was, and meekly go away and give in to his demands, then he was in for a shock.

Vivienne stood up. 'That's my flight being called. I can't believe you've chosen to try and end twenty-nine years of marriage like this, but believe me, Jeremy, I'll fight you every inch of the way. Move out if you must, but I don't want a divorce and I'm not selling the house to suit you and your lover.' She picked up her laptop and started to walk away before turning. 'This woman you're dumping me for? Is it someone I know?'

'Yes,' Jeremy said. 'I'm so sorry. You deserve to hear the truth from me. It's...'

Vivienne barely heard the name he whispered, but the shock must have registered on her face before she turned away for the last time and stumbled her way towards Departures. The name he'd spoken so quietly was the one person whom she would never ever have suspected Jeremy of having an affair with. This affair of Jeremy's was about to wreck her life in more than one way.

2

Maxine Zonszain had finished planting the last one of six cosmo plants into its place in her favourite ornamental granite pot by the front door of her cottage in the old town of Antibes, when her mobile buzzed with a text. Simone apologising but she couldn't do the airport pick-up for Madame Wilson that afternoon because one of the twins wasn't well. Maxine quickly typed a reply, saying she'd cover it, not to worry. Simone rarely let her down and, of course, an ill child must come first. It was a lovely late spring day, a drive along the bord de mer would be enjoyable.

Three hours later, she was easing her car into the traffic on the coast road and leaving Antibes behind. Collecting holidaymakers for one or other of the several holiday lets she managed was a rare occurrence for her. She didn't mind picking up clients from the airport but preferred not to do it on a regular basis. Besides, she knew that using people like Simone, who couldn't commit to a regular routine day job for various personal reasons, gave them some welcome additional money. Now, driving along the bord de mer rather than taking the busy autoroute out of town, Maxine hummed along to the eclectic playlist of Riviera Radio coming through the car speakers.

The Mediterranean on her right was glistening in the sunlight, several yachts and a cruise ship were making their way across the bay and there were even a few brave souls swimming in water that hadn't yet taken on its summer temperature. The opening bars of 'All I Really Want is Love' floated into the car as she sat waiting for the traffic lights at Villeneuve-Loubet to change to green. The last time she'd heard this song she'd burst into tears, unable to bear listening, and now her hand spontaneously moved to press the radio off button as Henri Salvador's unmistakable voice began to croon the opening words. but she snatched it back and gripped the steering wheel tightly.

Her emotions were surely more under control these days. The memories it stirred would be good ones. Happy ones. This was 'their' tune. The one that had truly epitomised their relationship and their love. Lisa Ekdahl had joined Henri now singing the lyrics and Maxine felt a small smile touch her lips. She and Pierre had bought the CD and the pair of them had tried to imitate Henri and Lisa, but Pierre couldn't hold a tune and she was too busy laughing at him to sing.

A sharp blast of the horn from the car behind brought Maxine out of her reverie and she hurriedly raised her hand in apology, took her foot off the brake and started to drive.

How different her life was now from those loved-up years after she'd finally met the love of her life, Pierre. She'd known from the moment he'd taken her hand as they were introduced by a mutual friend at a Parisian dinner party that this man was going to be a part of her life forever. After a whirlwind romance, they had married and Maxine knew this second husband of hers was her one true love and they were destined to grow old together.

Pierre dying nine months ago, just two days after their eighth wedding anniversary, had been an unexpected, seismic shock in her life. He'd gone off to his office on Friday morning promising to meet her at the airport later that day for their flight down south to spend their usual weekend in Antibes. Instead, his distraught PA Beatrice had phoned at eleven o'clock to tell her that Pierre was in hospital after collapsing in the office.

Maxine, rushing across the city to his side, arrived at his hospital bedside barely in time to hold his hand as he died. The following week had passed in a blur of officialdom, endless paperwork and, on the sixth day, the funeral. Pierre's son, Thierry, had supported her as she'd staggered down the church aisle in a zombie-like daze, detached from reality. She remembered nothing of the service, the tributes paid, the eulogy read by Thierry, the hymns they'd sung. The single thought in her brain going round and round in an endless circle, drowning everything else out, was the knowledge that having finally found her soulmate, he'd gone, leaving her floundering. If she grew old, it wouldn't be with him at her side, something that she couldn't bear the thought of.

It was Thierry's tight hold on her arm that prevented her from falling when her knees threatened to buckle as they stood at the graveside watching Pierre's coffin being lowered into the grave. At that moment, she wasn't sure she could summon the strength to carry on – or even if she wanted to – after this latest loss in her life. It was only when everyone had left after the wake and she was alone in the apartment that Maxine had allowed her memories and thoughts to chase each other around and around until she was exhausted. That night, though, as she had tossed and turned in her empty bed, she knew however much the loss of Pierre hurt, there was no alternative universe for her to run and escape into. Facts had to be faced. Once again she'd have to dig deep and find that almost superhuman strength that, years ago, she hadn't known she possessed, to carry on. She could only pray that she'd find it again.

Pierre's apartment in one of the iconic Haussmann buildings in the 7th arrondissement of Paris had been in his family for generations and Maxine had always known Thierry would inherit it. A day or two after the funeral, Thierry had gently told her she was welcome to stay there for as long as she wanted, but as the days slowly turned into weeks, she had realised she didn't want to be there. When Pierre had been alive, it hadn't mattered that it was full of mementoes of his family, his boyhood, his life before her, and she'd lived uncomplainingly with the fact that the ghost of his first wife still lingered in several of the rooms she'd redecorated when in residence there.

During those first weeks as she had grieved for the loss of Pierre, Maxine's thoughts had turned more and more to the mews house she and Pierre had bought together in Antibes. They'd bought it jointly soon after they were married, but Pierre had insisted it was registered in her name only. He'd wanted her to always be secure, just in case. Spending time there together had been some of the happiest times of Maxine's life and they'd often talked of the day they would eventually retire down there. One month after Pierre's death, Maxine had decamped to Antibes and shut herself away to grieve until she felt able to return to Paris and face her friends and the world again.

She and Thierry had spent that first Christmas without Pierre, together in Antibes. When, after a quiet and thoughtful day, Thierry had asked her, did she have any plans to return to Paris yet, she'd hesitated. The thought of returning to her old life in Paris without the presence of Pierre at her side made her shudder. Thierry had understood and gently told her that she had to do what was best for her and that the Paris apartment was hers to live in if she wanted to return and pick up the threads of her old life.

But, if not, then he'd like to make it his European base, a home to return to from his current job in Singapore. 'But there's no rush to decide,' he'd said. 'Take your time and make the right decision for you.'

After he'd left, Maxine had wandered around the streets and harbour of Antibes for hours, thinking about the future. Her future alone. The truth was, her old normal life had gone, never to return, and she had to acknowledge that, and create a new normal life for herself. Would staying permanently in Antibes make that a little easier than returning to Paris?

She had phoned Thierry on New Year's Day and apologised for selfishly keeping him out of his family apartment and told him she'd decided Antibes would now be her permanent home. Knowing that as an *immobilier* she could work anywhere – her professional 'estate agent licence' was up to date and she was already registered as self-employed – it seemed the obvious and sensible thing to do.

When they had realised she was staying, a couple of local friends from her life with Pierre, had asked her to manage their holiday apartments – organising the advertisements, the bookings, the cleaning, the refurbishment, the airport collections and dealing with any problems that might arise. Nobody had batted an eye at the prices she worked out she needed to charge. And slowly she'd started to rebuild a new life for herself.

Now, at the beginning of May, she was living a completely different life to the one she'd anticipated to be living at sixty-three, but it was becoming a busy life, if a little lonely, and it helped to keep the bouts of depression, which still overcame her occasionally, at bay.

Once at the airport, Maxine collected a ticket from the machine and parked as close as she could to the Arrivals Hall, before making her way back down to the concourse. A glance at the information board told her the plane had landed, so passengers with nothing to declare in customs should be coming through soon.

After writing the name 'Madame Vivienne Wilson' on the card she would hold up to catch the eye of the unknown passenger she was meeting, Maxine stood at the back of the small crowd that was waiting to greet friends and family. As people started to come through, there were shrieks of excitement and lots of hugs being exchanged. Patiently Maxine waited, holding her card aloft and searching for a lone woman amongst all the groups and couples spilling out into the foyer.

Two women walked through the doors together and one of the women was instantly accosted by a small child who ran towards her shouting, 'Gangan. We've come to get you.' The woman laughed and picked up the little girl before turning to her companion and saying something quietly and pointing in Maxine's direction. The woman glanced across and, as Maxine gave her a questioning look, nodded and pointed to herself.

Maxine waited as Vivienne said goodbye to the woman and walked towards her. She looked terrible, a defeated air hung over her and, having been there, Maxine recognised the symptoms of the walking wounded. Judging by her bloodshot eyes and smudged make-up, Vivienne Wilson was clearly in a state of shock.

Moving forward, Maxine grabbed hold of Vivienne's wheeled suitcase, worried that she was about to keel over at any moment. '*Bonjour et bienvenue sur la Riviera*. Do you speak French? *Non*? I'm Maxine Zonszain, the agent in charge of the apartment. You have a good flight? No screaming babies, I hope.'

'To be honest, I plugged myself into my laptop and shut everything out for the majority of the flight,' Vivienne said tonelessly. 'I wouldn't know if there were screaming babies or even drunken passengers.'

Maxine led the way to the car, paying the parking fee on the way, and opened the passenger door for Vivienne to get in while she put the suitcase in the boot. Stopping at the barrier on the way out, Maxine put the ticket in and waited for the barrier to rise.

'You have visited the Riviera before?' she asked as she drove towards the exit road.

Vivienne shook her head. 'No.'

'I take the scenic route along the bord de mer,' Maxine said. 'You see the sights.'

Vivienne shrugged. 'Whatever,' and she turned to stare out of the window.

As Maxine drove, she pointed out various landmarks and places of interest, but Vivienne didn't respond to anything. In the end, Maxine fell silent and, after giving Vivienne a quick glance, pressed the radio button and let Riviera Radio fill the silence.

Thankfully, rush hour was almost over and traffic wasn't too bad and it was a mere twenty-five minutes before she was pulling up on the coast road on the outskirts of Antibes Juan-les-Pins outside a pretty villa converted into two apartments.

'*Voilà*,' she said. 'Your home for the next eight weeks. Just two apartments in the villa and you have the top one with its wonderful views.'

'Will there be a refund if I have to leave early?' Vivienne asked quietly, turning finally to look at her.

'Perhaps,' Maxine said. 'We talk about it if it happens. *Bien*, we get you indoors and settled.'

Maxine had just unlocked the front door of the villa and the two of them walked into the hallway and were about to go up the stairs, when a young woman opened the door of the ground-floor apartment.

'Hi, Olivia,' Maxine said. 'This is Madame Wilson, your neighbour for the next eight weeks. Olivia lives down here full-time,' she added, turning to Vivienne, who gave Olivia a brief smile. 'And is the proud owner of the pink flower taxi, which I'm sure you will see around town.'

'I'll look out for it,' Vivienne said. 'I'm up here I take it,' and she turned and began dragging her suitcase up the stairs.

Maxine shot Olivia an apologetic look and whispered, 'I see you on my way out,' before quickly following Vivienne.

On the next landing, she unlocked the apartment door and ushered Vivienne in.

'*Cuisine, salle de bain*, sitting room and two *chambres*,' Maxine said before pointing to the wooden spiral staircase in the far corner of the sitting room. 'That leads to your roof terrace. And here's your key.' She placed the key on one of the kitchen work surfaces alongside the welcome basket of Provençal goodies and a bottle of rosé wine that was always left for new guests. 'There's also a welcome brochure with lots of information and here's my card. If you have problems, you give me a call and I do my best to sort things out for you. Sarah, the *femme de ménage*, usually comes on a Saturday at ten o'clock to change the bed linen, towels and to clean through. As you have come midweek, there is no need for her to come so soon. Unless you like for me to send her in two days.'

Vivienne shook her head. 'No, Saturday week will be fine. Thank you.'

'Is there anything else I can do for you today?' Maxine asked quietly, trying to hide the anxiety she was feeling about this woman.

'No, thank you. I have everything I need. You have been very kind.'

'Right. I leave you. Enjoy your stay,' and Maxine made her way thoughtfully downstairs to Olivia's.

'Coffee?' Olivia said. 'Please don't tell me I've got some weird woman living above me for the next two months.'

Maxine sighed. '*Non*, I don't think she's weird-weird, but I feel she's definitely hurting inside, as if something terrible has happened in her life recently. She already ask if there will be a refund if she leaves early.'

Olivia pulled a face at that. 'She's booked a long stay. Maybe her marriage is in trouble? Was her husband supposed to come with her? If she even has one.'

'*Non*, the booking was made in her name and for one person.' Maxine took a sip of the coffee Olivia had handed her. 'I know I generally step back once I've seen the guests in, but I think I call by in a couple of days and check on her.'

'You haven't told her about me? That I'm effectively her landlady.'

'*Bien sûr que non*. You ask me not to tell any of the guests and I understand. *Mais* if you see her, you will be friendly, won't you?'

'Of course. I'm out this evening, but tomorrow I'll be around in case of problems. Tonight I'm having dinner with my parents.' Olivia grimaced.

'James as well?' Maxine asked with a smile.

'No. Just me and the parents.' Olivia raised her eyebrows in despair. 'So we all know what the main topic of conversation is likely to be this evening, don't we?'

'Do give them both my regards. I've not seen them for far too long. I must catch up with Felicity soon. No sign of her softening towards James then?'

Olivia shook her head. '*Non*. You know how stubborn my mother is. Once she decides on something...' she shrugged. 'But she forgets I have inherited not only her stubborn streak but also Papa's determination.'

Maxine laughed. '*Peut-être* she meet her match in her own daughter then.'

Olivia gave Maxine a rueful look. 'But I'm beginning to suspect that she might be right about James not being the man for me – not that I'm going to tell her that any time soon.'

3

It was half past seven that evening when Olivia drove down into Monaco and parked her Mini Countryman in the underground garage of the block of apartments where her parents lived. The car, a twenty-fifth birthday present from her parents, spent most of its life in the big double garage back at the villa. Antibes was such a compact town, Olivia found it easier to walk around than to struggle with driving in the narrow streets, but the Mini was great fun to drive fast on the autoroute.

Making her way out of the garage, Olivia didn't immediately head for the main apartment entrance and the lift. Instead she wandered along by the main harbour, where despite it still being several weeks before the famous Monaco Grand Prix took place, barriers and other safety features were already being slotted into place. Olivia loved the buzz of Grand Prix time and always joined her parents to watch the race.

She strolled along enjoying, as she always did, the early-evening atmosphere of Monaco, the town where she'd been born after her parents had relocated to the Principality for tax reasons. At this time of day, the majority of tourists were back on the giant cruise ships or in the comfort of their French hotels, and the thousands of office workers, shop assistants, domestic staff and others who travelled into town for work had departed. Monaco, whilst pulsating with the glamour that it was renowned for, still somehow retained that small-town vibe of an evening.

Whenever she came home to see her parents, Olivia always made a point of walking along the old harbour, Port Hercules, as far as she could, but tonight she reluctantly turned back before she reached the modern extension that in recent years had brought more yachts and people into the Principality. Felicity, her mother, was very keen on punctuality and if she lingered too long looking at the yachts, she would be late and then there would be a fuss.

* * *

As Olivia stepped out of the lift into the hallway of her parents' penthouse, her heart sank as she heard voices. Once again, Felicity had failed to tell her there would be guests tonight at dinner. Olivia could only hope it was not another attempt on her mother's part to marry her off.

Her father, Trent, engulfed her in one of his usual body-crushing bearlike hugs. 'Good to see you, Tuppence,' he said, calling her by the family pet name that her mother hated. Felicity had declared that Olivia had outgrown the childish nickname on her sixteenth birthday and had forbidden the use of it. Neither her husband nor her mother-in-law had taken any notice of the order. Since Granny Mavis had died, Trent was one of two people left who were likely to use it these days and then only when her mother was unlikely to hear. But as Olivia's life had moved on from the other person who said it so warmly and had made her smile, she was unlikely to hear it again from him.

Olivia moved her head in the direction of the large sitting room. 'Who's here?' she whispered.

'Some new friends of your mother's, who I actually like for a change,' her father said. 'But, be warned, they have a bachelor son.' He grinned at her. 'How's James?'

'I'm seeing him tomorrow night. His boss is on board this week, so...' Olivia shrugged. 'Is the son here?'

Her father nodded. 'And this time it's me that's not so keen, despite your mother saying he'd be perfect for you. Too serious for you, I think!'

'It's going to be a long evening by the sounds of it. I drove over, so I can't even have a drink.'

'You know you can always stay the night. Your old room is always ready,' her father said.

Olivia gave a reluctant nod. 'I might just do that if the need for a drink overtakes me.'

'Come on let's take you in and introduce you.'

Harry, the son, was an economic advisor with an investment company, and Olivia instantly saw why her mother liked the thought of her daughter dating him. She also knew instantly that that would never happen. Harry was simply not her type. Her father was right – far too serious and full of self-importance for her. It was going to be a long evening.

Taking the bottle of rosé out of the gift box, Vivienne placed it in the freezer compartment of the fridge to cool it while she moved slowly around inspecting the apartment. Decorated and furnished in the Provençal style with terracotta tiles in the kitchen and hallway, the walls and furniture a mixture of pale greens and lavender, with the yellow silk cushions on the two cream settees in the sitting room providing a dash of sunshine, it looked exactly as portrayed on the website.

Any other time, Vivienne would have been thrilled with the thought of living and working in such a lovely environment for the summer, but right now she was emotionally drained and incapable of rational thought. Her brain was stuck with the final bombshell of Jeremy's affair going round and round like a squealing hamster on a wheel, unable to jump off. The repercussions behind that nugget of news when it became public knowledge, which it surely would, would be huge and wide. Nothing in their lives would ever be the same again.

And when the children heard how their family was about to be torn apart? What would happen then? It was unlikely that either Natalie or Tim would react with unadulterated happiness at the news of their father's affair. As for his mother Elizabeth, Vivienne could guess how she would react to the news. She and Elizabeth had tolerated the other's place in Jeremy's life as wife and grandmother to the children but had never been close. Vivienne had tried her best with the snobbish woman who had let her know from the moment they were engaged that she, Vivienne, was not what she'd wanted as a daughter-in-law, but there had been no softening in attitude towards her down the years. The news of Jeremy's affair was likely to increase, not decrease, that animosity towards her.

Grasping the handrail of the spiral staircase, Vivienne hauled herself up to the roof terrace and collapsed onto one of the sun loungers she found up there. This time yesterday her worries had been nothing compared to the ones she now found herself facing. For weeks she'd been increasingly uneasy about coming away on this working holiday, even if she had called it a retreat, and leaving Jeremy on his own, but the deadline on this new book was tight and she really needed the time alone to concentrate. Frustration and worry about the way she and Jeremy seemed to be drifting apart had worried her for months, but she'd never dreamt that her marriage could be in real danger of collapsing. That Jeremy would betray her like he had, especially with the woman he'd chosen.

In her naivety, she'd thought it was just a case of sitting down together and talking things through, getting back into the habit of doing couple things together and taking steps to reconnect with each other. Revitalise their relationship for the next stage of their married life. Vivienne grimaced. If only it could have been that simple. She should have realised when Jeremy refused outright to join her down here for a short holiday that something was seriously wrong.

And now she was a thousand miles away with no way of knowing what was happening, no way of influencing things, a mere spectator at the demise of her own marriage as she waited for events to unravel.

Sighing, Vivienne stood up. Unable to face food and drink, she'd refused both on the plane, but now her tummy was rumbling and she was in desperate need of a drink. She'd spotted some Brie and crackers in the welcome basket and hopefully the rosé would be cold enough soon to be refreshing. She paused before leaving the terrace – really the view along the coast was quite spectacular. She'd come up here tomorrow and work under the shade of the parasol she'd seen in the corner.

Ten minutes later, Vivienne was sitting at the small breakfast bar in the kitchen, Brie, crackers and grapes in front of her, a glass of rosé poured. Her phone, now switched back on after the flight, was in her hand and she scrolled through the two messages that flashed up. Jeremy's 'I'm truly sorry', she deleted. Being truly sorry didn't cut it in her opinion. The other message was from Natalie, checking that she had arrived. Vivienne quickly typed a reply, saying all was well, that the apartment was everything she'd hoped for and that she'd ring her tomorrow. She simply couldn't face talking to her tonight.

That done, Vivienne had a sip of wine before opening her laptop. Nothing from her editor or her agent, thank goodness, just a couple of spam messages, which she deleted before she closed the laptop down again with a feeling of relief. Idly, she picked up the card the agent had given her and tapped it on the granite work surface. Maxine Zonszains. Vivienne recalled her heart sinking as she'd caught her first sight of Maxine across the foyer at the airport – so casually French and all together in a way that felt slightly intimidating and one she couldn't cope with right then, so she'd brushed her aside with uncharacteristic rudeness.

Sipping her wine Vivienne felt a twinge of guilt. She owed Maxine an apology. And the girl downstairs, Olivia. She'd been less than friendly towards her too.

Vivienne topped up her rosé and stood up as a wave of tiredness swept through her body. An early night was called for. She'd take her wine through to the bedroom, close the shutters and try to sleep. As a more famous author than her had once written, 'Tomorrow is another day.'

4

Maxine spent a few hours the next morning working on her desktop computer making sure her diary was up to date with new bookings for the various apartments she took care of, noting who needed a car from the airport, and making sure cleaners were available before she turned to the accounts.

The town hall clock struck twelve as she printed out the last page of accounts to be added to the file of papers the accountant was waiting for. She ate lunch – a few slices of smoked salmon and a salad – sitting at the teak table under the shade of the vine growing over the loggia attached to the back wall of the house.

Inevitably, Vivienne Wilson came into her thoughts and Maxine found herself wondering how the woman had settled in and how she was today. It was too soon to go round and check on her, but tomorrow she'd wander along that way and see if there was any sign of her. She'd check with Olivia too.

This afternoon she was taking a couple to look at a villa near the golf club in Mougins. Afterwards, she might go for a swim down at Plage de la Gravette, the beach next to the ramparts – not quite wild swimming, but the water would be cold and refreshing

– and then, this evening, when it was cooler, she would spend time pottering in the garden.

Houses in the old town of Antibes rarely came with a garden, let alone a garden as large as the one she enjoyed. She and Pierre had both loved the house, but it was the private mews-type street it was situated in and the secluded garden that had clinched the deal for them. The two of them had worked hard creating a tranquil welcoming space where they could entertain their friends on a summer evening, filling it with plants that could withstand the heat of the Mediterranean. These days, pottering around the garden gave her some much-needed solace.

Before Maxine had moved here permanently, the house had just been number seven in the lane, but as she slowly came back to life she'd commissioned a local artisan potter to make her a nameplate that Pierre had designed just weeks before he died. And now the yellow and blue glazed pottery sign with its olive leaves framing the house name 'L'Abri' written across its surface was screwed into the old stone wall.

Never had a house been better named. 'The Refuge' had been their weekend escape from the city and was now truly her refuge and sanctuary. Maxine smiled every time she saw the sign as she walked towards home. Two bicoloured bougainvillea, white with edges of the palest pink, climbed the front wall of the house, whilst night-scented jasmine in pots framed the door on either side planted with daffodils and tulips that sprang up every springtime.

Inside the house, the kitchen doors at the back opened onto a small terrace with a loggia covered with a vine. The garden proper began in front of this with a stepping stone path, edged with terracotta and granite pots full of snowdrops, daffodils and tulips in spring, replaced with tumbling geraniums in summer, wound its way to the bottom of the garden. A small pergola-type archway overlayed with sweet-smelling blue plumbago covered the path for two or three metres, before it finished down by the fish pond with its dolphin fountain at the bottom of the garden.

Maxine loved working in the garden or attending to the pots and the other plants that framed the front of the house, but even now, all these months later, it was always in the garden that the knowledge that she was now truly alone and would be for however long she lived hit her. No family and no one close enough to comfort her and understand the pain she was in.

During the last long nine months, she'd discovered that most people, not knowing how to treat a recently bereaved person, reacted with embarrassment. When you were the walking wounded but with no signs of body damage or physical pain, people assumed you were fine and living a normal life and coping after your loss. But she missed Pierre so much, it literally hurt. Olivia, as young as she was, was the only person who seemed to instinctively understand how she felt, how hard she found living without Pierre. Thierry did, of course, but he was so far away living his own life, that they were both denied the chance to comfort each other.

Vivienne woke at her usual time of six o'clock the first morning in France, but it took her befuddled brain several moments to make sense of the unfamiliar room. Laying there not fully awake as the events of the previous day filtered one by one into her mind, she felt herself tensing at the realisation of what it all meant. The changes that were about to happen in her life, over which she had no control. However much she worried about Jeremy and his behaviour, however much she regretted the breakdown of her marriage, both those things were out of her control now. She had to focus on managing the things she could control if she was to survive the veritable maelstrom of horrible events that were circling around her, ready to tear her life apart.

Standing under the power shower letting the water pound her body at the highest temperature she could bear, Vivienne thought about her options. She was here for two months, eight weeks in which she could do what she had originally planned – research not only the Jazz Age for her new book and finish writing it, but also begin to trace her family history. But could she also start to try to come to terms with these sudden, unexpected and unwelcome developments at the same time? Or would it affect her writing? She was the only one who could take the tentative steps that were needed to sort out her own life. Concentration was going to be hard to come by, that was for sure, but she had to try to ignore Jeremy's devastating news, push it to the back of her mind, forget about it and leave dealing with all the consequences until she returned home.

Home. Would it still be her home when she returned? Or would Jeremy have taken the opportunity to move out – or move in his new love?

No, she couldn't bear to think about that happening. There was only one way she could deal with all this and that was to lose herself in a mammoth session of writing. Everything else needed to be pushed deep into the recesses of her mind to be dealt with later.

Decision made, Vivienne took a deep breath before bracing herself and reaching for the shower control to quickly turn the jets of hot water to cold – a ritual she did every day at home after reading how good it was for the body. Even in this beautiful French bathroom though, the cold water was still sheer agony and she turned it off within seconds.

Once dried and dressed, Vivienne made herself a cafetière of coffee and stood out on the balcony of the sitting room with her mug, looking at the Mediterranean sparkling in the early-morning sun, making plans for the day. The first thing she had to do was find a *supermarché* and buy some food and also a couple of bottles of decent wine to give Maxine and Olivia by way of apology. She wouldn't be able to settle down to write until she'd apologised for her rudeness yesterday.

And that woman on the plane. What was her name? She'd been so kind too. Cécile. She'd scribbled her email address and telephone number on a piece of paper and told her if she ever wanted to chat while she was here to give her a ring, she was a good listener. Vivienne resolved to drop her a thank you email later.

Vivienne rinsed her mug and left it on the draining board, grabbed her linen jacket from the bedroom, put the apartment key in her pocket, found her purse and went shopping.

The *supermarché* she found not far from the villa was small but packed with delicious-looking food. A fresh fish counter, a meat counter, a long cheese counter and a patisserie boulangerie full of the most wonderful-smelling bread and tempting cakes. Vivienne held herself in check, realising she could come and shop here every day if she wanted to, so she didn't need to go mad on this first morning. Today she'd simply buy bread, croissants, pain au chocolat, cheese, olives, cold chicken for lunch, wine and a coffee éclair for a treat.

It was when she reached the cash desk that she realised she'd stupidly forgotten to bring a bag to carry the shopping home in. Thankfully, there was a rack of large eco-friendly carrier bags at the end of the conveyor belt and Vivienne picked two – one with a picture of sunflowers, the other with scarlet poppies.

Back at the villa, Vivienne knocked on the door of the down-stairs apartment, hoping to see Olivia. But there was no reply, so

Vivienne carried on upstairs to her own apartment. She should have realised Olivia would be out at work during the day. She recalled Maxine saying something about a flower taxi in Antibes? Maybe she'd go back down this evening and apologise to Olivia for her rudeness yesterday. The only problem was she'd intended to ask her if she knew Maxine's address as she wanted to take a bottle of wine round to her as an apology too, but then, she would probably be out during the day as well.

Vivienne put her own wine in the fridge and left the other two bottles on the side, as she put the rest of her shopping away.

After making herself a coffee and enjoying both a croissant and a pain au chocolat whilst sitting out on the balcony, Vivienne fetched her laptop and phone before making her way up to the roof terrace. Time to start to get organised with what she was here to do.

Her phone pinged as she placed the laptop on the table. Natalie.

'Hi, darling. How are you?'

'Fine, but I've had a funny phone call from Dad. He wants Tim and I to meet him because he needs to talk to us. Says he can't tell us what he needs to over the phone. Any idea what it's about? He's not ill is he?'

Vivienne, determined not to do Jeremy's dirty work for him, smothered a sigh before answering. 'No, as far as I know he's not ill.' She ignored the first question and hoped that Natalie wouldn't repeat it.

'Honestly, he's frightened me a bit, Mum. He sounded so down and serious. Anyway, Tim can't make it on the evening Dad suggested, so it'll be a few days before we see him. I said I could make it, but for some reason he insists on telling us whatever it is together. Said it would be better for the two of us to be together to hear it.'

'Have you spoken to Granny Elizabeth?' Vivienne asked.

'No. I might ring her later and see if she has any ideas.'

'Please don't say anything that might worry her,' Vivienne said. 'You know how she worries about everyone.'

'Promise. Now tell me about your apartment. Do you have a proper sea view?'

Vivienne laughed. 'And some. I'm currently on the rooftop terrace that looks directly out over the Med. You'd love it here.'

'I'm determined to try to come for at least a weekend, hopefully longer, towards the end of your stay,' Natalie said. 'Don't want to stop the writer writing! Have you done anything about our French connection yet?'

'Give me a chance, I've barely been here twenty-four hours.'

'Sorry, but it's exciting. Got to go. Got cakes in the oven and the timer has just buzzed. Talk again soon. Love you.' And the line died.

Thoughtfully, Vivienne placed her phone on the table alongside the laptop. She knew with certainty that Jeremy had not given his mother the bombshell news of his affair since she'd left. If he had, Elizabeth would have rung her by now, placing the blame squarely at her feet for not being a good enough wife.

Vivienne opened the parasol before settling down underneath it in front of her laptop and bringing up the file titled 'My French Connection'. It wasn't a large file, consisting only of the two items she'd scanned in before leaving home. A black and white photograph and a photograph of a sealed envelope with something inside and a French name and address scrawled across it. The temptation to open the envelope had been strong but she'd resisted, deciding as it wasn't addressed to her she had no business opening it, unless she failed in her search for the addressee. She'd brought the actual items with her in the hope that they would help in her search. They were still in her suitcase for safekeeping.

So little information – would it be enough to help uncover a secret from the past? Vivienne sighed. She was here to work. Searching for answers to secrets from the past would have to wait a little longer.

She closed the file and brought up her email programme. She'd write that quick thank you to Cécile now before it got forgotten. She'd been so kind to her on the plane.

As the email whooshed off into cyberspace, Vivienne resolutely opened the document that contained her latest book. She needed to stop procrastinating and get to work. This morning she'd read through the chapters she'd already written, make a list of the things she needed to research and the places she needed to visit, and then sketch out a plan of action.

5

Her parents were still sleeping when Olivia crept out of the apartment early the next morning. She'd not made it past the entrées last night before deciding she definitely needed a drink to get through the rest of the evening. Standing out on the balcony with nibbles and a glass of non-alcoholic bubbly, she'd chatted to her mother's new friends until Harry had claimed her attention and both sets of parents had moved away as if by tactical agreement. Her first impression of Harry proved to be only too correct. It wasn't just that he was far too serious and seemed to have had a sense of humour bypass, but he also turned out to be a firm believer in mansplaining. Sat next to him at dinner, the final nail in the coffin as far as she was concerned was his presumptuous rudeness about her job.

'I'm assuming you're not in finance? You don't look the type,' he'd said, raising an eyebrow at her.

She was tempted to mention her BSc from Keble College, Oxford in Economics and Management but decided she couldn't be bothered. He'd clearly decided she was a blonde airhead so she played along with it.

'Goodness, no. Far too boring for me. You may have seen a pink London taxi driving around Antibes and occasionally Monaco? Olivia's Flowers and Champagne Taxi. That's me.'

Harry had given a considered nod. 'Good to have a hobby that gives you some additional income, but it's not a proper job, is it?'

Olivia had seen her father, who was seated opposite her, glance across the table and she'd picked up her empty wine glass. 'Please.'

Smiling, her father had picked up the bottle of Château Margaux and poured her a glass. '*Santé.*'

Olivia had swallowed her murderous thoughts along with a large gulp of her wine and from then on had struggled to talk to Harry without being downright rude.

Following her mother out to the kitchen to help carry in the main course, she'd tried to forestall the criticism about her behaviour she knew Felicity would launch into the moment they were alone by saying, 'Maxine sends her love and apologies. Says it's far too long since she saw you both. I think she's planning a lunch with you soon.'

'I'll give her a ring in the week and we'll arrange something,' her mother had replied. 'Could you please try a little harder to be polite to Harry? He is a guest here. I thought you and he might—'

'Please don't finish that sentence,' Olivia had interrupted. 'You have to stop this matchmaking, because a) I'm not currently looking for a husband, I'm happy on my own. And b) your idea of a suitable husband for me is miles away from the kind of man I like.'

'Well, you seem unable to find a suitable man yourself,' her mother had snapped back. 'Are you still seeing that deckhand?'

Olivia had smothered a sigh. Monaco had briefly been the home port for the yacht James was a senior deckhand on and early on in their relationship she'd driven over to meet him a few times of an evening. On one of those occasions, not wanting her mother to hear from friends that she'd been in town and not called in, she'd taken James home to meet her parents. Her father and he had got on at that initial meeting, mainly because of their common interest in F1, but her mother had grilled James about his prospects before deciding he wasn't good enough for her daughter. It was a meeting that Olivia would rather forget and didn't plan to repeat in the near future. She knew deep down that James was not a keeper, but he was good company and she needed her mother to realise she was a big girl now and would make her own decisions and mistakes.

'Yes, I'm still seeing him. He's fun and definitely not like Mr Up Himself out there.'

'Here, you take these plates in and then come back for the meat,' her mother had said, thrusting six warm dinner plates at her. 'I blame Daphne for your current attitude. Ever since she left you that silly pink taxi and the villa, you've changed.'

Taking the plates, Olivia had opened her mouth to protest that it wasn't a silly pink taxi but a flourishing floristry business, but closed it again. It had not been the time to argue with her mother.

Now as she drove up out of Monaco and approached the A8 in the early-morning light, Olivia thought about her mother's words – had she changed that much since the unexpected inheritance from Aunt Daphne, her godmother? It had never occurred to her that her mother's widowed and childless older sister would leave everything she possessed to her. If she'd given it even a moment's thought, she would have assumed her mother would have been the beneficiary of her sister's will. But it was an inheritance she, Olivia, would be eternally grateful for. It had given her the independence she'd started to crave: the freedom to choose how she lived her life, where she lived and, importantly, the freedom to be herself.

She'd known from an early age that she wanted to make her own income, not to be dependent on her parents, who'd given her the best possible start in life, for which she would be forever grateful. She knew she was lucky at twenty-seven to have been able to jump off the financial services rat race roundabout of living to work and to allow the French mantra absorbed in to her DNA as she grew up, of simply working to live a good life, run free.

Returning to live in France as an independent woman after university and five years in England was the first big change that Daphne's inheritance had given her. The second change was learning to be her own boss. It had been a steep learning curve, but now she couldn't imagine working for anyone else ever again. She loved that she had total responsibility for everything to do with the business. It was up to her, no one else, to make it a success.

Daphne had been a popular woman and, as her niece, Olivia had always been made to feel welcome when she'd helped out with flower arrangements and bouquets at weekends and during school holidays. When she'd inherited the business, she'd realised that that had been Daphne's plan all along. Olivia had signed up for an intense course of floristry, she'd worked for free at the Cours Saleya flower market in Nice for some more real hands-on experience. She'd studied every video she could find online about the art of flower arranging: wedding flowers, buttonholes, large urn arrangements, wreath making, vase arrangements, posies, bouquets. Several of Daphne's customers had stayed loyal, giving her a base to build on, and these days she supplied flowers for a variety of events, as well as selling in Antibes market and supplying several of the luxury super yachts.

Despite her mother saying it was the wrong thing for her to be doing, Olivia loved the life she lived now. It was, she knew, an intrinsically happy life because flowers were so universally loved and people invariably smiled at her and the pink taxi when they saw her out and about.

As the kilometres flew past and the sign for the exit to the large wholesale flower market at Nice St. Augustin approached, Olivia smiled to herself. She'd take advantage of the unexpected stopover in Monaco and visit the market. Buy a few extra flowers for tomorrow – her day for delivering weekly flower arrangements to the luxury yachts moored in Port Vauban marina, Antibes. She always made a few impromptu sales to chief stewardesses from visiting yachts who saw her and bought mixed bunches to arrange themselves back on board.

After parking the car, Olivia walked into the large flower hall and inhaled deeply as the heady perfume hit her nostrils. She felt so at home here. Although still early, the place was busy and Olivia waved at several of her florist friends as she made her way round the stalls. But everyone was intent on buying supplies, not chatting. It didn't take long for her to buy a box each of daffodils, tulips, variegated carnations and a smaller box of early peonies, ready for Antibes market later in the week. Next on the list were red and yellow roses, some lilies and boxes of cut jasmine and eucalyptus leaves to mix in with arrangements.

As Olivia loaded them carefully into the boot of her car, her mobile pinged with a text message. James. Sitting in the car, she read his short message.

Sorry. Boss wants to go to Corsica. Back in a week – maybe.

Olivia heaved a sigh of disappointment. James was rarely in

harbour these days and when he was, the owner seemed to be on board, which limited his time away from the yacht.

Quickly she typed a reply.

Was looking forward to seeing you. Enjoy Corsica.

Thoughtfully, she dropped the phone into her bag. It was at least a month since they'd managed to spend more than an hour together. And with the summer season coming up, Olivia knew James would be at sea for most of it, port-hopping around the Mediterranean.

Olivia sat for a few moments deep in thought. Would she ever meet that special somebody? She had to believe that she would. It would be nice to have a land-based boyfriend, someone who kept to the arrangements they made, someone who didn't take her for granted, someone who made her feel special. Actually, it was a long time since James had done that.

Enough was enough. Time to move on. Accept that it was over. The next time she saw James, she'd tell him it was over – if he hadn't totally ghosted her by then. At least her mother would be pleased.

Driving back to Antibes along the A8 as the early-morning commuter traffic increased, Olivia decided her plan for the summer would be to grow the business and to work on getting more of a social life.

Once home, she parked up in the garage and, taking the boxes out of the boot, she went into her flower room – originally the utility room for the villa. Now filled with her floristry paraphernalia and a floral fridge unit, it was the coldest place in the house. Shelves lined one wall filled with floristry equipment: floral tape, pin frogs, water tubes, cutting tools, vases, chicken wire, floral foam, paddle wire, cellophane paper, decorated paper and small cards for messages. There was a sink on the far wall, in the middle of the room the long wooden table with a metal top that Daphne had invested in years ago and an air-conditioning unit fixed to the wall ready for action in the height of summer. Planning to come down later and make a start on the arrangements for the morning, Olivia simply placed the boxes on the table and went upstairs. Time for a coffee and breakfast.

As she poured coffee into her favourite mug, her phone pinged with a text. Olivia smiled as she read the message from Maxine inviting her to aperitifs that evening if she was free. Just what she needed. Maxine might be old enough to be her mother, but unlike her mother she was fun to be with. However, the suggestion at the end of the text that if she saw Vivienne to bring her too was awkward. The woman had been so abrupt yesterday that Olivia wasn't sure whether or not she'd be rude to her. She could sense muted movement in the above apartment, so she could at least tell Maxine that Vivienne was alive and kicking. Footsteps coming down the stairs confirmed that too – and then there was a knock at the door.

Hesitantly, Olivia opened the door.

'Good morning. I'm sorry to disturb you so early but I wanted to catch you before you left for work,' Vivienne said, holding out a bottle of wine. 'Please accept this as an apology for my bad manners the day I arrived. It's not an excuse, but it wasn't a good day for me.'

'Thank you,' Olivia said, taking the wine. 'I'm sorry for your bad day.'

'I need to apologise to Maxine as well. Could you tell me where she lives please?'

'I can do better than that,' Olivia said. 'She's invited me for aperitifs this evening and said if I saw you to ask you too, so I can take you there. If you're free of course?'

'Definitely. What time?'

'Seven thirty, here?'

'See you then. And thank you.'

Olivia closed her door as Vivienne left to return upstairs and, picking up her phone, sent Maxine a text to tell her the good news.

6

Maxine smiled as she read the text message from Olivia.

See you later. Weird woman is nicer today and is coming tonight.

Pierre had introduced Maxine to his old friends, Trent and Felicity, the first time he'd brought her down to the Riviera. He and Trent had met at university and despite their careers taking different paths, they had remained good friends ever since. Trent had openly admitted to Maxine in the weeks after Pierre died how much he missed him and that his death had been a personal wake-up call for both himself and Felicity. Maxine found Felicity difficult on occasions and sometimes had to bite her tongue to stop herself from responding to a particularly old-fashioned snobbish remark – one that usually concerned Olivia's lifestyle and her lack of a husband. But Maxine and Olivia had soon become firm friends despite the difference in their ages.

Maxine knew that Olivia would not only ask her advice about things but would also talk to her woman to woman in a way she couldn't with her mother, and whilst Maxine wouldn't dream of burdening Olivia with the dark thoughts that still crept up on her in the middle of the night, she did talk to Olivia about how much she missed Pierre. Last year, after a particularly difficult exchange with her mother, Olivia had called in to see Maxine and Maxine, sensing that Olivia needed a hug, had simply opened her arms to her and held her tight.

'Thank you, I needed that,' Olivia had said. 'If there were more of us, we could regularly have a group hug.'

'Any time you need a hug just say "needy",' Maxine had instructed.

'Only if you promise to do the same,' Olivia had replied, and Maxine had nodded.

'I miss Pierre's hugs,' she'd admitted.

And that was how the phrase 'I'm needy' become code for whenever either of them wanted the comfort of a hug from someone who cared.

More and more, Maxine found herself thinking of Olivia as the daughter she'd longed to hold for so many years. Too old now to ever hold a daughter of her own, she'd started to regard Olivia as a wonderful substitute – a daughter by proxy. Of course she'd never voice that thought to Felicity.

It was a lovely spring evening and Maxine checked the rosé in the fridge before placing glasses and a few nibbles in a covered dish on the table and lighting a couple of citronella candles to keep the insects away. Finding her favourite jazz playlist on Spotify, she pressed the button and soon the gentle sounds of a Miles Davis track was drifting around the garden.

Maxine heard Olivia call out 'Cooee, we're here,' from the front door and she went into the house to greet them.

She was pleased to see that Vivienne had a smile on her face. The miserable, distant person she'd collected from the airport had vanished. Replaced by a happy-looking woman who was holding out a bottle of wine.

'Thank you so much for inviting me this evening. This is by way of an apology for my behaviour. I know I was way out of order. My only excuse is that I had some upsetting news at the airport and, of course, I spent the entire flight brooding about it, leaving me not only shattered, but in a foul mood.'

'*Merci* for the wine,' Maxine said, accepting the bottle. 'The rude mood? It is forgotten. We all have the days like that. I hope whatever it is has been sorted.'

'I wish,' Vivienne shrugged. 'It's a long story that can only get longer.'

'The garden it is this way,' Maxine said, sensing that Vivienne wasn't going to enlarge upon what the story was.

'I love your house,' Vivienne said as she followed her into the garden. 'As for your garden,' she stopped as she stepped out onto the terrace. 'What a wonderful place.'

'It is unique,' Olivia said. 'Nobody ever expects to see a garden like this in the old town.'

'Pierre, he did the design and the hard work,' Maxine said. 'And, of course, I try to keep the garden as beautiful as he would want. I miss him so much, but when I'm working out here, I feel as if he is still around and I talk to him. It is comforting and difficult at the same time somehow.'

Vivienne glanced at her.

'Pierre was my husband. He died nine months ago.'

'I'm sorry to hear that,' Vivienne said.

'Thank you. Now, you two have a wander while I fetch the rosé and the rest of the food,' and Maxine turned away and hurried into the kitchen before Vivienne saw the tears she could feel welling up in her eyes.

When she returned a few moments later, she was pleased to see Olivia and Vivienne down by the pond watching the fish and chatting away happily.

As Maxine poured the rosé, the other two strolled back up the garden and, within minutes, the three of them were sitting companionably under the loggia enjoying the various nibbles Maxine had placed on the table – warm garlic bread, cheesy biscuits, olives, a plate of charcuterie and another with small slices of quiche arranged on it.

'Can someone please tell me why the food here tastes a million times better than the food I eat back in England, even though I buy and eat similar things?' Vivienne said. 'This is so simple and so delicious.'

Maxine laughed. 'No idea. Perhaps it's the air? The sunshine? We're better cooks than the English?' She gave Vivienne a cheeky smile. 'You're on holiday and relaxed?'

'Could be any one of the first three, I suppose,' Vivienne said, helping herself to another slice of quiche. 'Although my daughter Natalie, who is a chef, would be up in arms at that put-down of English cooks. As for the last one...' She shook her head. 'I'm not on holiday and I'm definitely not that relaxed.'

'You'll be relaxed after eight weeks here,' Olivia said confidently. 'Antibes has that effect on people, it's such a laid-back town. If you're not on holiday, though – why are you here?'

'I'm having a one-person writing retreat. And once I'm on course to meet my deadline and have some time left...' Vivienne took a deep breath. 'I'd like to try to trace my paternal family roots.'

'You have the French relations? How wonderful,' Maxine said. 'You know much about them?'

'No, hardly a thing. I suspect it's going to be like looking for the proverbial needle in a haystack.' Vivienne shook her head. It was too complicated to try to explain her family life and history right now. 'Anyway, enough about me – how do you come to be running a pink florist taxi?' she asked, looking at Olivia.

'My godmother aunt left it to me when she died,' Olivia answered. 'Which, according to my mother, was the worst thing that could have happened. Apparently I'm not the same girl I was before I became a florist – no, sorry, being a florist is fine. It's the pink taxi that is the real problem. She thinks it's common.' Olivia took a mouthful of wine. 'All she wants is for me to marry a suitable man and have a family. Not going to happen any time soon, especially if she keeps insisting on introducing me to men who are just not my type. Harry the other evening was typical of how desperate she is to marry me off and start producing grandchildren.' And Olivia made them both laugh with her description of Mr Up Himself.

Maxine gave Olivia a sympathetic look before changing the subject. 'This book you write? What is it about?' she asked Vivienne.

'It's a time-slip novel about a woman who finds herself involved with the jazz scene down here in two different eras. Listening to the music you are playing here, I guess you like jazz?'

'I do. I adore the Juan-les-Pins Jazz Festival in July, the atmosphere is amazing. Pierre and I always go.' Maxine fell silent, realising that this year she'd be going alone. If she even went.

'What a shame I'll have left by July,' Vivienne said wistfully. 'I should have timed my retreat better. Perhaps I'll try to have a return trip.'

'Pierre had quite a collection of books about jazz down here in the twentieth century, you're welcome to borrow any that will help,' Maxine said, jumping up. 'Come and take a look. His study I have not changed.'

Minutes later, Vivienne found herself standing in front of a bookcase full of jazz related books, most in French but a few were in English. Some she had read, some she had heard of but had been unable to find copies of and others that were unknown to her. 'Are you sure you don't mind lending me a book or two while I'm down here?'

'Not a problem,' Maxine said, shrugging.

'Can I borrow these two? I promise to take care of them. *Jazz Cleopatra*, the story of Josephine Baker and *The Mistinguett Legend*. I plan on featuring both Baker and Mistinguett in my novel.'

'I fetch you a bag,' Maxine said.

As they went to return to the garden through the sitting room, Vivienne noticed Maxine's collection of silver framed photographs on a small highly polished table and she moved across to take a closer look.

'This is you and your husband?' she asked, pointing to one and catching her breath. Maxine, looking lovely in a long silver evening dress that was clearly couture, was standing face to face and holding hands with a tall, debonair man in a black-tie evening outfit. Their body language indicated that the camera had caught the couple at the exact second they'd drawn apart after a kiss and were exchanging a look that positively sizzled with loving intimacy.

Maxine nodded. 'My favourite photograph of the two of us. The fact that it is also the last one of us together makes it extra poignant for me.'

'And this one,' Vivienne said, indicating a black and white photograph of a young woman and a small girl. 'Is that you too?'

But Maxine had already turned away to pick up a paperback. 'I promised to lend Olivia this book when I finished it. The writer she is English. *Peut-être* you have heard of her?'

Vivienne looked at the book Maxine held up to show her and smiled when she saw the author's name. Jill Mansell 'Yes, she's well known and very popular in England.'

Olivia gave a happy sigh when Maxine handed the book to her. 'Thank you. I love Jill's books.'

The aperitif hour extended into the evening as the three women started to bond, sipping their wine and chatting. Olivia even relaxed enough to tell the other two her decision to finish with James.

She glanced at Maxine. 'Please don't mention it to my mother, otherwise she'll be lining up even more men she considers eligible.' Olivia shook her head. 'There are times I think my mother allows her desperation to be a grandmother to grab at any likely male she meets – either that or she doesn't know me at all.'

'Well, I too know some delightful young men,' Maxine said mischievously. 'I could introduce you.'

Olivia held up her hand. 'Don't you dare, Maxie. I'm going to try to resurrect a social life and enjoy summer on my own terms.'

It was almost ten o'clock when Olivia and Vivienne left and Maxine wandered between the garden and the house, loading the dishwasher, tidying cushions. It had been a lovely evening. Olivia had seemed in good spirits and Vivienne had turned out to be way more friendly than she'd expected when they first met.

But now she was alone again, the depressing thoughts that were always circling in her brain were trying to descend and engulf her.

Maxine picked up the photograph she'd pretended not to hear

Vivienne asking about. Even after all these years, it was impossible to ignore the maelstrom of emotions that the photograph always stirred inside her. It was only by sheer force of will that she'd recovered from those years that the photograph represented the end of, while at the same time it marked the beginning of a truly dreadful time in her life. Thirty years had passed since the photograph had been taken, but the pain had never been forgotten and never would be.

She'd often thought about hiding the photo in a drawer, shutting it away out of sight, but could never bring herself to do that. It had happened and she would always remember. Whilst she could acknowledge that it was a part of her life that had gone, never to return, she knew the memory could never be shut down completely. Denying the past was not an option.

Replacing the photograph on the table, Maxine's thoughts turned to Vivienne. There had been a couple of times during the evening when Vivienne had quickly changed the conversation when her husband had been mentioned. Did he have something to do with the upsetting news Vivienne had received before she arrived? Perhaps when they knew each other better, Vivienne would confide in her. But then again, maybe not. Perhaps Vivienne's secret, like her own, was not for sharing.

7

The morning after aperitifs at Maxine's, Vivienne got up at 6.30 and showered before walking to the boulangerie for a baguette and croissants. Returning to the apartment, she took her breakfast coffee and croissant up to the roof terrace, which was rapidly becoming her favourite place in the apartment.

Last night sitting out in Maxine's beautiful garden drinking wine and talking about everything under the sun, Vivienne had realised how much she missed having close female friends. She'd never been one for girly nights out but had enjoyed the camaraderie of other mothers as the children grew, and a couple of closer friends like Lisa and Dawn. Otherwise, it was a quick coffee with the other mums while the children were at after-school club, swimming and any PTA event she'd been roped in to help with.

But life had changed over the years. The children had grown, primary schools had become senior schools, people had divorced, moved away and slowly the whole network of friendly female support had disappeared. Lisa had been the last to leave, for a new life in Australia. Now, working from home as a writer, Vivienne realised she rarely met up with anyone outside of the family or

Jeremy's colleagues at the newspaper. She met with both her agent and her publisher once or twice a year for lunch, but that was about it. Spending time with Maxine and Olivia last evening had been an unexpected but welcome surprise. She felt as though she had made two new friends – friends that she would keep in touch with when she returned home.

Down below her, Antibes was waking up for the day. The Mediterranean waves were gently lapping the beach in the early-morning sunlight, there were people walking their dogs, others going for a swim, runners jogging past, and cyclists whizzing down the road before the traffic began to increase as shop and office workers headed into town.

Vivienne gave a sigh. Sitting there under a clear blue sky with a warmth to the early-morning air, it was all too easy to forget and push her problems to the back of her mind. To believe that life, even if not perfect, was at least filled with good things. Her books were selling well, Natalie and Tim were happy with their chosen careers – Natalie with her catering business and Tim a recently qualified paramedic working with the fire service. Elizabeth was enjoying a busy social life as her seventy-fifth birthday approached and Jeremy...

Vivienne's enjoyment of the terrace and its view vanished as thoughts of Jeremy and his affair flooded into her mind once again. His news was about to wreck everything they'd spent their married lives believing in. Even if they did manage to work through this crisis, nothing would ever be the same again. How could it be?

She closed her eyes and took several deep breaths, trying to pull herself together, wishing her adoptive mum was still alive and she could talk to her. Ask her advice on how she could cope with the changes that were coming her way. Jacqueline Lewis had always guided her with wise words and kindness. Indeed, kindness summed up Jacqueline. She'd spent her life being kind, saying it was impossible to be too kind.

Fourteen months after her death, Vivienne still ached with the hurt of losing the woman who had adopted her at two weeks old and had been such a loving and supportive presence in her life. Always there at school open evening, sports days, school outings. Her childhood, filled with love and happiness, had been wonderful.

She remembered too the pride and the joy they'd shared when her first book had been bought by a publisher ten years ago. Together they'd danced around the sitting room before Jacqueline had insisted on opening the bottle of champagne that she'd bought in readiness for that day. Their mother-daughter bond had been strong and Vivienne knew how lucky she'd been to have Jacqueline as a mother. She was the reason Vivienne had never been tempted to ask questions about her birth mother. It would have felt grossly disloyal.

Even after Jacqueline's death, Vivienne didn't feel the need to discover the truth about her birth mother. As far as she was concerned, Jacqueline was her mother and there was no way she would taint her memory by searching for the woman who had given her up, even if there had been extenuating circumstances beyond her control. All Jacqueline had been able to tell her was that her mother, Deidre Hewitt, had shamed her family by becoming pregnant after a holiday romance in France and they'd disowned her, insisting the baby be put up for adoption. After the birth, there was no question of Deidre keeping the baby and, two weeks later, Jacqueline and her husband Oscar had adopted her.

But things had altered when Vivienne, clearing out the bureau in the sitting room after Jacqueline's death, had discovered what she'd dubbed 'The French Connection'. In an envelope with her original birth certificate with its 'father unknown' statement, she'd found real evidence of her beginnings. A black and white photograph of a young couple whom she took to be her birth parents, with their arms around each other standing in front of the statue of Eros in London. And a sealed envelope with the ink-faded name Pascal Rocher, followed by the postcode and name of a French village in the Alps-Maritimes in the south of France, handwritten across it. Why had Jacqueline never told her about the existence of these things? Why had she never even shown them to her?

Once she'd discovered them, Vivienne had kept picking up the photograph and studying it every spare moment she had, trying to discern if there was any likeness between herself and either of the people in the photograph. Impossible to tell, she decided the image wasn't sharp enough to give information like that. But Vivienne's thoughts had gone round and round in circles. She knew the name of her birth mother – did the name on the envelope belong to her birth father?

The sealed envelope intrigued her. The name Pascal Rocher written in unfamiliar capital letters. Why was it in with Jacqueline's papers? Should she open it? Should she post it? Even deliver it personally? Strangely, searching for her birth father wouldn't feel like a betrayal of her adoptive father, Oscar Lewis, like it did with her mum.

Thirteen years older than Jacqueline, he'd never been unkind, never raised his hand to her and Vivienne knew he had loved her in his own undemonstrative way, but he had been a more remote father figure than a hands-on one, unable to express his emotions to anyone other than his wife, and even then it was never with over-the-top expressions of love. A bunch of flowers on her birthday, an unexpected box of chocolates. For Vivienne, it was a pat on the head, a 'Well done' for a school report. An arm around her shoulder for a quick hug. Tactile Jacqueline made up for it, though, never needing an excuse to pull Vivienne in for a quick hug.

Vivienne sighed. Both Oscar and Jacqueline were gone. It would make no difference to either of them if she searched for this Pascal Rocher, living in a village in the countryside behind Nice. In all probability, he too would be dead by now.

Breaking off a piece of croissant Vivienne chewed thoughtfully. For the next few days, she needed to concentrate on reading through the thirty-five thousand words she'd already written, thinking of possible scenes and plot lines and making notes of the various places she needed to visit to get a proper feel of the Riviera atmosphere. This was the first time she'd set a book on the Côte d'Azur and she was determined to get it right. And then she needed to get into a writing routine.

Once she was settled into her minimum two thousand words a day, she'd ask Maxine if she knew the best way to get to the village behind Nice. It seemed silly not to at least find the place whilst she was so close here in France.

Vivienne drained the last of her coffee, inwardly telling herself off for not telling both Maxine and Olivia who she was last night. She'd felt so comfortable in their company, and there had been the perfect opportunity when Maxine had given Olivia the Jill Mansell book to tell them about the books she wrote, the awards she'd won and the popular TV series adapted from one of her books, but the moment had passed quickly. She'd grown so used to hiding behind the anonymity of the pen name both Jeremy and her agent, Sadie, had suggested her using when she began writing that it was hard to admit to anyone outside of her immediate family that she was actually quite a famous writer.

But now her life was about to change, now that she would have to be an independent woman, perhaps it was time she started admitting to strangers and the world at large exactly who she was.

8

Olivia too was up early the next morning, needing to put the finishing touches to the arrangements she'd created yesterday afternoon, before loading them into the pink taxi.

Marina delivery day was her favourite day of the week. She loved driving around Port Vauban marina – one of the largest in Europe – parking up and then greeting the yacht crew who came to pick up the individual orders. First, today she had six large arrangements to deliver to different yachts moored on Billionaires' Quay before returning to the main marina. Billionaires' Quay had been specifically built to accommodate the super yachts that frequented the Mediterranean and were too big to moor in any of the other nearby ports.

Afterwards, she drove back to the main marina and enjoyed slowly pootling along the numerous quays with their moored boats delivering her flowers. She always carried extra flowers too for impulse purchases by people who were surprised to see her but loved the quirkiness of buying flowers from a pink London taxi for their boat. Her last stop was always at the Capitaine's large building at the edge of the marina with its spectacular 360-degree view of the surrounding area and the Mediterranean. Every week, she always dropped off an arrangement there as a thank you. The harbour master had assured her it wasn't necessary, but she was grateful for the business that the marina generated.

Finally, all the commissioned arrangements had been delivered and Olivia had sold several rapidly made-up bouquets to impulsive customers and she was ready to leave the marina. Driving past the last quay, she was surprised to see James's yacht moored there when he'd told her he was off to Corsica. Slowing down, she searched for any sign of life on board but saw none. Should she stop and see if he was around, find out if he'd lied to her? Perhaps it was just an unexpected change of plan by his boss and he hadn't lied intentionally. Or maybe he had? Maybe he'd come to the same conclusion as her, that it was time to end things between them. Fingers crossed she wouldn't have to tell him face to face it was over, they would just drift apart.

Thoughtfully, Olivia drove past.

Back in the centre of Antibes, she found a parking space at the market and prepared to hopefully sell most, if not all, of the remaining flowers before the market closed. There were still people milling around the various stalls and the unusual sight of the pink taxi with its flowers brought lots of smiles in her direction.

Olivia was starting to think about packing up and calling it a day when Vivienne stopped by.

'I love your taxi,' she said. 'Such a great idea. Like a pop-up shop on wheels. May I buy a bunch of twelve mixed tulips for the apartment please?'

'Of course,' and Olivia began to gather the various coloured tulips together. 'Are you on your way back to the apartment? I'm almost finished here for today. Fancy a drink before we both go home?'

'Make that a cold drink, and yes please,' Vivienne said, handing over some euros in payment. 'I'm not used to this heat.'

'If you go and grab a seat over there,' Olivia said, pointing to one of the market cafes, 'I'll join you in about five minutes. Leave the tulips here for now.'

* * *

Sitting there waiting for Olivia to join her at the pavement cafe, Vivienne looked around, breathing in the atmosphere of the market. The stallholders were starting to pack up, but there were still people milling around, carefully placing green peppers, tomatoes, strings of garlic, rounds of cheese, bottles of rosé into their capacious straw shopping baskets. The smell from the lavender stall with its oils, dried lavender, candles, perfume, sachets and soaps mingled with the lunchtime aromas starting to drift out from the various cafes.

Vivienne watched as a woman made her way confidently past several stalls before stopping in front of the olive oil stand. The woman, slim and dressed simply in white jeans and the ubiquitous Breton top, her sunglasses pushed to the top of her head, was casually chic in a way that Vivienne could only admire, albeit with a twinge of envy. How did French women retain that almost indescribable air of just being? The old French cliché saying that they all seemed to embody *'je ne sais quoi'* sprang into her mind. There were similar white jeans and a striped top in her own wardrobe, but she was sure as hell she'd never managed to pull off that chic look when wearing them.

'I definitely want one of these baskets,' an English voice interrupted her thoughts and Vivienne turned to look at the shop next door to the cafe. With its door opening straight out onto the pavement, there was no real need for a stall in the market itself. Baskets that had been piled up and arranged neatly at the beginning of the morning were now all higgledy-piggledy and almost tumbling onto the market floor. A teenage girl was busy trying to gather them up and replace them in an orderly manner. Other baskets with their colourful weaving hung suspended from various poles fixed to the stone wall of the shop, out of reach of customers.

Olivia joined Vivienne just then as a waiter approached the table. '*Deux verres de rosé s'il vous plaît,*' she said, smiling at the man, who immediately turned around to fetch the order, before pulling out a chair and sitting down.

Vivienne, about to protest about drinking wine at midday, gave a mental shrug. Why not? The words hadn't been flowing this morning, which was why she was down here, soaking up the atmosphere of the market, hoping for inspiration to strike rather than back in the apartment struggling to find the right words. A drink might help her this afternoon when she was writing the next chapter. After all, traditionally, everyone expected writers to like a drink, using the excuse it aided the imagination.

The cold rosé which arrived almost immediately was deliciously refreshing and Olivia gave a contented sigh after taking a sip or two. 'That's better.'

'Busy morning?' Vivienne said.

'No more than usual, but I saw James's yacht. When he cancelled our date, he told me he was off to Corsica for at least a week, but he is still in port,' Olivia said, giving a small shrug. 'It shouldn't matter because our relationship is clearly over, but it hurts that he probably lied to me. I have zero tolerance of liars,' she added.

'Maybe there was a change of plan?' Vivienne suggested.

Olivia shook her head. 'I think it was easier for him to lie than to tell me face to face. Or give me the chance to dump him.'

Vivienne gave a sympathetic nod. 'Men can be devious creatures, can't they? Something I've only found out to my cost recently.' She shook her head as Olivia gave her a concerned look. 'Another time.' Vivienne sipped her wine before moving the conversation on. 'It was a lovely evening yesterday. I love Maxine's house, and as for that garden, it's so beautiful.'

'She and Pierre worked hard on it. So sad when he died. They were so in love, such a shame they had such a short time together.' Olivia finished her drink and stood up. 'Come on. Let's get Daisy.'

'Daisy?'

'My pet name for the pink taxi. I'll give you and your tulips a lift back home.'

Vivienne gave a small chuckle as they headed over to the pink taxi.

Olivia drove them sedately along the coast road. The pink London taxi was definitely not built for speed. She was like some outdated blowsy actor still bowing to her admirers as she drove by. The number of people who smiled as they saw her and waved was astonishing. Vivienne was tempted to wave back like the Queen but left Olivia to do the acknowledging with a gracious wave of her hand and the occasional toot of the horn when she saw a friend.

Back at the villa, Vivienne took her tulips, thanked Olivia for the wine and the lift home and, humming happily to herself, climbed the stairs to the apartment. As she arranged the tulips in a jug she found in the kitchen, her mobile rang. Caller ID flashed up. Jeremy. No way was she ready to talk to him. She had planned a simple cheese and baguette lunch and then an afternoon writing up on the terrace. Talking to Jeremy would only disrupt that plan and she had no intention of allowing him to do that. She let the phone ring, hoping that he'd hang up when she didn't answer.

She froze as the voice message kicked in and Jeremy's voice filled the silence. Listening to his words almost broke her resolve not to talk to him. She desperately wanted to scream abuse at him.

When Jeremy finally finished speaking and the phone clicked off, Vivienne opened the fridge. Her hand was shaking as she grabbed the bottle of rosé and splashed some into a glass.

To hell with not drinking at lunchtime. Right now, she needed something to take away the pain of Jeremy's news. News which she had no idea how to deal with or how to tell the children that in a few months they would have a new sibling.

9

Maxine wandered down through her garden, absently pulling a weed here and there, smelling one of the early roses, bending to gently stroke a velvety grey leaf of the lamb's ears plants that edged the path. Evening was her favourite time of day in the garden and tonight was a perfect late spring one. Still warm with the full heat of summer yet to arrive and everything was flourishing. Perfect and ready for their annual garden party.

Ever since they had owned 'L'Abri', she and Pierre had organised a garden party for their friends during the Cannes Film Festival. Pierre had always loved playing the genial host, welcoming his friends, spoiling them with good food and wine. Last year's party had been one of the best ever. The thought of organising one without him at her side was unbearable. And yet deep down she knew Pierre would have been disappointed in her if she didn't do it. Maybe a smaller party – fewer people would make it more intimate and people would understand.

Maxine gave a sigh. It was so hard rebuilding her life without him. She also knew that, in truth, she should host the party for herself. Another act of normality in her different world.

Standing by the pond watching the fish gobble up the food she'd thrown on the surface, Maxine forced herself to think about the Cannes Film Festival, starting in just a few days. Time to make a decision was running out. Maybe she could have a supper party instead. That way, she could limit numbers to just close friends, and reinstate the party next year when she would hopefully be feeling stronger.

She dangled her hand in the pond water and smiled as an inquisitive fish swam across and nibbled her finger before darting away. Mentally, she started to tally up the people she could invite for supper. Reaching twenty, she gave a short unladylike snort. Pierre had always reckoned that twenty-five was the ideal number for a garden party, so twenty was almost a full party already. It was definitely too many for supper. It would have to be a party or nothing. Decision made.

Strolling back to the house, Maxine thought about which day would be best. The first Saturday of the festival opening week had always worked well, so she'd stick to that date, which gave her seven days to invite people and to organise things. Keeping extra busy would at least stop her thinking too much.

Back indoors, Maxine emailed invitations to her friends.

A day later replies were pinging into her inbox. Eighteen acceptances to date, three 'with regret' refusals.

Maxine frowned. One of the refusals was from Vivienne, saying thank you but no. Maxine tapped her fingers on her laptop. She liked Vivienne and had a feeling that, given the chance, they could be good friends. How could she get her to change her mind? And, importantly, did she have time before the party?

* * *

Vivienne closed her laptop with a satisfied sigh. It had been a good writing day and she was back on target with the book. Jeremy's phone call twenty-four hours ago had shaken her, but she'd been determined to push it into the 'deal with later' file at the back of her mind.

Time for a quick shower before Maxine arrived. She'd messaged early that afternoon, saying she had something for her and could she pop around this evening? Vivienne, grateful that Maxine hadn't turned up without warning when she was busy writing, had happily messaged back to say she was looking forward to spending the evening with her.

Vivienne had just finished smoothing some foundation under her eyes in the hope that it would conceal the dark smudges when Maxine arrived.

'Hi. Come on in,' Vivienne said. 'I thought we'd sit up on the terrace – no garden, but at least we can sit outside and look at the view. There's a bottle of rosé in the fridge, but if you'd prefer something else? Coffee? Tea?' Vivienne looked at Maxine questioningly.

'A glass of wine would be lovely. You are okay? You have the look of working too hard.'

Vivienne laughed the remark off, realising that the foundation concealer had failed. 'That's because I have been today.' No way was she going to admit to not sleeping because of that phone call.

'How's the writing going?' Maxine asked.

'When I stop looking at the view, it's fine,' Vivienne said.

Once they were settled on the terrace, glasses of wine on the table in front of them, the bottle in a terracotta cooler, Maxine reached into her handbag and pulled out a book. 'You missed this one the other day, it was in the bedroom. *The Wonder of Jazz* – it is, I think, an important book in the history of jazz.' She held it out to Vivienne. '*Peut-être* it help your research?'

'Thank you,' Vivienne said, flicking through the pages.

'But I have another reason for coming this evening to see you. Please come to my garden party. You will enjoy it and meet more people. *Peut-être* you have ideas for your story too.'

Vivienne sighed. 'I'm sorry. I didn't pack any clothes suitable for going to a glamorous party for one thing. And for another, I'm not very good with parties where I don't know anyone.'

'Pff. All that is nonsense. I take you shopping for a dress. Not expensive – or expensive if you like. You know me and Olivia. My stepson Thierry has messaged to say he is coming, so already there is three people you can talk to. Felicity and Trent, Olivia's parents, are coming also. You can help me keep the peace between Olivia and her maman!'

Vivienne laughed. 'You're not exactly selling me the idea of coming to the party with that job offer. As for shopping for a glamorous dress, I'd probably only wear it once. My life in England isn't remotely glamorous.' No need to tell Maxine that it was a life that was about to descend catastrophically into chaos when she returned with even less use for a glamorous dress.

'All the more reason to seize the opportunity to go to a glamorous party while you are on the Riviera,' Maxine said. 'So we go shopping? *Oui*? I know a little boutique. I get you a good price. I arrange and then afterwards we have lunch.'

Vivienne laughed. 'Okay, I know when I'm beaten. I will buy a dress and come to your party, thank you.'

'*Bien*,' Maxine said. 'You and I will have fun shopping. *Santé*,' and she raised her glass in Vivienne's direction.

Before Vivienne could acknowledge and respond, her mobile rang. Natalie.

'My daughter, will you excuse me, but I need to answer this. Hi, darling, I'm a bit busy right now, can I ring—' Vivienne stopped as she heard the sound of sobbing. 'Natalie, are you all right?'

'No. Tim and I have just been to see Dad.'

'Ah.'

'How can he do this to you? To us.'

'Sadly, it happens to a lot of people. Are you at home now?'

'Yes. How come you are so laid-back about it? And why didn't you tell me what was going on?'

'Because I have no intention of making life easy for your father,' Vivienne said. 'Try to put it out of your mind for a while. Maybe a cup of tea, glass of wine, might help to calm you down. I have a friend here right now, but I'll phone you later this evening and we'll talk then. Okay?' She heard Natalie sniff and take a deep breath.

'Promise?'

'Of course.'

Vivienne's shoulders sagged as she pressed the off button. She gave Maxine a rueful smile as she asked, 'Problems at home? You like me to leave so you can phone your daughter back right away?'

'No, please don't leave yet. Have another glass of wine,' and Vivienne picked up the bottle and topped up both their glasses before looking at Maxine. 'Jeremy, my husband, drove me to the airport for my flight down here and decided it would be a good time and place to tell me, minutes before I boarded, that he's been having an affair, intended to leave me and wanted a divorce.' She took a large drink of her wine. 'He also seemed to think I'd help him break the news to not only his mother but also our children. I declined and told him to do his own dirty work. Apparently he has now done so, to the children at least. I'm not sure he's told his mother yet.'

'*Mon Dieu*, Vivienne, what a bastard,' Maxine exclaimed. 'I hope you punch him on the nose. I'm so sorry your marriage has ended in such a way. No wonder you were in a bad state when you arrived.'

Vivienne laughed. 'I'm far too British to do something like that in public, but oh how I wanted to. I simply turned my back on him and walked away and haven't contacted him since, although there have been a couple of messages which I've ignored.' She sighed, remembering the last one. Had Jeremy passed that information on to Natalie and Tim as well? His mother? She pushed the thoughts away.

'Your daughter, she is upset with her father too?'

Vivienne nodded. 'I think when it all begins to sink in, she's also going to be extremely angry with him. As for Tim, my son, I'm sure he will be the same.'

'But it is not like it is their marriage that has imploded,' Maxine said gently. 'They are young and resilient, they will surely be hurt because of his behaviour but in time, they will become used to what he did, become used to their parents living separate lives. It will become the normal way their family is. It is you who will be most affected. I know how hard divorce is, after even a short marriage.'

Vivienne glanced at her, surprised.

Maxine gave her a rueful smile and shrugged. 'My first marriage, it was a mistake. I was too young and too stupid to realise that he was a control freak and he also had a serious mistress – alcohol.' Maxine pulled a face. 'The bruises faded. I recover. You will recover – but it may take some time because of the close family ties that exist between the two of you and bind you together. And because...' She paused. 'Because it is hard to recover from emotional pain however old one is, but in mid-life...' Maxine sighed and closed her eyes, shook her head before opening them and saying sadly, 'I have to warn you, the future can look bleak for a long time.'

10

―――――

After Maxine left, Vivienne returned to the terrace, took a deep breath and phoned a still tearful Natalie.

'I just don't understand, Mum, how you can sound so calm. How long have you known about it? Is that why you decided to go to France, to get away from it for a while?'

'No, I didn't know about it before this week,' Vivienne said and told her daughter how Jeremy had broken the news to her.

There was a stunned silence at the other end of the phone for several seconds before Natalie exploded with anger. 'Bastard. What a horrible, cowardly thing to do.'

Vivienne opened her mouth to tell Natalie not to call her father that and closed it again. The name calling was justified.

'Well, he needn't think he's going to get any sympathy from me because "he didn't mean it to happen", as if that absolves him of blame. Who is she anyway?'

'Didn't Dad tell you her name?'

'Nope, simply said we'd learn it all in good time as things progressed, but he'd just wanted to tell us he and you were divorcing before the fallout became gossip and somebody else did.'

Vivienne sighed. 'I told him he had to tell both you and Tim as well as Elizabeth the truth about everything, so I'm not going to tell you either.'

'Mum!' Natalie's exasperation was clear.

'As for divorcing, that is months away. How did Tim react?'

'Oh, you know Tim. Didn't say much. I didn't either really. We just sat there together listening to Dad apologising over and over, saying it didn't make any difference to his feelings for us. But it sure as hell makes a difference to mine for him.' Natalie sighed. 'In the end, we just thanked Dad for telling us himself and we both left. I did get the feeling, though, that it wasn't entirely a surprise to Tim, but he'd gone before I got the chance to quiz him. But I will. He did say to give you his love and he'll ring you as soon as he gets a chance – but I shouldn't hold your breath. You know what he's like.'

'Was Granny Elizabeth mentioned?'

'Dad was having supper with her tonight. Mum?' Natalie paused. 'Are you okay? I mean, I guess you're not okay with the whole sordid business, you must be hurt and reeling from it, but you are so far away...' Her voice trailed anxiously away. 'I want to give you a hug and I can't.'

Vivienne took a silent deep breath before answering. She didn't want Natalie to get even more upset on her behalf, which was one of the reasons she'd insisted Jeremy told Natalie and Tim who his lover was. 'I'm coping. I'm glad I'm away, to be honest. If I was at home, there would be no escaping from the problem – it would probably be row after row, which will no doubt happen when I return. But, right now, it's like a bad dream that's happening to someone else that I don't currently have to deal with.'

'Can you write? Or are you too stressed to concentrate?'

'I have to concentrate I have a deadline to meet,' Vivienne said, not wanting to confess how far behind she'd slipped. 'Now I've settled in a bit, I do have a routine emerging.'

'You said you had a friend there earlier?'

'Maxine, the agent for the apartment. She's lovely. Olivia who lives downstairs permanently is about your age and is nice too. You'll meet her if you manage to come over next month.'

'Oh I'm definitely coming,' Natalie said. 'I've blocked a possible week out in the diary. And if you haven't cracked our French connection by then, I'll be cross.'

Vivienne laughed. 'I'll do my best.' When the call ended a few moments later, she was relieved that Natalie no longer sounded tearful.

Vivienne picked up the book that Maxine had brought her and flicked through the pages before putting it down and opening her laptop which she'd left up on the terrace table. Checking her email, she smiled. Céline had answered her, saying it was lovely to meet her and any time she came to Cannes she was welcome to call in and she'd put her address below. Vivienne flagged the email. She might well take Céline up on that offer before her holiday was over.

She glanced at the time. Nine thirty. She'd do a read-through of the chapter she'd written earlier in the day, correct any typos, maybe write a few more sentences before going to bed.

When her phone rang half an hour later, Vivienne was so deep into her story that she absently picked up the phone and pressed the button without checking caller ID first.

'Well, I cannot in all honestly say that I'm surprised that Jeremy has finally found someone else more suitable for him. The surprise is that it took him so long,' her mother-in-law's accusatory voice with its perfect Home Counties accent jolted Vivienne out of her concentration. 'But how I am to face everyone at the WI, I don't know. My only consolation is that my friends have always wanted the best for Jeremy, he is such a popular person, they will understand, that, in the end, he really had no choice.'

'Good evening, Elizabeth,' Vivienne said. 'Your son is not as popular as you think he is, and he did have a choice. He chose to have an affair and end his marriage.'

'And I wonder why that is? If you'd been a proper wife, paid more attention to him, rather than spending all your time scribbling the rubbish you write, perhaps it would not have happened.'

Vivienne took a deep breath. 'Perhaps it was more a case of "like father, like son"?' she said, her patience with Elizabeth snapping at the mention of her writing. Early on in their relationship, Jeremy had told her that his father had once had a short fling with a work colleague at a conference, which, once Elizabeth learnt about it, was rapidly ended by her threatening divorce and naming the woman as co-respondent. Back in those days, outward respectability was required of everyone in the law firm Jeremy's father worked for and hoped to became a partner in. Jeremy had made Vivienne promise she'd never let his mother know that she knew about his father's 'little indiscretion', as his mother had apparently termed it. 'Goodnight, Elizabeth,' Vivienne said into the sudden silence that had descended and ended the call. She refused to feel guilty about her 'like father like son' jibe to the woman who had always been so mean-spirited towards her. Along with all the changes that were happening in her life, it was definitely time to lose all the bad karma Elizabeth had thrown at her down through the years.

Tiredly, Vivienne turned and went downstairs and made for her bed.

* * *

A day later, Vivienne stood in front of the wardrobe wondering what to wear from her limited selection of clothes for lunch with Maxine and dress shopping. Maxine had asked if she could be at L'Abri at ten o'clock today ready for a drive out of town to Valbonne, where her friend had a boutique. Vivienne wanted to look smart but also needed something easy to slip on and off for trying on dresses. In the end, she settled for an old favourite, a terracotta shift dress and her cream linen jacket with its pretty embroidery, and hoped it would do.

Maxine was standing by her car when Vivienne turned into the mews-like road L'Abri was situated in and a mere five minutes later they were on their way through Antibes, heading out into the back country.

Vivienne, watching the suburbs of Antibes blend into urban and then open countryside, gave a sigh.

Maxine glanced across at her. 'You are okay?'

Vivienne smiled. 'Yes, very happy actually. I'm in the South of France, the sky is an amazing blue, the sun is shining, the scenery is wonderful and I'm having a day off with a new friend,' Vivienne answered. 'It's a day to forget my problems and enjoy.'

'Sensible woman,' Maxine said. 'I do the same and we have fun. Valbonne is a lovely medieval village. You will like it, I think.'

Thirty minutes later, Maxine pulled into a car park and they made their way to the centre of the village.

'You have seen the film *French Kiss*?' Maxine said. 'It was very popular a few years ago.'

'Yes. Natalie and I saw it together. We both loved it.'

'This is the square where the fight between the brothers was filmed. We have lunch here at the restaurant,' and Maxine pointed to the table and chairs with their parasols already open. 'But first we shop. My friend Giselle she designs and makes the clothes. I think you will find something you like.'

Vivienne, walking alongside Maxine through a labyrinth of narrow streets, gazing at the artisan shops selling jewellery, paintings, clothes and local delicacies all jostling together in ancient buildings, longed to slow down and have a proper look. Maxine, though, was on a mission. She must have sensed Vivienne's longing as she said, 'After we buy your dress, we have lunch and then we will take a look at the shops. I take you to the English bookshop too if you like?'

'Please,' Vivienne said, briefly wondering if she would find any of her books there. If she did, she'd buy one to give to Maxine as a thank you for today.

Maxine finally stopped outside a tall narrow house, with its brightly painted red front door held open with a terracotta pot full of sunflowers and a short rail of dresses placed on the other side. '*Voilà*,' and pushing aside the mosquito net curtain, she stepped inside.

Vivienne followed and found herself in a veritable Aladdin's cave of feminine clothing.

After the obligatory hug and cheek kisses, Maxine pulled Vivienne forward to quickly introduce her, telling Giselle that Vivienne needed at least one party dress. Vivienne squirmed inwardly as Giselle looked her up and down before nodding thoughtfully.

Standing there with these two chic French women, Vivienne felt positively dowdy. What on earth was she doing here? She didn't need a glamorous party dress. She was a middle-aged English woman with no real sense of style who was happy to dress comfortably and live a quiet life. Had she become boring? Happy to live in the world of the stories she wrote? Was that why Jeremy had looked elsewhere? Maybe. But she wasn't going to take full responsibility for their current situation. She might have ignored the signs that their marriage was in trouble, but it was Jeremy who had decided to play away, when sitting down together and talking might have made all the difference. But today was not the day to think like that and Vivienne made a determined effort to push those thoughts away.

Giselle, moving across to a rail, asked, 'Is there anything here that appeals? Any of these dresses would be perfect for summer parties. If you need something more formal, the outfit on that model would suit you,' and she pointed to a sequinned off-the-shoulder evening dress on a nearby mannequin.

'No, nothing as formal as that,' Vivienne said hastily, moving across to the rail to have a closer look at the clothes hanging there. But it seemed she wasn't allowed to browse for too long.

'This would suit you,' Maxine said, taking an ivory floral-print wrap midi dress with a V-neck and cap sleeves off the rail. 'Go try,' and she held it out Vivienne.

'Here try it on with these sandals,' Giselle said, handing her a pair before pulling a curtain aside and revealing a small changing room.

As she changed, Vivienne could hear Maxine and Giselle chatting quietly. Once she'd tied the wrap dress in place, she slipped her feet into the high-heeled sandals and glanced at herself in the mirror before pulling the curtain back. 'I feel good in this, but is it glamorous enough for the party?' she asked Maxine anxiously.

'Yes, but try this one,' Maxine said, handing her a green midi dress. 'This is truly a party dress.'

Vivienne went to protest, but both Maxine and Giselle waved her into the cubicle. She looked at the green dress on its hanger – a Bardot neckline, with straps around the upper arm for sleeves, small red flowers scattered over the bodice and the hemline of the skirt which had a slight flare. This was so not her. She just knew that it was a waste of time trying it on.

Opening the curtain, she stepped out into the shop without even looking at the mirror in the changing room and was totally unprepared for both Giselle and Maxine's reaction. 'Now that is truly glamorous. I insist that is the one you buy. *C'est parfait.*'

Giselle nodded in agreement. 'I think I design and make it knowing you would be coming to buy. It has your name written all over it.'

'But I never wear green or anything with bare shoulders.' Vivienne shook her head and caught a glimpse of herself in the shop mirror and stopped to take a proper look as the flared skirt swished around her legs. 'And I'm too old for a dress like this.' If Jeremy were here, he'd be shaking his head at the sheer folly of her even trying on such a dress at her age.

'Nonsense,' Maxine said sternly. 'Me, I'm too old for it, but you are the perfect age for it.'

'A dress like this is completely out of my comfort zone. I'm happiest in trousers, if I'm honest. What about a trouser suit?'

Wordlessly, Giselle walked over to a rail at the back of the shop and took a terracotta trouser suit off the rail. 'Try it on. You could glam it up for Saturday night with some accessories. Down here, anything really goes for evening outdoor parties. It tends to be very relaxed.'

'Thank you,' Vivienne said, relieved that the discussion over the Bardot dress was over.

Back in the cubicle, she stood in front of the mirror and tried to look at herself and the dress dispassionately. It was a lovely dress; beautifully cut and made, it fitted her perfectly. She even liked the vibrant colour. The neckline was actually quite flattering, not as low-cut as she'd expected it to be. No cleavage on show. The straps around her arms were comfortable. Were Maxine and Giselle right when they said it was the perfect dress for her?

Carefully, she took the dress off and hung it back on the hanger and put on the trouser suit. Once again, everything about the outfit was good – the linen material was lovely and the fit was perfect. She had some jewellery – a bracelet, earrings and a large topaz ring – that would jazz up the ensemble for Saturday night. As an outfit, it would certainly get more wear and be more useful than the green dress, that was for sure. Jeremy would approve.

Vivienne pushed that thought aside before it could register. He wasn't here. The days of taking his feelings into account were over. As a married couple, it was only natural to ask each other's opinion, but as a separated woman she was on her own for choosing how to dress. It had been a long time since she'd had to rely solely on her own judgement, which was a scary thought. Fleetingly, she wished Natalie was there to voice her honest opinion but she wasn't. Maybe it was now time for her to start making her own decisions about how she dressed. Decisions about everything actually, not just her clothes.

Dressed once again in her shift dress and linen jacket, Vivienne took all three hangers with the outfits off the hook and resolutely pulled the curtain back. Time to start trusting her own judgement.

Giselle was showing Maxine some of her design sketches for her autumn collection and Maxine was oohing and aahing over a velvet evening cape. They both glanced up as Vivienne joined them.

'Which one is it to be?' Maxine asked.

'In the end, I couldn't decide between them. So, please may I take all three,' Vivienne said. 'And the sandals too.'

'Only if you promise to wear the green dress to Maxine's party on Saturday night,' Giselle said.

'*Oui*, I agree,' Maxine echoed, looking at Vivienne.

Vivienne smiled. 'We'll see.'

Maxine wagged her finger at her. 'Not good enough. You need to promise.'

'Okay, I promise I will wear the green dress on Saturday to

your party,' Vivienne said, placing her credit card in the machine to pay.

After thanking Giselle and inviting her to join them for lunch, which she regretfully declined, Vivienne and Maxine made their way back to the restaurant on the main square. After ordering their lunch, Vivienne took a few sips from her glass of cold rosé and Maxine pulled a face at her non-alcoholic glass of wine.

'Giselle is one talented lady,' Vivienne said. 'Her clothes are amazing. I never impulse-buy clothes like I have this morning. Too many disasters in the past.' The thought, would the green dress turn out to be an expensive disaster, slipped into her mind. Worn once this Saturday and then left to languish in her wardrobe?

'Giselle – her clothes are an investment, you will wear them time and time again.' Vivienne could only smile at Maxine's confident attitude, whilst inwardly wondering whether she would indeed wear any of the clothes again when she returned home.

Lunch was delicious. They'd both decided against a starter, Maxine choosing *moules marinières* in white wine with French fries for her main course, and Vivienne, not being fond of mussels, opting for a croque monsieur served with Bechamel sauce and a small side salad. Afterwards, they both gave into temptation and ordered profiteroles with home-made vanilla ice-cream, hot dark chocolate sauce and whipped cream.

'Too many treats like this and I won't be able to fit into my new clothes,' Vivienne said, swallowing the last mouthful of sauce and cream.

After coffee, Vivienne insisted on paying the bill and they began making their way to the English bookshop. This time, as they wandered through different narrow streets, they passed an ancient fountain and more artisan shops selling a multitude of different goods.

As they turned into Rue Grande and Vivienne saw the open

doors of 'Niche Books', she smiled. This looked like the perfect bookshop where she could easily spend a couple of hours.

Maxine too seemed happy to browse for a while, picking up a Veronica Henry book, *Thirty Days in Paris*.

'You like to read in English?' Vivienne said.

'Yes, sometimes there are books I want to read and some authors I like do not always have the French translation.'

They both wandered across to a 'Summer Reads' display of paperbacks and Vivienne gave a small smile as she saw half a dozen copies of her own latest book. Maxine picked up a copy with a delighted sigh. *'J'adore cet auteur.'*

Vivienne gently took the book out of her hands. 'Please let me buy it for you as a thank you for introducing me to Giselle.' She waved Maxine's *'C'est pas nécessaire'* protest aside. 'I insist.'

Ten minutes later as they left the bookshop and made their way back down to the car park, Maxine's mobile rang.

'Hi, Olivia,' she said with an apologetic look at Vivienne, who shrugged off the unspoken apology with a shake of her head.

Maxine's quick-fire French conversation with Olivia as they walked was mostly lost on Vivienne, but she did pick up a few words. *Cinema sur la plage* – cinema on the beach. It was when she heard her own name, she turned and gave Maxine a puzzled look.

'Olivia has suggested the three of us go to the cinema on the beach in Cannes tomorrow evening,' Maxine said as the call ended. 'As part of the film festival, they feature films from the past on several evenings. Tomorrow it is *Thelma and Louise*. I accept Olivia's offer for us to go with her. We go to Cannes tomorrow at five o'clock. *D'accord?*'

Vivienne gave her a bemused nod. *'D'accord. Thelma and Louise* is one of those cult feminist films I've always wanted to see but never have.' She'd have to burn the midnight oil every evening to get back on schedule with the book. But what the heck, she was allowed to enjoy life down here as well as write.

'*Bon*. Now we go home. I have a party to finish organising.'

As they settled into the car, Vivienne took out the copy of the book she'd bought for Maxine, found a pen in her bag and started to write a message on the book's title page.

'What are you doing?' Maxine asked.

Vivienne finished writing, closed the book and handed it to Maxine before saying. 'The other evening I simply told you I was a writer. Well, this is my latest book and I've just signed it for you.'

'This is you?' Maxine looked at the book and then back at Vivienne. 'You are a famous writer. Why do you not use your own name so that everyone can congratulate you?'

'Jeremy thought it would be good to create a bit of a mystery around who exactly the author was.' Vivienne shrugged. 'It worked to a degree and I'm happier meeting new people as me, Vivienne, rather than them having expectations of what I'm like before meeting me.'

'I can understand that,' Maxine said. '*Mais* now I shall tell everyone I have a friend who is a famous writer but I'm not allowed to talk about her.'

11

Late the next afternoon, Olivia's sigh of relief was echoed by Maxine and Vivienne as she finally spied a space in the big subterranean car park in Cannes and was able to park. Olivia slipped the parking ticket in her bag and the three of them made their way out into the fresh air.

The Croisette was heaving with people, especially around the Palais des Festivals. 'Do we have a plan for the next couple of hours?' Maxine asked.

'I've booked a table for seven o'clock at one of the smaller restaurants by the harbour,' Olivia said. 'I thought before then we could just have a wander, give Vivienne a brief glimpse of Cannes, soak up the atmosphere and see if we can spot a celebrity or two.'

'What time does the film start?' Vivienne asked.

'Nine thirty,' Olivia answered. 'But we need to get there early to grab a decent seat.'

'Come on, let's make a start looking at the posh shops,' Maxine said. 'We can cut through up into Rue d'Antibes and then come back down to the harbour.'

* * *

By seven o'clock as they made their way to the restaurant by the harbour, the three of them were tired. It was Vivienne who voiced what she suspected they were all feeling.

'I'm sorry,' she said. 'I'm sure Cannes is lovely, but today the place is just so crowded with too many people fighting to see things for me. I'll have to come back another day when it's quieter, I think, to see Cannes at its best.'

'I'd forgotten how busy it always gets for festival time,' Maxine said. 'Food and a glass of wine now will revive us. The beach will be quieter later – and so will the Croisette once we get past all the paparazzi outside the Palais des Festivals.'

An hour later, refreshed and looking forward to the cinema on the beach, they made their way slowly past the barricades close to the iconic red-carpeted steps, where, as Maxine had said they would be, the paparazzi were busy snapping away at celebrities and film stars arriving for the evening's film.

Once down on the beach, they found three deckchairs together, four or five rows from the front of the big screen, and sat down gratefully.

Sitting there, listening to the murmur of voices around them, the waves lapping the beach and the night sky slowly darkening, Vivienne felt her spirits lifting as she let her mind drift over certain things. She was in the South of France, sitting on the beach with two new friends, wearing a lovely new trouser suit and she'd been invited to a party at the weekend. If she were honest, everything at this particular moment in time couldn't be better.

Vivienne closed her eyes and, sniffing the sea air, took a deep breath. Okay, she knew that she would have to make lots of decisions in the next few months, decisions forced on her by Jeremy creating problems she'd never expected to face, but that was life throwing an unexpected curveball in her direction. In a year's time, everything would have sorted itself out and she would be living a different life – a life of her own choosing. Where that would be she had no idea, but Jeremy would be in the past and she would be a single woman living life on her own terms.

An hour and half later, the credits rolled and the three of them stood up and made their way back to the underground car park. With the crowd leaving the beach and the Palace des Festival also emptying, it was difficult to stay close enough to each other to talk as they walked back to the car.

Once they'd all strapped themselves in, Olivia drove the car up several floors and out onto the Croisette. The three of them were silent, each lost in their own thoughts looking at the palm trees with the coloured lights wound around their tall trunks, couples with arms around each other strolling along, overhead lights sparkling, some stretched across the Croisette with their 'Welcome to Cannes' messages. A film set in its own right.

Rounding the bend and passing The Palm Court at the far end of the Croisette, where ordinary street lights took over from the gaudy decorations, it was Olivia who finally broke the silence.

'Well, it might be a landmark feminist film, but those two women made some terrible decisions.'

'Didn't they,' Vivienne said. 'It was very well acted and funny at times and really action packed, but also heartbreaking. And I can't believe how young Brad Pitt looked.'

Olivia laughed. 'You're right. But I'm glad I've finally seen it, although I think it was showing its age. Definitely from another era as far as women are concerned, don't you think?'

'We certainly have more choices these days,' Vivienne said.

'But don't you think they were out for revenge rather than advocating feminist values?' Olivia asked.

'Don't we all want revenge on a man at some point?' Maxine asked quietly from the back seat.

'Maybe, but I don't think many of us in real life would sink to such extraordinary actions, would we?' Vivienne said. 'Admittedly, their options were not great. I mean, I'm more than furious with Jeremy at the moment, but I haven't started plotting to kill him. Although I might kill him off in the next book,' she added, laughing.

'The phrase "It's a man's world" is still true, though, in certain cultures where women have to fight for their rights,' Maxine said quietly.

'Thank goodness we've moved on from that outmoded attitude,' Olivia said.

'We haven't totally. It's still out there alive and kicking.' Maxine shrugged when Olivia glanced at her in the rear-view mirror and Vivienne turned to look at her questioningly. 'It might be a different world where we have more rights and freedom, but not all men have changed. Equality still has a way to go in some cultures.' And Maxine turned her head to look out at the moon shining down on a darkened sea.

The journey along the coast road was relatively free of traffic and within ten minutes they were on the outskirts of Antibes.

'No need to drive me to my door, the corner of the street will be fine,' Maxine said as Olivia drove towards Maxine's cottage. 'Merci for this evening and see you both on Saturday.'

'We'll wait until you are indoors,' Olivia said.

Vivienne and Olivia watched as Maxine walked to her door and waved as she disappeared inside, before Olivia drove away.

* * *

Once indoors, Maxine checked her phone to find a message from Thierry. She gave a happy sigh as she read.

Arriving Friday evening. Okay to stay with you?

Ever since Thierry had accepted the invitation, she'd worried that he wouldn't make it, that something would crop up, preventing him from leaving Singapore. The fact that he would definitely be here for the garden party filled her with delight. He was the one person she needed to be there; this first party without Pierre would be easier with Thierry by her side.

Maxine quickly typed her reply.

Where else would you dare stay! See you then.

12

Saturday morning and Maxine was pottering around the garden having fed the fish, waiting for Thierry to return from the boulangerie with baguettes and breakfast croissants. As promised, he'd arrived late last evening and the two of them had sat companionably at the table on the terrace under the light of the moon, drinking a glass of the very good red wine that Thierry had brought and making final plans for the party.

As they'd talked, Maxine had told him how she'd very nearly decided not to bother with the party this year. 'I'm so pleased you decided to come for it. It will be different and hard without Pierre, but having you here will make it so much easier.'

'Everyone adores your parties,' Thierry had said. '*Peut-être* you worry too much. Everybody who comes will be an old friend who is happy to see you getting back on the horse, so to speak.'

Maxine had laughed. 'I have a new friend coming too, Vivienne, she is a writer, and is staying in Olivia's top apartment to write her next book.' She'd taken a sip of wine and changed the subject then. 'Enough about me for now – what is happening in your life?'

There was a pause before Thierry had said quietly, 'I am back in France for good.'

'What, forever?' She had tried hard to keep the surprise out of her voice but knew she'd failed.

'Definitely for the immediate future.'

'What's happened?' Maxine had asked.

Thierry had shrugged. 'Too soon to talk about it, but I will tell you – only not this evening.' And he'd deftly changed the subject back to asking how she truly was. She'd smiled, shrugged and made light of her feelings, telling him keeping busy was helping. He clearly had some problems in his own life. He didn't need to know about the nightmares his stepmother still suffered on a regular basis. Thierry was her stepson, not her counsellor. Maxine had been relieved to hear the town hall clock striking midnight which had been the signal to send them indoors and to bed. She would, she decided, control her feelings and make a determined effort not to burden Thierry with her sad thoughts this weekend – or ever, in fact. Instead, she would try to get him to open up to her about his own problem and see if she could help him.

'J'arrive,' Thierry called and Maxine began to walk back up through the garden.

Five minutes later, they were both sitting at the terrace table, coffee and croissants in front of them.

Maxine glanced at him. 'I have a question. If you are in no hurry to return to Paris, will you stay with me longer?'

'If I may,' Thierry said.

'Now you make me cross,' Maxine said. 'You are my family and family is welcome any time. There is no need to ask.'

'Merci,' Thierry said, pushing his chair back and standing up. 'Désolé. I forget. I have some post for you from the Paris apartment. I'll go and fetch it.'

Maxine sipped her coffee thoughtfully, wondering what had

happened to bring Thierry back to France from his high-powered investment job in Singapore. Pierre had been worried about him in the months before he died, telling her that he suspected Thierry was not happy in his chosen career, and had tried to get him to talk about it, unsuccessfully. He'd even suggested that he did something different, but Thierry had insisted all was well.

Thierry returned at that moment with the post and Maxine flicked through it after he'd handed her three envelopes. Two white and small, the third one white and A5 size. She'd stopped the redirection of mail at La Poste after six months, figuring that she'd informed all the authorities and all the contacts in her diary and that Thierry would let her have any stray missives like these. The two small letters, she could see, were end-of-year subscription renewals to magazines she'd decided to cancel, but the third official-looking white one gave her an unexpected shiver.

Thierry looked at her. 'You okay?'

Maxine forced herself to give him a bright smile. '*Oui*. Fine. I'll open them all later when I have more time to read them. We've got a busy day getting the garden ready for the party.' She stood up. 'I'll just take these upstairs and then we make a start, *d'accord*?'

'Ready when you are.' Thierry gave her an anxious look as she went into the house, before he started to clear the breakfast things away.

Up in her bedroom, Maxine threw the two smaller envelopes on the dressing table and stood looking at the third one. What was it about this envelope that had caused her to shiver uneasily? A typed address label, no handwriting to give her a clue, the date on the postmarked English stamp was smudged – how long had the letter taken to reach its Parisian destination, and how long had it sat there? It felt quite padded as she fingered it thoughtfully. More than a single letter inside. Maxine turned the envelope over and her heart skipped a beat as she recognised the name of the legal firm she'd had dealings with over thirty years ago stamped on the back.

She took a deep breath, squared her shoulders and resolutely placed the letter with the other two on her dressing table. Today was on track to be a fun day, if a difficult one, and she didn't want any more trauma hovering around her to spoil things. Opening the letter would be like opening a can of worms. She knew that Thierry, like his father Pierre had been, was intuitive and, if she wasn't careful, would pick up on the fact that something had happened. She'd open the letter after the party – maybe this evening when she came to bed, or tomorrow morning.

Vivienne was in the kitchen Saturday morning, drinking her second cup of coffee and planning her day. Despite losing writing time over the past week by having lunch and clothes shopping in Valbonne with Maxine, as well as going to Cannes for cinema on the beach, she'd managed to snatch a few hours in the evenings and up her word count. This morning, she'd decided to walk into Antibes for a mooch around, treat herself to a new lipstick and possibly a new tube of foundation from the beauty shop she'd seen in one of the main streets. Tonight, she planned on having a leisurely bath before getting ready for the party, so buying a bottle of her favourite bubble bath was also on the list. She'd have lunch up on the terrace and then an afternoon of writing before getting ready for the party.

Sipping her coffee, Vivienne thought about the party. It would be the first time in years that she had gone out socialising by herself on a Saturday night and the nerves were already starting to kick in. Was it too late to cancel? Or just fail to turn up? Always more of an introvert than an extrovert, she never felt at her best meeting new people. The female guests tonight were sure to be like Maxine, trés chic in a typical French way, they'd all know each other and she'd be the object of curiosity. Maxine, though, was lovely, so hopefully her friends would be too – although Olivia's mother did sound difficult.

An unexpected knock on the apartment door brought her out of her reverie. Expecting to see Olivia when she opened it, Vivienne stared in surprise at a young woman standing there.

'*Bonjour,*' Vivienne said.

'*Bonjour. Je suis Sarah, la femme de menage.*'

'Oh.' Vivienne had completely forgotten about Maxine telling her the cleaner would arrive on Saturday mornings. Because she'd arrived midweek, she'd said it wasn't worth the cleaner coming when she'd only been there for two and a half days. Today was the first time. '*Entrez.*'

While Sarah set about the sitting room, Vivienne went into the bedroom to make sure drawers were closed and clothes were hanging in the wardrobe rather than simply thrown onto the chair. Picking up her bag and phone, she returned to the sitting room to tell Sarah she was leaving her to it.

'*Au revoir,*' she said, smiling her goodbye as she let herself out of the apartment.

Strolling along the coast road and onto the ramparts as she made her way towards Antibes old town, Vivienne thought about the past ten days. So different to the way she'd been expecting to spend her time – much nicer in fact. Although, having said that, Jeremy's unexpected bombshell at the airport had left her reeling, her happy preconceptions of the weeks to come shattered, engulfing her in gloom and despondency. Now, standing looking down over the rocks towards the curve of Plage de la Gravette to the left, Vivienne realised how good the past week had been. And that was down to Maxine in particular but also Olivia. The two of them had offered her unconditional friendship despite her initial behaviour towards them.

Vivienne watched as sun worshippers down on the beach spread out their towels and set up windbreaks for privacy rather than to keep the gentle breeze coming off the Mediterranean at bay. With the day already heating up, the on-shore breeze would be more than welcome by mid-morning. Vivienne followed the progress of a two-masted yacht for a few moments as it sailed slowly across the bay in the direction of Nice or perhaps Monaco, while further out at sea a giant cruise ship was moving in a westerly direction. Closer inland, there were smaller boats – dinghies and canoes – enjoying the calm sea conditions.

A tour group of Japanese tourists, led by a tall man holding a large sunshine-yellow umbrella high above his head, began to jostle their way past Vivienne en route to the Grimaldi museum. Conscious she was in the way, Vivienne turned and began to walk down the incline towards the bottom of the market.

The market was crowded and she quickly made for a small street that she hoped would lead her in the general direction of the beauty shop she wanted. Passing a women's hairdresser, Vivienne paused and read the notice in the window. 'Rendez-vous are not always necessary'. She peered through the window. There were a couple of clients in chairs with hair being blow-dried or cut. Other chairs were empty. Staff not working with clients were busy at the reception desk checking through some paperwork. The whole place looked very professional.

Almost before she realised what she was doing, she'd walked inside, and after a brief conversation with Samantha the receptionist in fractured Franglais which made them both laugh, Vivienne found herself enveloped in a swish black cape and sitting before a sink having the best hair wash and head massage ever. A short consultation with Samantha over a picture book of styles and five minutes later head stylist Gaspard was wielding a pair of scissors over her hair. Vivienne closed her eyes and gave herself up to a strange, liberating feeling as she sensed chunks of her hair falling past her to litter the area around the chair.

Sometime later, when the scissors stopped flashing around her head and Gaspard said, *'J'ai fini.* You like?' Vivienne opened her eyes and silently stared at the woman's reflection in the mirror. A woman she didn't fully recognise for several seconds, but when finally she did, she turned to Gaspard with a huge smile on her face.

'Merci, bien, merci,' she said before turning to look at herself again. A pixie cut that back home she would have refused to even contemplate had replaced her normal longish bob and wisps of hair now framed her face, highlighting her eyes and cheekbones.

After thanking both Samantha and Gaspard and paying the bill with a generous tip for both of them, Vivienne almost skipped out of the shop with a happy smile on her face.

A street away she found the make-up shop and bought lipstick, foundation and a wickedly expensive bottle of bath bubbles. On the way home, passing a snack bar in one of the streets in the old town selling delicious-looking *pan bagnats* stuffed full of salade Niçoise, she stopped and bought one.

Sarah had left by the time Vivienne let herself back into the apartment and she quickly put her things away. Pouring a glass of rosé and picking up the *pan bagnat,* she climbed the stairs up to the terrace to eat her lunch.

Half an hour later, she was busy tapping away on her laptop.

* * *

After Vivienne put the finishing touches to her make-up and put on the green dress, she stood in front of the wardrobe mirror gazing doubtfully at this strange new version of herself. The new hairstyle had been a drastic change in itself, but coupled with the green dress, was it a transformation too far? The flared skirt of the dress swished, skimming her calves as she turned from side to side looking at herself from every angle. Could she live up to this new image of herself that she was presenting to the world? Tonight she was about to find out.

As Vivienne turned to pick up her bag, there was a knock on the apartment door. A glamorous Olivia was standing there when she opened it.

'Wow,' Olivia said, stepping back and taking in Vivienne's changed appearance. 'You look fabulous. Love the hair and that dress is beautiful. Did Maxine take you to Giselle's by any chance?'

'Thank you. And yes, this is a Giselle dress.'

'Maxine was worried you wouldn't turn up to the party on your own so she suggested I collected you and we walk there together.'

'You don't know how close that came to being the truth earlier,' Vivienne said, laughing.

13

The door of L'Abri was open as Vivienne and Olivia walked down the mews-like street, where perfume from the pots of night-scented jasmine either side of the door was filling the evening air. Maxine had chosen a playlist of music from the big band era of the 1930s to set the mood for the evening and currently a Glenn Miller tune was wafting through the cottage out into the street.

Vivienne hung back, letting Olivia take the lead into the cottage as they both heard laughter and conversation drifting out. Once they'd accepted glasses of champagne from one of the waiters circulating amongst the guests with laden drink trays, they stood for a few moments on the terrace taking in the scene before them.

Solar lights were popping into action all around as the sun set. Candles were already lit in tall vintage metal holders with decorative glass panels placed in the flower beds at strategic places, as well as a couple hanging from the trees at the bottom of the garden. Glamorous-looking people were poised around the garden like statues that unexpectedly came to life as they laughed or raised their champagne flutes to drink. It was a scene that Vivienne had never imagined being a part of, a scene that she needed to memorise every detail of to write about later.

'Hello,' Giselle said, joining them on the terrace. 'Vivienne, I recognised the dress before you. You look so different. Love the new hairdo.'

'Thank you,' Vivienne said. 'I promised to wear the green dress but the new haircut was unexpected and to tell you the truth I hardly recognise myself this evening.'

'That's good. We all need to shake things up a bit sometimes. It's good for my business, if nothing else,' Giselle said, smiling.

As Giselle moved away to talk to someone else, Olivia saw Maxine standing down by the pond and caught her breath at the sight of her companion. What was Thierry doing here? The last time Maxine had mentioned him he'd definitely still been in Singapore doing something financial and scandalously profitable. She'd never so much as dropped a hint that he would be here tonight.

Because of Trent and Pierre's long friendship Olivia had known Thierry all her life. Five years older than her, he'd tended to treat her as his annoying young sister, teasing her affectionately, but never unkindly, whenever the two families got together. He'd always been the first person she turned to whenever she needed to talk something through, or to rant about her mother's latest interference in her life.

Not anymore. Their old easy-going friendship that had developed between them as she grew older, and something Olivia had taken for granted would always be there, had been fractured nearly three years ago, when Olivia accused Thierry of not exactly jettisoning his principles for his current job, but definitely stretching them to accept some of the less than favourable aspects. The resulting argument had driven a distance between them that time had done nothing to close. Olivia missed his presence in her life but had grown used to the empty space he'd left behind.

She had, of course, gone to Pierre's funeral with her parents and she'd also sent a personal message of condolence to Thierry. Her father had told her Thierry's visit back for his father's funeral would be a fleeting one and she'd made sure they didn't meet up face to face on that occasion by leaving immediately after the service. She doubted that Thierry had even realised she was there. He and Maxine, as Pierre's only family, were united in their grief, and from the state of Maxine on that day, Olivia suspected she'd never have got through the service without Thierry at her side.

'Shall we join Maxine?' Vivienne asked, breaking into Olivia's thoughts and looking down the garden towards the pond. 'Do you know the man she is with?'

'Thierry, her stepson.' Hearing her mother's tinkling laughter as she approached the terrace, Olivia began to walk towards Maxine. 'Come on then.' At least this way she wouldn't have to face Thierry alone.

* * *

'I do wish your father was still here,' Maxine said, looking at Thierry. 'This was one of his favourite nights of the year.'

'I struggle to believe sometimes that he's gone,' Thierry said. 'I keep wanting to phone him to tell him something that has happened. Ask his advice. Talk to him. I've even picked up the phone to do just that. But then,' he shrugged, 'I remember.'

Maxine hooked her arm through his. 'I know. It's hard. We just have to cling to the hope that it will get easier with time. How much time we need, though, is open to question,' she added quietly.

Thierry squeezed her hand in sympathy.

'It is good having you back in France,' Maxine said. 'Although I am curious as to why you've returned.'

Thierry took a deep breath and exhaled before saying. 'Losing Papa so unexpectedly has made me re-evaluate certain things in my life. Suddenly, all those so-called important business meetings I was involved in became an irritating waste of time, energy and resources. I couldn't find it in me to care about anything. I decided I needed some time, some space, to work out what is important to me, how I wanted to live my life. I wanted to come home. To be with old friends, people who know me. So I quit.'

'A little drastic?' Maxine said quietly.

'*Peut-être*, but I had to get away.'

'I understand that feeling only too well.' Maxine gave Thierry's arm a sympathetic pat.

'I've only been back a few hours and already I feel lighter, more optimistic, so promise no worrying about me, okay?' Thierry gave her an affectionate look. 'Things will work out.'

Maxine nodded. 'I promise, but don't forget you can always talk to me.'

'Thanks. Now enough about me. Who is this coming with Olivia?'

'Vivienne Wilson, my new writer friend I told you about, staying in Olivia's apartment,' and Maxine smiled in welcome at the two women. 'Vivienne, you look amazing. I adore the new hair. I'm so pleased you kept your promise to come tonight. This is Thierry, my stepson. No need to introduce you, Olivia, you two are old friends.'

'Long time no see.' Olivia's voice had a cool edge to it as she looked at Thierry. 'Two? Three years?'

'I guess it must be.' Thierry nodded, his voice equally subdued.

Maxine, sensing the strained atmosphere between the two of them, gave them both a quick glance as the silence lengthened.

Something was wrong here. These two had always been so easy with each other. Felicity had mentioned something about the two of them falling out ages ago, but surely they'd made up by now?

'Have you introduced Vivienne to your parents yet?' she asked, turning to Olivia, who shook her head. 'In that case, I do it now. We leave you two young people to catch up with each other. I think you have lots to talk about.'

Trent and Felicity had moved to the side of the garden and were admiring the white rambling rose that Maxine had trained along the stone wall dividing the garden from the neighbour.

'Felicity, she can be a little difficult at times and she asks a lot of questions, it is the way she is. I tell myself she doesn't mean to be rude or unkind,' Maxine said as she and Vivienne made their way towards them. 'Pierre, he always say she's impossible and that Trent deserve many medals for staying married to her.'

After she'd introduced Vivienne as a new friend who was staying in Antibes for several weeks to write her next book, Felicity asked, 'What do you write? Will I have heard of you?'

'It rather depends on the kind of books you read,' Vivienne answered. 'I write contemporary women's fiction.'

'Oh romance, something I never read,' Felicity said.

Vivienne opened her mouth to protest, but Maxine beat her to it. '*Non*, not pure romance. Relationship stories about families, sisters, friends. Maybe you try one sometime. I will lend you a copy.'

But Felicity was intent on asking questions. 'Where are you staying in Antibes?'

'In the lovely apartment above Olivia, that's how we met.'

'I can never understand why Olivia doesn't live in it herself. It's far nicer than the bottom one.'

Surprised, Vivienne turned to look at Maxine. 'Olivia owns the villa? She's my landlady?'

Maxine nodded. 'Yes. Something we never tell guests. It is easier to have a go-between in case of problems. I think Olivia would tell you soon. Olivia, she never mixes with the guests, but you two have become friends in a short time, yes?'

Vivienne nodded. 'She and my daughter are about the same age, I think.'

'Your daughter, she is married? Are you a grandmother?' Felicity demanded.

Vivienne laughed. 'No, I'm not a grandmother. Natalie isn't married. Too busy making a success of her catering business. Like Olivia is doing with her flower taxi.'

Felicity made a noise that Vivienne could only think of as a dismissive ladylike snort. 'They'll both miss out if they are not careful. Biological clocks only tick for so long.'

'I'm sure both Olivia and my Natalie are aware of that,' Vivienne said. 'In any case, the way they live their lives is their decision.'

Felicity shrugged. 'I can't stand by silently and watch my daughter leave it too late to have a family.' She held up a hand. 'I know Olivia resents me trying to matchmake and some other people' – turning, Felicity glared at Trent and Maxine – 'think I interfere too much, but I only want the best for her.'

'We both do, but this party is not the place to discuss it,' Trent said firmly. 'So let's change the subject.' He looked at Maxine. 'Thierry arriving was a surprise. Is he okay?'

'I think so. He's staying with me for a short time while he sorts some things out. He misses Pierre like I do, so much. Maybe you could...?'

Trent understood what she was suggesting immediately. 'I'll arrange a get-together soon, see if he wants to talk.'

'You know, I've always thought Thierry would make a good catch for Olivia,' Felicity said, glancing down the garden. 'Lovely person, excellent job with good prospects. Look at the two of them now. Don't they look good together? Perhaps I—'

'Felicity! Stop right there.' Trent's voice was firm, daring his wife to argue. 'Why don't we go and find some of the delicious food Maxine has provided,' and he held out his hand to Felicity, the look on his face daring her to refuse.

* * *

It was Olivia who broke the silence that continued between herself and Thierry for several seconds after Maxine and Vivienne left them.

'Well, that was pretty undiplomatic of Maxine, taking off like that,' she said, giving Thierry a small smile. 'But it is good to see you.' There was no point in denying it even to herself, because it was good to see him. 'A flying visit as usual?'

Thierry shook his head. 'Not this time. I'm back in Europe permanently.'

Olivia's eyes widened in surprise. 'Truly? I thought you'd found your niche over there in Asia.'

Thierry gave a shrug. 'Turns out I prefer to live in France.'

'Pierre would have been pleased to hear that,' Olivia said quietly, remembering how close father and son had been before Thierry's career took him halfway around the world to live.

'Sadly it is too late for that, Tuppence, *mais oui*, I hope somehow he knows.'

Olivia, smiling at his use of her childhood pet name, one she'd never thought to hear him use again, took it as a sign that he was no longer angry with her. Perhaps now would be a good time to try to mend things between them? Apologise for behaving badly and saying things that would have been best left unsaid. Get their friendship back. But before she could speak, Thierry was speaking again.

'Maxine tells me the flower taxi business is blooming?' His lips twitched as he looked at her.

'I'm getting there – petal by petal,' Olivia said, trying not to laugh.

'Did you hear about the flower that never bloomed? It was a bud omen.'

Olivia groaned. 'Still the master of terrible jokes then?'

'I've been saving them up especially for you,' Thierry shrugged. '*Moi*? I can take them or leaf them.'

And just like that they were laughing together, friends once more.

Olivia knew though she wanted to say sorry to Thierry at some point. Their falling out had been mostly her fault. She'd had no right to say the things she did, no wonder he'd responded angrily. Now, as the two of them laughed and chatted, she promised herself that at the first opportunity that presented itself, she'd apologise to him. Tonight wasn't the right night, but soon.

14

A crescent moon was silver in the light-polluted starless sky as Vivienne made her way up to the terrace, taking a glass of water and her mobile with her. Still buzzing after an evening of socialising, ten minutes sitting looking out over and listening to the gently dancing waves of the Mediterranean lapping the shore would help calm her down and hopefully the water would banish any chance of a hangover in the morning. Not that she'd drunk too much, she never did, but champagne always tended to give her a headache for some reason. Probably the bubbles, she reasoned.

The party had been fun and she'd enjoyed herself far more than she'd expected. Maxine had introduced her to so many of her friends and made sure she wasn't left alone, or without a drink. Olivia too had kept an eye on her, and later on in the evening she'd spent time with her and Thierry, whom Vivienne had liked instantly, thinking that they made an attractive couple. She'd noticed that after saying hello to her parents at the beginning of the party Olivia had kept her distance from them. Vivienne gave a small smile. Who could blame her when Felicity was so clearly still in helicopter mother mode despite Olivia being an adult. As she and Olivia had thanked Maxine for a wonderful evening before they left together to walk home, Vivienne had impulsively suggested supper at the apartment on Wednesday evening to the two of them. 'My way of saying thanks to both of you for making me feel so welcome.'

Picking up her phone that she'd left behind for the evening, Vivienne began to scroll through a list of messages and missed calls. Damn she'd missed a call from Tim. Too late to call him now, she'd send him a quick text, make sure he was okay. With the exception of one 'How are you?' message from Natalie, the remaining four messages with their demanding 'Phone Me. Very important.' were all from Jeremy as were all the missed calls. She quickly sent Natalie a text message with a thumbs up sign and saying she'd ring in the morning. As for all those messages from Jeremy, she certainly wasn't going to phone him at this time of night, so she deleted them all. She'd deal with whatever it was in the morning. Nothing could be that urgent. Right now it was time for bed after a lovely evening spent with new friends.

'I think your party was a terrific success, felicitations,' Thierry said as he and Maxine wandered through the garden after all the guests had left, blowing out the candles that were still alight.

'*Merci*, Thierry.' Maxine glanced at him. Would he think her a crazy old woman if she told him she'd had a strong sense of Pierre's presence tonight in the garden? Had even imagined she'd seen him standing there, once in the shadows by the pergola benevolently surveying the scene. The second time he'd been down by the pond watching the fish. Something he'd done every evening when they were in L'Abri. It made her feel happy thinking his spirit had been here in the garden tonight, as if he was giving her his blessing for going it alone.

'Although it wasn't the big ordeal I expected – you being here made it easier, thank you for coming.' She smothered a sigh, pushing her imagined sightings to the back of her mind. 'It's another first survived without Pierre at my side,' she said. '*C'est la vie.*' Time to change the subject. 'You and Olivia are friends again? Felicity told me she thought the two of you had an argument before you went to Singapore.'

Thierry nodded. 'Yes, we're friends again.'

'*Bon,*' Maxine said, waiting and hoping he'd say more, but his next words changed the subject.

'The candles are all out,' Thierry said, glancing around the garden. 'Would you like me to lock up while you go straight to bed?'

Maxine nodded, unable to speak. In that moment, Thierry had looked and sounded so like his father that it had taken her breath away. Managing to murmur a quiet '*Bon nuit,* I'm so happy you are here,' as she kissed his cheek, she left him in the garden and went straight to her room.

After the nightly ritual of cleansing her face and cleaning her teeth, Maxine sat on the dressing-table stool and stared at the white envelope she'd placed on the glass top of the dressing table hours ago. Hesitantly, she picked it up and studied it again. Rereading the name of the legal firm who had sent it instantly brought back memories of those terrible days years ago.

She knew without a doubt that opening the envelope, reading the letter that would be enclosed, whatever it said, good or bad, it would bring all the hurt, resentment and bitterness back up to the surface. Could she bear to open it? Relive the total disillusionment when somebody she had believed herself in love with had cut off all contact and disappeared out of her life, separating her from the one person she'd loved more than life itself.

But how could she choose not to open it? She knew with absolute certainty that she'd be devastated once again if it failed to give her the news that she'd longed to receive for so many years. But there was a slim chance surely that the letter would contain welcome news? She couldn't take the risk of not opening the letter and missing it.

Knowing that she was in an impossible situation – sleep would evade her despite her tiredness if she didn't open the envelope, but the chances were she wouldn't sleep once she'd seen and read the contents of the letter – Maxine took a deep breath. Carefully opening the envelope, she pulled its contents out slowly. An official-looking typewritten letter was folded in half around a smaller, sealed white envelope with her name handwritten across the face of it. Staring at the word with its loopy and exaggerated curves, Maxine felt her heart quicken. Was he finally going to give in after all these years? She placed the sealed envelope on the dressing table. Taking a deep breath, Maxine unfolded the official letter and began to read:

Dear Maxine Zonszain, it is with regret that we write to inform you...

15

The persistent ringing of the phone on her bedside table, coupled with her usual morning alarm call, broke through Vivienne's deep sleep at six thirty the next morning. In a daze, stretching out her arm to reach the phone, her hand fumbled around and knocked it on to the floor, where it noisily carried on ringing.

Groaning, Vivienne leant over the edge of the bed and, finally locating the phone, grabbed it and sat up. Knowing instinctively who it would be, she didn't bother to look at caller ID, she simply pressed the button. Immediately, Jeremy's voice was loudly berating her. It was far too early to cope with one of his tantrums, so she disconnected the call and switched the phone off. Throwing herself back onto the mattress, she lay there for some minutes thinking murderous thoughts about Jeremy before throwing off the duvet and making for the shower.

Half an hour and a strong coffee later, Vivienne picked up her phone and called Jeremy, braced for another outburst from him. As soon as she heard him on the line, she interrupted him. 'If you start yelling and shouting at me, Jeremy, I shall hang up and block you. So tell me what it is you want.'

'What I want is for you to come home and sign some papers so we can both get on with our lives.'

'I'm getting on with my life quite happily,' Vivienne answered. 'Anyway, what papers?'

'House papers. The estate agent has been and the house is ready to go on the market, but he needs your signature on the for-sale agreement papers as well. He has several people already lined up to view. Reckons it's a desirable property and will sell quickly. So if you come home Monday or Tuesday, we can get it done.'

'Stop right there. First, I am not coming home next week. Secondly, I haven't agreed to sell the house yet. If and when I do, you can scan the papers to me for my signature.'

'But we have to sell so we can both move on.' Jeremy said angrily.

'There is no "have to" about it for me.'

'You're just being difficult.'

'Did you really expect me to agree to you getting your own way over everything? You chose to have the affair with that person I can't bear to name but you expect me to pay the price and give up my home instantly because you want to move on. I'll sign those papers when I have a plan in place for me – and not before.'

'Bitch.' And the line died before he could have heard Vivienne muttering a quiet, retaliating 'Bastard' at the man she'd once loved but now hated.

Vivienne closed her eyes and shook her head. What had their marriage become? Where had the man she'd been married to for so long gone? She'd never known Jeremy to behave like this before. He'd always been prone to a short temper when stressed but had been reasonably quick to calm down. At the airport when he'd told her he was leaving, he'd done it in a sad but composed way, blaming himself, but now she was refusing to make life easy for him by agreeing to sell, he claimed she was being difficult. Perhaps it would be better if she simply gave in and signed the papers, try to stay civilised for the sake of Natalie and Tim. And sort her life out afterwards. But that would be tantamount to giving in to his bullying and she'd always hated bullies. No, she would sign the papers eventually, but she would hang it out for as long as possible.

Once the divorce happened, and happen it would, she had no doubt about that now, and the house was sold, she'd be a free woman to go wherever she wanted. Free to create a new life for herself. A life on her own terms. The only questions were, what would she do and where would she go?

Maxine dragged herself out of bed late Sunday morning after a restless night with very little sleep. A shower revived her somewhat and she made her way downstairs hoping Thierry wouldn't notice the dark circles under her eyes that she'd done her best to conceal. There was no sign of him as she walked into the kitchen. A note was next to a bag of fresh croissants alongside the coffee machine.

Unexpectedly meeting an old friend for breakfast. See you later, T.

Maxine exhaled a deep sigh of relief. As much as she adored Thierry, and she truly did, she was grateful for his unexpected absence from the cottage this morning. She needed time alone to assimilate the contents of the two letters and to decide what to do about them. If anything.

The official letter with its unexpected, but also, if she were truthful, welcome news, was easy enough to deal with. Daiva

Toussaint was dead. The man she had grown to hate with every fibre of her body was finally, permanently, out of her life.

It was the second letter in the smaller envelope that had truly blown her mind as she'd read it last night. That letter had the ability to turn her life completely upside down. Currently, though, her mind was in a whirling turmoil as to whether that would be a good or a bad thing. Was it thirty years too late? Would it be better not to respond? Importantly, did the person whom it concerned the most, even know it had been written? Let alone what it was proposing?

Before taking her coffee and a croissant outside, Maxine ran upstairs and fetched the white envelope with its letter to reread as she ate her breakfast under the loggia.

Maxine, if you are reading this you will have been informed that I am dead. I have no expectations that you will mourn me. This letter is to legally confirm permission and to instruct you to contact Leonie Tous-saint. I hope you will put aside any reservations you may harbour and do the right thing even after all this time. She will need you. The lawyers will need to see this letter before they give you the contact details. Daiva.

Maxine placed the letter on the table and closed her eyes in despair. Only Daiva could have penned such a letter. Short, to the point and completely devoid of any emotion. The phrase 'do the right thing even after all this time' made her want to scream. He was the one who had originally done the wrong thing and then prevented her from doing anything about it. Anything. Right or wrong. But, as usual, there was no admission of guilt or an apology from Daiva. He'd told her once that his Indian mother had chosen his name because it meant 'by the grace of god'. Maxine had never met anyone who deserved the name less.

Drinking her coffee, she wished, as she did so often these days, that Pierre was still alive. He'd know how to deal with this bombshell from her past. Help her decide what was the right, the best, thing to do. Her first instinct might be to take a leap into the unknown, make contact and hang the consequences, but so much could go wrong. Contacting Leonie Toussaint would mean opening up old painful wounds and Maxine wasn't at all certain that her heart would physically survive another damning emotional attack that would surely reopen all the old scars that had left her permanently damaged.

'That was so delicious,' Olivia said, swallowing the last of her breakfast bruschetta. 'Thank you for suggesting it. I know it's simple to make, but somehow the Italian cook here turns tomatoes and mushrooms on sour dough toast into a real treat. I can't remember the last time I had bruschetta here in the market. Probably with you before you went away. Talking of which, I need to apologise to you. I am sorry. I shouldn't have needled you about your job. It was nothing to do with me.' There, she'd apologised.

Thierry shook his head. 'No apology needed, Tuppence. You were looking out for me, concerned that I was doing the wrong thing. If an apology is due, it's from me to you. I can admit now that you were right. It wasn't the job for me, but at the time chasing the big money...' He shrugged. 'It seemed the thing to be doing. Papa, he didn't want me to take the job either,' Thierry admitted quietly. 'He told me several times that I wasn't living the life he wanted for me. The one that would make me happy.'

'I was so sorry about Pierre. I loved him too.' Olivia reached out to touch Thierry's hand resting on the table and he gave it a squeeze as he grasped it. 'Do you have any plans for finding a job that will make you happy?'

Thierry shook his head. 'I have a couple of ideas that I need to check out. There's no rush. I have savings, and since Papa died...' He shrugged. 'Let's say I can take my time deciding what to do. I know one or two things that I don't want to do and the first is I don't want to live in Asia any longer, and secondly...' He took a deep breath. 'I don't want to be a player in a high-powered business world anymore. But as to what I do want.' He gave her a quizzical look. 'Not quite sure.'

'Inheriting Aunt Daphne's flower business got me out of the rat race that I hated,' Olivia said quietly. 'Being a florist wasn't something I'd ever thought about doing, but I love being back in France and running the flower taxi. Maman isn't so thrilled and seems to be increasing her efforts to find me a rich husband so I can give it all up and settle down to give her the grandchildren she is apparently desperate for. But the men she keeps introducing me to are not my type at all. I'm pretty sure you'll meet one of them, Harry, at the Grand Prix next Sunday. Maman is sure to have invited his parents and him.' She turned to look at Thierry. 'You are coming to that, aren't you?'

'Of course. Family tradition. Papa, he always insist we spend race day with Trent and Felicity.'

'It will be hard for you this year,' Olivia said. 'But I know Dad will make sure you're okay and I shall rely on you to rescue me from Harry – not to mention from my mother.'

* * *

Vivienne spent the rest of Sunday writing and managed to push all thoughts of her future into a deep recess in her mind after 'that' phone call with Jeremy. She'd think about the future another time. Today she would concentrate on the book.

It was four o'clock when her mobile rang, breaking her concentration, and she quickly glanced at the caller ID before smiling in relief. Natalie not Jeremy.

After the usual pleasantries, Natalie said, 'I've spoken to Tim and I was right. He did suspect that Dad was playing away. He and the team had answered a call on the outskirts of town just after Christmas and he got a brief glimpse of him walking along, with his arm around the shoulders of a crying woman.'

'Why didn't he say something to you or even to me?'

'Apparently he tackled Dad about it the next time he saw him and Dad assured him he was just comforting a friend who'd had some bad news. Tim did say he wasn't sure he believed him at the time, but he didn't have any evidence to call him out on it.'

'Did Tim recognise the woman?'

'Nope. Said the patient they'd picked up was critical and they had the blue lights and the siren on so they were going too fast and he was too busy after that.'

'Have you spoken to Dad recently? Has he told you her name yet?'

'No to both questions. Have you heard from him?'

'He bombarded me with messages yesterday evening. I'd gone to a party and left my phone here, so I didn't pick them up. He was very cross with me when he rang at six thirty this morning,' Vivienne said. 'Especially when I refused to do what he wanted me to do.' She quickly went on to explain to Natalie about the house sale. 'Told me I was being difficult because he wants to get on with his new life as quickly as possible. And then he called me a rude name and hung up on me!'

Natalie was silent for a second or two. 'Dad might be keen to get on with this new life he wants, but do you have any idea yet what you're going to do with your new life? When it's all settled down?'

'I truly have no idea at the moment,' Vivienne answered. 'For the immediate future, I am going to concentrate on what I came down here for, writing my next book. Oh, can you switch into video mode?' she said, pressing the video button on her own phone. Time to change the conversation. 'Look what I had done yesterday.'

'Mum! I love it. That style really suits you. So how was the party last night?'

'It was great. Maxine's friends were all welcoming and next Sunday a couple of them, Felicity and Trent, have invited me to a party in Monaco to watch the Grand Prix.'

'Tim will be totally envious when I tell him that,' Natalie said. 'Any news on our French connection?'

'No, sorry. I haven't had time to do anything with that yet, but I will soon, I promise.'

'Okay, I'd better go, cakes to make for tomorrow. When I talk to Dad next, I shall make a point of telling him that you are having a ball down there,' Natalie said, laughing as the call finished.

16

Vivienne thought about the conversation with Natalie as she prepared a salad and poached egg for her supper. Tim's confession that he'd seen Jeremy all those months ago made her wonder how many other people knew that her husband was having an affair and had chosen not to mention it to her? In a way, she could understand Tim not saying anything to her, especially after Jeremy's glib explanation. He'd been preoccupied with a patient and had had only a brief glimpse of his father with an arm around a woman. Nothing more than that. Besides, who wanted to accuse either of their parents of cheating? Would she have believed Tim back then anyway? She was conscious at the time that she and Jeremy were going through a rough patch but had thought it was nothing that couldn't be sorted by sitting down together and talking. If Tim had said something, perhaps it would have spurred her into taking action to demand the truth about their marriage from Jeremy. On the other hand, it had probably been already too late to save their marriage.

Sitting up on the terrace to eat her lunch, Natalie's question about what was she going to do with this new life of hers popped into Vivienne's mind. A question she'd given the only possible answer to at that moment: concentrate on writing the new book. Otherwise, it was an impossible question to answer until she'd figured out what she wanted to do. Life as a single woman would take some getting used to. So many decisions to be made before a new normal life could resume. The biggest decision she had to make was where would she live once her home was sold? Could she bear to stay in the same town and know everyone was talking about her and Jeremy? Risk the chance of bumping into him and her in the supermarket or even simply walking down the street or in the park.

No, she'd have to move away. She hadn't asked for this sudden disruption, but she was the one who had to pick up the pieces of her life and try to create a new order out of the mayhem. At least Natalie and Tim were adults. It wasn't as if they were children who would be traumatised by the whole thing. Maxine had been right when she'd pointed out that while the two of them would obviously be upset at the family breaking up they would accept and move on with their own lives quicker than she would be able to. Vivienne was the one whose whole existence had been thrown up in the air and was currently crashing around her in pieces. And she was the only one too who could pick up the pieces and rearrange her life to give her a happy future by letting Jeremy and the past go.

Finishing her wine, Vivienne loaded the supper dishes into the dishwasher and opened the French connection file on her laptop. This was something from her past that she needed to investigate before she could consign that to history along with Jeremy. She stared at the two items. Jacqueline had left her tantalisingly little to go on. A sealed envelope, with the name Pascal Rocher and his address in Puget Theniers, in the Alpes-Maritimes, and a photograph of a couple who might, or might not be, her birth parents.

Vivienne took a deep breath. She'd start by googling a map to find the location of the village in the countryside behind Nice and then work out a way to get there.

* * *

Maxine spent the next couple of days at home, thankful she had no meetings with holidaymakers for any of the apartments, or clients for house viewings. The weather, all blue skies and sunny days, allowed her to spend the mornings gardening, leaving her subconscious mind to wander over and over the decision she needed to make as she pulled weeds and deadheaded flowers, in the futile hope the right decision would arrive in her brain in a flash, ready-made. With the temperatures hitting the high twenties by midday, Maxine was happy to head indoors for lunch and to spend the afternoons trying to read in the coolest room in the cottage: her bedroom.

Living in the same house, it was impossible to avoid some contact with Thierry, especially at mealtimes. He had clearly noticed she was quieter than usual when they met up – usually for dinner as she'd decided to skip breakfast most days – but so far, beyond a concerned '*ça va?*' he hadn't pushed, for which Maxine was grateful.

Part of her longed to talk to someone about her problem. Thierry would have listened and tried to help she knew, but she also knew she couldn't bring herself to tell him how stupid she'd been and all the circumstances that lay behind the decision she now had to make. Pierre had been the only person she'd ever talked to about Daiva Toussaint, and that had been difficult enough. No point in burdening Thierry with the knowledge as well. Of course she'd have to tell him the truth if she did make contact with Leonie, but until that happened there was little point in mentioning it.

By Wednesday afternoon, Maxine was close to making a decision and settling on a plan of action. When she was absolutely certain it was the right thing to do, she'd get in touch with the lawyer, send him a copy of Daiva's letter and obtain the contact details. She didn't have to do it immediately, she could wait until she was totally certain it was the correct thing to do. She could still decide against using the contact details when the solicitor sent them and consign all the Toussaints to her past.

Thierry was in the sitting room scrolling through his phone when she went downstairs ready to go to Vivienne's for the evening.

'You are going out?' Thierry asked. 'You feel better?'

Maxine nodded. '*Oui*, I'm having supper with Vivienne and Olivia.' She hesitated. Thierry had obviously been more worried about her than she'd thought. 'I am *desolé* if I've been a little off since the party, but normal service resumes *maintenant*,' and she smiled at him.

'*Bon*. I have to admit I was worried. It is not like you to be so quiet,' Thierry said.

'*Merci*. It was just the party, it was you know... a little overwhelming. I'll see you later.' And Maxine quickly left, hoping she'd said enough to stop Thierry worrying and not to probe further the next time they talked.

Olivia spent Wednesday morning down in Port Vauban Marina delivering flowers and commissioned arrangements to the various yachts. Driving the pink taxi home at midday, she thought about her plans for the rest of the week. Grand Prix week was always a busy one for her. A couple of arrangements to create this afternoon for two of the large yachts moored in Monaco, plus the one she always did for her parents' sitting room ready for the Sunday party. Timing was everything during the week because Monaco roads were closed at different times for practice and qualifying for the various road races that would take place over the weekend. Working out a timetable if you needed to get in and out of Monaco and sticking to it was crucial during Grand Prix week.

As she signalled to turn down the narrow lane that led to the villa's garage entrance, Olivia saw Thierry standing on the corner. She gave a quick toot, coupled with a wave, and smiled as he began to make his way across the road to the garage.

'Hi. Have you got time for a coffee or even lunch?'

'A baguette from the beach snack bar would be great,' Olivia said. 'Give me a few minutes to put the leftover flowers in the cold room and I'll be with you.'

'I'll give you a hand,' and Thierry lifted up the nearest urn with its lilies and effortlessly carried it in while Olivia followed with two boxes.

Five minutes later, they were buying cold drinks and salad baguettes from the snack van on the beach and settling down to eat their lunch on one of the benches.

Halfway through his baguette, Thierry gave a contented sigh. 'I've missed this so much,' he said.

'I'm sure you could have got a salad baguette in Singapore if you'd looked in the right place,' Olivia said lightly. 'But that's not what you meant, is it?'

Thierry shook his head. '*Non.*' He gestured around him. 'It's all this. I missed down here more than I missed Paris.'

'Well, when you decide what you're going to do next, you'll have to ensure you can do it from here,' Olivia said.

'You make it sound easy.'

Olivia gave a shrug. 'It might be, it might not, depends on what you decide to do. You did say you had a couple of ideas?'

Thierry nodded. 'I've done a bit of research on one, which has shown it's a no-go. I'll have to see what happens with the next one.'

'Why not talk to Papa? He still seems to have fingers in lots of pies, as they say. He may have a suggestion or two.'

'Good idea. I'll have a word with Trent after this weekend. See if he has any ideas.'

Olivia finished her baguette and brushed the crumbs away. 'I have to get back. Lots to do this afternoon before supper with Vivienne and Maxine. It will feel strange being a guest in my own apartment.'

'Will you let me know how Maxine is please? Since the party she's not been herself and I have the feeling she is avoiding me. I do worry about her.'

'I think perhaps the first garden party without Pierre must have been more difficult for her than we realised,' Olivia said thoughtfully. 'I'll message you if I'm worried about her tonight. Otherwise I'll see you in Monaco on Sunday. Thanks for lunch.'

17

Vivienne spent all Wednesday morning and most of the afternoon up on the terrace writing. Lunch was a quick cheese sandwich, eaten still hunched over her keyboard. At four o'clock, happy with the day's work, she gave a deep sigh and closed her laptop. Time for a shower, a quick dash to the supermarket to buy food for supper and then an evening with Maxine and Olivia.

A couple of hours later, Vivienne gave the terrace a quick sweep and tidied the cushions before putting plates and glasses on the table. In the supermarket earlier as well as food, she'd bought four citronella candles in terracotta pots and, after lighting them, she placed one in the centre of the table and dotted the others along the terrace wall. Hopefully, they'd serve to keep the mosquitoes at bay as well as looking pretty.

Olivia and Maxine arrived together, minutes after Vivienne had finished carrying the food up to the terrace. Olivia with a posy of flowers, which she handed to Vivienne with a smile, and Maxine handed over a bottle of already chilled rosé, also with a smile.

'You didn't need to bring anything,' Vivienne protested.

'Supper is my way of saying thanks to you both for everything. But thank you anyway.'

Vivienne poured glasses of rosé and the three of them stood by the terrace wall looking out at the view.

'I try to angle my chair to just see the Med when I'm working up here,' Vivienne said. 'I'm so easily distracted by the people on the beach.' She glanced at Olivia. 'I think I saw you with Thierry earlier today.'

'You did. But please don't mention it to my mother on Sunday. She'll immediately start planning our wedding and that would be exasperating because, in the scheme of things, that's not going to happen.' Olivia laughed. 'Thierry has always been in my life and it's good to have him back. He's like my big brother really, he always used to tease me mercilessly when I was younger. Now we're good friends and he just tells me awful jokes.'

'He's a good man,' Maxine said quietly. 'Like his father. I'm glad he's back too.'

'Shall we eat?' Vivienne asked. 'I would like to ask your advice about something.'

As they all tucked into the platter of cold meats and cheeses, olives, mozzarella salad and slices of baguette, Vivienne told them what she knew about her 'French connection'.

'My birth mother came down here on holiday and apparently had a brief romance and returned home pregnant. Her parents sent her away to a mother and baby home and two weeks after I was born, my parents adopted me.' Vivienne paused. 'When Jacqueline, my adoptive mum, died, going through some of her papers, I found my birth certificate, a photograph and a sealed envelope with a man's name written across it and the address of a village in the countryside behind Nice where he lived.'

Vivienne paused and took a deep breath. 'I believe that man to be my birth father and I would like to find him. I've googled and found the village – Puget Theniers – but there doesn't appear to be an easy way of getting there. Do either of you have any ideas how I get there – other than hiring a car? And if that's the best option, I'll probably wait until Natalie gets here and we can go together.'

'Hiring a car, it is the best way,' Maxine said. 'There is a small train to take you to Puget, but then you have the problem to find the address. Perhaps it's in the commune and not in the village itself. I'm happy to drive you. We make a day out and I show you the countryside.'

'Really? That would be wonderful.'

'I might even be tempted to come with you,' Olivia said. 'If you go on a day when I'm not busy. Next week is mostly quiet for me!'

'One day next week it is,' Maxine said. 'I'll sort a day out, probably next Wednesday.'

Olivia glanced at Vivienne. 'May I ask you something? Did you always know you were adopted? And how did you feel about it?'

'Mum and Dad never made a secret of the fact that I was adopted. They always said they had chosen me, which made me feel special, and I didn't question the circumstances. They never said my mother didn't want me. They simply said it was impossible for her to keep me and she wanted a better life for me than the one she could give me. And they gave me that. I had a happy, stable childhood with loving parents.'

'So why the need now to find a man who's never been in your life, and probably doesn't even know of your existence and who, by the way, might be dead? How are you going to feel if he turns out to be...' Maxine shook her head in irritation. 'Oh, I don't know. Someone you wouldn't want to be associated with?'

Both Vivienne and Olivia stared at Maxine, startled at the vehemence behind the sharply spoken words.

'Put like that, I suppose it does seem selfish and silly,' Vivienne finally said. 'But this man is a part of me, whatever he turns out to be like. If he is still alive, surely he deserves to know he had a daughter? To meet her? As much as I have the right to know about my heritage.'

Maxine nodded. 'True. But it is not always good to know the truth. Sometimes the past should be left in peace. Your life, his life, are not part of one of your stories. They are for real. Promise me that you will be careful in case you are lifting the lid on a Pandora's box that will turn out to be uncontrollable.'

'I promise to be careful,' Vivienne said, deciding she needed to change the subject but uncertain as to how to do that. She smothered a sigh of relief when Olivia spoke.

'I'm taking some flower arrangements to a couple of yachts in Monaco tomorrow and then staying with my parents until Monday. It's going to be a busy weekend.'

'I can't believe my first visit to Monaco is for the Monte Carlo Grand Prix,' Vivienne said. 'It's something I never expected I'd do. Tim is going to be so jealous.'

'Parking will be impossible, so we'll go by train early on Sunday morning,' Maxine said. 'I'll organise the tickets.'

'Thank you. How much money do I need to give you?'

'Don't worry about it. You can buy me breakfast at my favourite cafe in Monaco.'

'Fair enough.' Vivienne smiled, glad that the atmosphere had lightened a little. She but couldn't help wondering what exactly had made Maxine so uptight this evening. She hoped it wasn't anything she'd said or unintentionally done.

18

It was late Thursday afternoon before Olivia drove along the lower Corniche to Monaco, the pink taxi filled with a couple of arrangements and some extra flowers for her mother. Traffic, as she'd expected, was busy and she breathed a sigh of relief when she finally drove into the underground garage and parked. She grabbed her overnight case and one of the flower arrangements and took the lift up to the foyer. Crossing to the concierge desk, currently empty, she placed the basket on the desk but didn't push the bell for attention. Ruby, the concierge, was probably taking a quick well-earned break. She'd know who the flowers were from as Olivia brought an arrangement every year for Grand Prix weekend. It was something that Aunt Daphne had done and Olivia was happy to carry on the tradition.

As Olivia stepped out of the lift into the hallway of her parents' apartment, her father opened the door. After enveloping her in one of his trademark hugs, he took her overnight bag from her.

'I've got some flowers to bring up for Maman,' Olivia said. 'I'll fetch them from the car.' And Olivia went back down to the garage.

When she returned with the flowers, her mother was out on the balcony watching the activity in the pits down below. Olivia placed the arrangement on the table in the sitting room and joined her mother on the balcony.

'There's just something in the air during GP week,' she said leaning on the balcony alongside her mother. 'Even now when the cars are in the pit garages with the mechanics and the electronic teams and nothing is out on track, there's a sort of extra energy in the atmosphere giving the place an exciting buzz.'

Felicity nodded in agreement. 'I miss the old days when we used to host team sponsors here for the three days of the weekend. Nowadays, it's just friends and friends of friends for race day.'

'Those race weekends were fun but jolly hard work though,' Olivia said. 'Entertaining strangers is harder than feeding friends. You never quite relax in case anything goes wrong. I enjoy the race and Sundays so much more now. And hiring a couple of waiters to circulate with the food means that you can relax knowing that people are being served.'

'Yes, that certainly helps. I forgot to tell you, we've got an invitation from a friend of Papa's for drinks on one of the yachts tonight,' her mother said.

'Do I have to come?' Olivia questioned. 'I've got a couple of deliveries to do and also the other two arrangements for you.'

'It's not until nine o'clock. You can do the arrangements, we'll have an early supper, and then we can drop off the deliveries on our way.'

Olivia couldn't face arguing with her mother at the beginning of the weekend, so she shrugged. 'Okay. I'll go and make a start on the arrangements now,' she said before turning to leave.

'Have you seen Thierry since the party?' her mother asked.

'Why would I?'

'You used to be such friends, go places together. He'd be quite a catch.'

'Maman, how many times do I have to say it – I'll find my own husband and if I don't, that's my problem, not yours. So stop trying to interfere in my life.' And Olivia walked back indoors before her mother could respond.

Working on the arrangements in the kitchen, Olivia hoped and prayed her mother would not embarrass either her or Thierry, by trying to push them together on Sunday. There was no way she would admit to anyone, least of all her mother, how happy she was to have Thierry back in her life. She might have had a teenage crush on him years ago, but knowing that he was unlikely to ever reciprocate the feeling, she'd made sure she'd left it behind with the rest of her childish dreams when she left for university. After the row they'd had over his job in Singapore and the ensuing horrible silence that had existed between them afterwards, she'd settle for being friends and keeping her opinions about his work to herself.

Thursday evening went according to Felicity's timetable, something Olivia had given into as inevitable. After supper, the three of them went out *en famille* to deliver the flower arrangements to the two yachts that had ordered them and were, thankfully, moored close together in the overcrowded harbour. Trent's friend welcomed them on board his boat and Olivia found herself unexpectedly enjoying herself when one of the guests turned out to be a girl she'd known at university. It was nearly midnight before they said their goodnights to everyone and made their way home.

Friday was as busy as Olivia had expected, helping her mother do the food shopping for Sunday and then preparing and cooking the various dishes that would be the cold buffet on Sunday. Qualifying, on Saturday afternoon, was watched from the balcony in between organising the apartment ready to accommodate twenty-plus people, making sure there were enough glasses and crockery, small tables on the balcony, and dashing down to the nearby *supermarché* for extra crisps, olives and bottles of water.

It wasn't until six o'clock on Saturday that Olivia remembered her promise to phone Thierry about Maxine if she was worried about her. When her father suggested aperitifs on the balcony for the three of them, she said, 'Great idea. You two go ahead. I need to make a phone call. Two minutes, I promise.' She sensed that her mother was itching to ask who was so important, but Olivia went into her bedroom and closed the door.

'Hi, it's me,' she said when Thierry answered. 'I'm sorry I didn't ring before, but it's been all hands to the galley here.'

'Not a problem.'

'I think maybe you are right to be worried about Maxine,' Olivia said. 'She got very agitated on Wednesday evening when Vivienne said she was looking for her birth father. I've never seen Maxine so uptight about something that is nothing to do with her.'

'What did she say?'

'She basically told Vivienne that it wasn't a good idea to look for a man who probably didn't even know about her existence. She also said something along the lines of sometimes the past should be left in peace, which, to be honest, from the way she said it, sounded like it came from personal experience.'

'Mm,' Thierry said thoughtfully. 'I'm having supper with her tonight. I'll try to winkle out what is upsetting her because something definitely is. Thanks for ringing. And you, how are you?'

'Bit tired but looking forward to tomorrow.'

'Me too. I'll see you then.'

* * *

Vivienne gave a happy sigh as she sat on the terrace Saturday evening, watching people stroll along the seafront below her and the lights coming on along the coast. She'd been busy writing for the last two days and had finally hit the halfway mark of her book. Two days of not seeing anyone and no interruptions had been so productive. Still lots to do of course, but she was happier overall now with the way the story was going.

It had been strange at first knowing that Olivia was away and she was alone in the house. Even though she and Olivia rarely saw each other during the daytime, it had been comforting at night knowing that there was someone else around. But it had brought home to her that after her divorce she'd need to get used to living on her own, something she'd not done since her early twenties before meeting Jeremy.

Thankfully, Jeremy had been quiet over the past days, which was a relief. Hopefully now that it was the weekend, he'd be too busy with his lover to harass her tomorrow about selling the house. Vivienne, determined to focus on happier things, pushed away all thoughts of her soon-to-be ex-husband, letting her thoughts drift instead back over the last few weeks. After she'd arrived in Antibes as somewhat of an emotional wreck, she had to acknowledge that whilst those weeks hadn't been the easiest of times, the complete change of pace, of country, had helped her to process and survive Jeremy's behaviour and news. The almost constant blue skies and sunshine down here contributed to a laid-back holiday-vibe lifestyle, which was just what she needed. She'd been lucky too, meeting up with Maxine and Olivia.

A sigh escaped Vivienne's lips as she thought of Maxine. She was clearly putting a brave face on things and struggling to come to terms with the loss of her beloved Pierre. Knowing nothing but time was going to help Maxine overcome that particular hurdle, Vivienne remembered her outburst the other evening. Her short-tempered outburst warning Vivienne to be careful had been spoken with such feeling. Was there something in Maxine's own past that she'd wanted to forget but in truth had never forgotten? Whatever it was, Vivienne promised herself that starting tomorrow whenever she saw Maxine she'd make a real effort to keep the conversation light-hearted and away from things that might unknowingly be a trigger for her.

Vivienne gave a small smile at the thought of tomorrow. Not only was she going to Monaco for the first time, she was going to watch one of the most exciting Grand Prix in the world. Tim had been a keen F1 fan growing up and the street race had been one of his favourites to watch on TV. She and Jeremy had even, on a couple of occasions, taken him to watch the British Grand Prix at Silverstone. Maxine had assured her they would have an unparalleled view of the starting grid from Trent and Felicity's apartment and huge TV screens were in strategic places on the circuit streaming the race. She was definitely going to take a couple of photographs from the balcony and send them to Tim.

Thinking of Tim, Vivienne wondered whether this evening would be a good time to catch him. They had still not managed to actually talk, although there had been a couple of missed calls from him. She desperately wanted to check that he was okay. Quickly she typed a text.

Are you free to talk right now?

A minute later, her phone buzzed. 'Tim. How are you doing?'

'I'm fine. I'm sorry I haven't rung before, my shifts have been all over the place. How are you, Mum? I'm sorry about all this business with Dad. You don't deserve it. Did Nats tell you I think I saw him? I did tackle him about it, but he said it was someone from work who'd had some bad news. I didn't mention it to you because I thought he was telling me the truth and there was no point in upsetting you needlessly.'

'I'm sorry it put you in a difficult position. At least it's all out in the open now,' Vivienne said.

'We'll talk properly when you get back,' Tim said.

'Has Natalie told you where I'm off to this weekend? Monaco for the Grand Prix.'

'She has, and I'm as jealous as hell! Make sure you take some photographs. Mum, I'm sorry, I have to go, I'm on duty in a few minutes. Love you. Take care of yourself.'

Maxine had declined Thierry's invitation on Saturday afternoon to book a table for dinner in a new restaurant in the centre of town, suggesting instead they stayed home.

'Shall we have a barbecue in the garden? Pierre bought one of those small round ones with a lid last summer, but we barely used it. Maybe if I get it set up and leave it out, I'll use it more.'

'Sounds like a fun idea,' Thierry said. 'Love barbecue food. I'll go and buy a few bits and pieces and come back and set it up. I'll buy some charcoal too.'

At eight o'clock, the charcoal was glowing a perfect red and Thierry deemed it to be the right temperature. He put a couple of small steaks, pork chops and sausages on the grill rack and carefully turned and rotated them, closing and opening the lid, until they were cooked. Maxine placed a green salad, slices of baguette, plates and glasses of red wine on the table, watching Thierry as he skilfully cooked their meal.

'You are now officially the champion barbecuer of L'Abri,' Maxine said, toasting him with her glass of wine as Thierry placed the meat on the table. 'Pierre, the first time he used it, managed to burn everything. This is all delicious, thank you.'

They ate in companionable silence for several moments when Thierry glanced across at Maxine. 'May I ask you something?'

Maxine nodded. 'Of course.'

'Earlier this week, you avoided me for a couple of days, saying the garden party memories overwhelmed you, but you've not truly been yourself since I arrived. The post I brought from Paris – was there something there that upset you?' Thierry paused, clearly choosing his next words carefully. 'Something maybe from Daiva Toussaint?'

Maxim's fork slipped through her fingers, clattering onto her plate. 'You know about him?'

'*Oui*. Papa wanted me to know in case there came a time in the future when that man attempted to re-enter your life and Papa was no longer here to protect you. He wanted me to be able to step into his shoes. For you to have someone on your side.'

Maxine pushed her plate away. Her appetite gone. 'Did he tell you everything?'

His eyes full of compassion, Thierry gave a slow nod. 'He also said he was breaking his promise to you by telling me but hoped that you would forgive him. He felt he had no real choice as you have no other family you can turn to. I think your need has happened far sooner than he could have anticipated.'

Maxine took a deep breath. 'One of the letters was from a London solicitor telling me that Daiva had died.'

'How do you feel about that?'

'Relieved that he is no longer around to cause problems. Still angry about his behaviour and the way it caused me such unhappiness. I won't be mourning him,' Maxine said, staring at Thierry, a defiant note in her voice. 'But even in death he tries to control the situation,' she added quietly, standing up. 'There was a letter from him enclosed with the solicitors. I'll fetch it and you can read it.'

When she returned with the letter, Thierry had cleared the table and placed two slices of tarte au citron on the table. 'Dessert. Still a favourite, I hope?'

Maxine nodded as she handed him the letter.

There was a short silence as Thierry read the letter.

'Are you going to do what he wants?'

'One moment I think yes, the next *non*.' Maxine shrugged helplessly. '*Mais*, rationally I don't see I have a choice if I want to live in peace with my actions for the rest of my life. I can either reach out and try to right the wrongs of the past by putting the truth out there, whatever the result. Or I can take the easier option and ignore the letter – leave the past and its hurt buried forever.'

Thierry's mobile rang at that moment, breaking the tension in the air. He held the letter out to Maxine before taking out his phone and glancing at the caller ID. 'It's Trent.'

'Go ahead, answer him. Give him my love,' and Maxine went into the study to put the letter down on the desk there.

Thierry was sat waiting for her at the table, the two slices of tart had been joined by a pot of crème fraiche, when she returned.

'Shall we eat dessert? Shame to waste these.'

'Trent and Felicity okay?' Maxine asked, spreading some crème on the top of her tart.

'They've offered me a bed for the night tomorrow. I might just take them up on their offer if that's okay with you?'

'Of course.' Maxine hesitated. 'But you won't talk to them about...' She let the unfinished sentence linger in the air as she gave him an anxious look. 'Pierre is the only person I've ever told.'

'It's your business, Maxie, no one else's. Just remember I'm here if you ever want to talk something through, *d'accord*?'

'*Merci*.'

* * *

Later that evening before going upstairs to bed, Maxine went into the study, picked up the letter again and studied it thoughtfully. Decision time. Sitting at the computer, she wrote an email to the lawyer asking for Leonie's contact details, scanned Daiva's letter into the computer and attached it to the email. Several heart-thumping seconds passed before she slowly and deliberately pressed the send key.

There, the first step had been taken. Whether she would be brave enough to take the next all-important one remained to be seen. But knowing Thierry was at her side, willing to help if she needed it, made her feel stronger and ready to right the wrongs of the past, whatever it might take her.

19

Although the early train to Monaco from Antibes that Sunday was crowded, Vivienne enjoyed the ride along the coast. On her right, the Mediterranean glistened in the early-morning sunshine, and through the carriage windows on her left, she caught glimpses of the towns that lined the coast and the villas up in the hills. Some stations, bright with hanging baskets, the train powered through, others they came to halt by platforms crowded with people jostling their way onto the train. Names of places she'd only ever read about – Eze, Villefranche-sur-Mer – flashed by in a blur. When the train entered the tunnel at Cap-d'Ail which would take them into the centre of Monaco, Vivienne marvelled at the unexpected length of it. And the huge cave-like station carved out of the rock almost took her breath away as she stepped onto the platform at journey's end.

Maxine, familiar with the station layout, led her to the moving walkway that would take them out of the station. 'The other exit and entrance means a longer walk down to the harbour,' she explained as they stood on the moving pavement. 'Besides, my favourite breakfast cafe is nearer this way.'

Walking down the hill towards the harbour, Vivienne gazed around her, trying to memorise everything she was experiencing. The huge TV screens, the harbour packed so tightly with large yachts, the red Ferrari flags alongside Monaco red and white national flags, all flying from apartment blocks and other tall buildings. The place was buzzing with activity, noise and a general air of excitement under a brilliant blue sky with its golden orb already warming the day up.

After an indulgent breakfast of waffles with maple syrup and cream and a large pot of coffee in a little cafe in a quiet side street, they began to make their way down to Trent and Felicity's apartment overlooking Port Hercule. Passing a stall selling Ferrari souvenirs, Vivienne stopped and bought a Ferrari sweatshirt for Tim. No point in buying Natalie anything with Ferrari or F1 emblazoned across it, she wasn't that keen on motorsports. Vivienne would buy Natalie something cookery-related another day.

Not yet eleven o'clock and already the Principality was heaving with people. Both Maxine and Vivienne heaved a sigh of relief as they stepped into the cool of Trent and Felicity's apartment block and pressed the button for the lift to take them to the tenth floor.

Olivia was waiting to greet them and quickly took them through to leave their things in the small cloakroom before leading them out to the balcony, where Trent broke off his conversation with Thierry and poured them both a glass of champagne.

'We are the first to arrive?' Maxine asked.

'Yes, we've said twelve o'clock to everyone else, but old friends are different,' Trent said, leaning in and kissing her on the cheek, before turning to Vivienne and kissing her cheek too. 'Welcome to Monaco, new old friend.' He turned and handed them both a lanyard with a pit pass attached. 'Put these around your necks and when you're ready, I'll take you down for a quick look at the pit lane.'

Standing on the balcony, sipping champagne, watching all the activity of race preparation down below, Vivienne, grown-up woman that she was, couldn't help but feel a little out of her depth. It was a surreal experience being on a balcony in Monaco, but one she was determined to make the most of. She took a couple of photos on her phone and WhatsApped them to Tim.

Half an hour later, Maxine having elected to stay in the apartment, Trent was guiding Vivienne along a crowded pit lane pointing out the different cars and celebrities and even introducing her to Toto Wolff, head of the Mercedes F1 team, who was apparently a friend of his from 'the old days'. He didn't explain about those days and Vivienne didn't like to ask.

'The time to come down here is after the race – it's really buzzing then, especially around the winning team,' Trent said. As they dodged around journalists and cameramen, Trent looked at his watch. 'We'd better make our way back to the apartment ready for the race.'

As they walked back along Boulevard Albert 1er, they passed the podium where later that afternoon the winner would be presented with his trophy by one of the Monaco Royal family, usually Princess Charlene.

'Tim, my son, is going to be incredibly jealous of me when I return home and show him all these photographs,' Vivienne said, taking another quick photo on her phone, this time of the pristine podium before the champagne was sprayed everywhere.

Back at the apartment, more guests had arrived and the sitting room was crowded. The catering assistants Felicity had hired were busy placing the lunchtime food on the table, alongside more champagne in ice buckets, crockery and cutlery. Vivienne spotted Maxine out on the balcony talking to Felicity and made her way over to them.

'You trust the catering assistants to do their job, why can't you trust Olivia to find herself the right husband?' Maxine was saying quietly as Vivienne joined the two of them.

'It's not the same thing at all. These people are professionals, good at their job. Olivia...' Felicity shrugged. 'I'm just trying to guide her in the right direction. She is her own worst enemy as far as choosing men is concerned.'

Maxine laughed. '*Non*, she is not. You have to stop interfering in her life.'

Felicity turned to Vivienne. 'You're a mother, I'm sure you're the same with your daughter, worried that she will make a bad choice and then have to live with it for years. As a mother, you can see instantly the men they like are not right for them.'

'Natalie has had a few dud boyfriends, for want of a better description, but she always sussed them out by herself in the end. You do have to trust them,' Vivienne said, hoping that agreeing with Maxine wouldn't upset her hostess.

She needn't have worried because Felicity simply sighed as she looked into the sitting room where Thierry and Olivia were standing chatting to several mutual friends. 'Look at them. Thierry would be absolutely perfect for her. Why can't she see that?'

'Probably because you keep telling her?' Maxine suggested. 'If you're not careful, you are going to drive a big wedge between both them and the two of you. Let's change the conversation.' She peered over the balcony before straightening up. 'Shall we go and get some food? Some of the cars are coming out to take their places on the grid. We need to have lunch out of the way before the race starts.'

The atmosphere out on the balcony as race start time got closer was jovial. There was a lot of light-hearted banter, especially amongst the men about who people hoped the eventual winner would be. Local boy Charles Leclerc driving for Ferrari and starting from third on the grid was clearly a favourite and people were hopeful that he would finally win his home race. But the general feeling was that this season was proving to belong to Max Verstappen, who was once again in pole position on the grid, and that it would be the Red Bull driver who crossed the line first. Again.

Two hours later, Max Verstappen stormed past the finishing line in first place as expected, with Charles Leclerc finishing in sixth place. Everyone crowded into the sitting room to watch the presentation by Princess Charlene on the TV. The podium, being virtually next to the apartment block, was in their blind spot and was impossible to see from the balcony.

Afterwards, people began to say their goodbyes to Felicity and Trent, keen to join the jubilant crowds, and hoping to see a few celebrities.

Vivienne, standing with Maxine out on the balcony watching normal traffic moving again along the front and up towards the Monte Carlo Casino, wondered what time they would be leaving.

Maxine, as if sensing her thoughts, glanced at her. 'Tonight Monaco will be Party HQ for the locals, and *peut-être* one or two of the drivers who live here, everyone else will either have left or be busy packing things up. We stay a short time for the evening party here, yes? We leave after eight? The train should be a little quieter by then.'

'Felicity has another party here tonight?' Vivienne said.

'Not a party-party, just friends hanging out and watching everything going on down below. Like I said, there will be many parties going on all over Monaco and on the yachts. Most people will want to be down there where the action is, hoping to see some celebrities enjoying themselves.'

20

Vivienne and Maxine said their goodbyes and thank yous to Felicity and Trent shortly before eight o'clock. When Thierry saw they were leaving, he said he'd walk them to the station. Maxine glanced at him, only to receive a warning glance from him, and she smiled understandingly. Olivia came across to say goodbye before following her mother to talk to two guests still out on the balcony, and the three of them rode the lift to the ground floor.

Maxine waited until they were outside the apartment block before looking at Thierry. 'So chivalrous of you, Thierry, but I suspect you have an ulterior motive? You will not be walking us to the station, will you?'

'Guilty as charged,' Thierry said. 'I'm meeting an old friend in, hopefully, about ten minutes.'

'When that old friend can get away without her maman noticing?' Maxine inclined her head at him. 'You didn't want to alert a certain other person to your plan in case she got the wrong idea.'

'Life could get complicated if a certain person got the wrong idea.'

'Mmm, true. But I have to tell you she's on your case already.'

Thierry shrugged and smiled. 'It's not a problem for me. I'm just trying to shield Olivia a little from her mother's unnecessary matchmaking.'

'Good luck with that,' Maxine said. 'See you back at L'Abri tomorrow.' But she couldn't help wondering, as she and Vivienne left him, whether Thierry was fonder of Olivia than he was admitting.

* * *

Leaving Maxine and Vivienne to make their own way to the station, Thierry turned and made for the Quai Antoine 1er, where he hoped Olivia would meet him soon. Twenty minutes later and the two of them were mingling with the crowds walking along the quay.

'How much time have we got before you have to leave?' Olivia asked. 'Or are you in town over tonight?'

'If you remember, Papa and I always used to stay after the Grand Prix,' Thierry said. 'Felicity has offered me a bed for the night. Said she doesn't see any reason to change that arrangement.'

'Of course she doesn't,' Olivia said, smiling. 'My maman will stop at nothing to force me to spend time with any man she thinks suitable in the hope that she can marry me off and, I'm sorry, but she clearly thinks you're a suitable candidate. Providing a bed for you for the night is no problem.'

'Maxine's already warned me she's on the case.'

Olivia groaned. 'I knew it. Somehow we have to get her to accept that she's wasting her time. That we're just good friends, like we've always been. I'll tell her, but she never listens to me, especially when she's got an idea into her head, so you're going to have to tell her too.'

'I'll tell her not to get her hopes pinned on me,' Thierry agreed.

'And I'll point out that you're currently unemployed and plan on becoming down and out rather than jumping back on the career ladder and, with luck, she'll back-pedal so fast, we won't see her go.'

'The phrase down and out should do it,' Thierry said, laughing. 'But I seriously hope it doesn't come to that.'

'Well, if you want a lift back to Antibes early tomorrow morning,' Olivia said, 'Daisy and I will be leaving about eight o'clock.'

'Perfect timing for me, thank you.'

Olivia gave a happy sigh as they walked further along the quay. 'I love the evening atmosphere after the Grand Prix,' she said. 'Everyone is happy and in a party mood. Tomorrow it will all begin to get back to normal.'

'Thierry. Olivia,' a voice shouted from the deck of one of the yachts. They both turned and saw a mutual friend, Alexander, holding up a champagne bottle. 'Come on board. Join the party.'

'Would you like to?' Thierry said. 'We can politely refuse and keep walking.'

'We don't have to stay long, but it could be fun,' Olivia said, waving hello to Alexander.

Five minutes later, they were on board, each holding a glass of champagne. Olivia's heart sank a little as she realised Alexander wasn't the only person she knew. There were also a couple of women she went to school with. Women whose mothers knew Felicity and often met up on the 'ladies who lunch' circuit. Felicity was sure to be interested in hearing Thierry and her daughter had been at this particular party together.

21

Felicity insisted on giving Olivia and Thierry breakfast before they left Monaco on Monday morning, ignoring Olivia's protests.

'We were going to have breakfast when we got back to Antibes.'

'Well, you can have it with your father and me instead,' Felicity said. 'Pierre and Thierry always had breakfast with us the Monday morning after the Grand Prix. Finished the weekend off nicely. They usually stayed on for lunch too. Why don't you—'

Knowing what was coming, Olivia interrupted. 'No. I can't. Thierry has asked me for a lift back, but if he wants us to stay for breakfast, that's fine. I'm not staying for lunch.'

Olivia closed her eyes and gave a heavy sigh. Her mother was impossible and totally out of order, but there was zero chance of her taking no for an answer to them staying for breakfast.

'Breakfast would be great, Felicity, but unfortunately I too have to get back, so lunch is a no-go today. Another time maybe?' Thierry said, flashing her a disarming smile.

It was an hour before they were able to say goodbye and make for the underground garage.

Thierry placed his overnight bag in the pink taxi and looked at Olivia questioningly.

'What?' she asked.

'I've never driven a London taxi. It would be something to put on my new CV.'

'You want to drive Daisy back to Antibes?' Olivia shrugged. 'Why not. But promise you'll be gentle with her, she's a bit of an old lady. Doesn't do the autoroute.'

'Thanks,' Thierry said, sliding into the driver's seat. 'I'd forgotten London taxies were right-hand drive. This should be fun.' He adjusted the rear-view mirror and grinned at her.

'I'm sorry about my mother,' Olivia said as Thierry edged Daisy into the traffic on the main road.

'No worries, Tuppence. Remember I've known your mother a long time – longer than I've known you, in fact. And I do know how irritating she can be. Papa always said we had to remember her heart was in the right place.'

'It might be, but I wish she'd stop interfering in my life,' Olivia muttered. 'Do you really have to get back or was that you being diplomatic?'

'Me being diplomatic,' Thierry confessed with a grin.

'Thought so, but thank you for getting us off the lunch hook. Anyway, let's change the subject. Did you have a good chat with my papa? I saw the two of you huddled together yesterday evening.'

'He has given me a few ideas and a couple of interesting and possible leads for me to check out. One sounds really good, but unfortunately it's in the UK and I really want to stay in France. I think I'll check out the others first and keep that one as a last resort.'

'Yes, no point in coming back to live and then leaving again almost straight away,' Olivia said.

'I'm planning on checking out one of Trent's suggestions later this week. Want to come with me? Your opinion would be good to hear. Near Tourrettes-sur-Loup. We could make a day of it. Have lunch in the village. If you're not busy with Daisy, of course.'

'Love Tourrettes,' Olivia said. 'Haven't been there for so long. I'd love to come. How are you getting there?'

'Maxine has said I can borrow her car any time she's not using it. Otherwise I'll hire one.'

'We can take mine. The Mini, not Daisy though. I'll even let you drive if you're good. But there is a condition attached to me coming with you.'

Thierry glanced across at her. 'I think I can guess what that is.'

'You do not mention our day out together to my maman,' Olivia said. 'If she hears we're spending time together, she'll really make our lives a misery. Okay?'

'My lips are sealed,' Thierry said. 'You will be my secret friend.'

Vivienne treated herself to a lie-in on Monday morning, deciding to give herself some time off to recover from the excitement of the weekend. She'd spend the day quietly in the apartment, pop out to the *supermarché* for a few bits and pieces, have lunch on the terrace, read one of the books Maxine had lent her, maybe go for a walk, phone Natalie, write Felicity and Trent a thank you note and, importantly, try to organise her thoughts about the future. The last one would be the hardest, but she couldn't put it off forever.

She was eating her lunch when her laptop pinged with an incoming email. She sighed as she took a quick glance at the sender's name. Jeremy had passed the buck to the estate agents.

The email was businesslike, pointing out it was imperative she signed before they could proceed to market the house. They would like to point out, too, that there had already been keen interest in viewing the house and they envisaged a quick sale. Although Mr Wilson had assured them that the house was definitely for sale, her signature was a legal requirement. They politely asked her to electronically sign and return the for-sale authorisation form which they'd attached, ASAP.

She knew trying to delay the sale until she returned home was pointless. Much better to get on with it. It was everything else that was going to be set in motion that she needed to get her head around. Being down here away from Jeremy and all the aggro, it was all too easy to shut out what was happening back in England. Even to optimistically hope it would go away before she returned. Which was a stupid thing to do. Jeremy had effectively killed their marriage, leaving no hope of reviving it, even if she wanted to. Which she realised, with a jolt, she didn't. She might be on her own, except for the children, for the rest of her life, but the future as a single woman would be hers to live as she pleased. The more she thought about it, the more she began to look forward selfishly to a future with only herself to please.

The phrase 'I have a cunning plan', taken from the popular TV programme *Blackadder*, popped into Vivienne's head and made her smile. 'I have a cunning plan', would become her mantra. Not that she had a cunning, or even, a plan yet, but she was now determined she would have a plan in place before she returned to the house she could no longer call home in a month's time.

Pulling her laptop towards her, she opened the estate agent's attachment, followed the instructions, signed the form electronically and returned it. But Jeremy shouldn't think that he was the only one who would be dictating or controlling things in the future. Selling the marital home was a big step that would take months to finalise, months in which she promised herself she would quietly work towards making sure she and the children received everything that they needed for their new lives.

Picking up her lunchtime glass with a mouthful of rosé left in it, Vivienne raised it up and toasted, 'To my future.'

22

Wednesday morning and Vivienne was up at her usual time preparing for the day ahead. She and Olivia were meeting Maxine for a coffee in town before they drove out into the countryside. She could feel the butterflies starting in her tummy already. Which was silly really. This was only the first foray into discovering something about her paternal family and it was highly unlikely that she was going to learn anything today, let alone meet the man himself or anyone connected to him.

After her shower, Vivienne pulled on her jeans and a short-sleeved Breton top. She'd take her lightweight denim jacket in case it was cooler inland, which it generally was. Everything else she needed she placed in her canvas tote bag, including her laptop, with the scanned items. She thought briefly about taking the actual envelope and photograph but decided against it. She wasn't expecting to meet up with Pascal Rocher today, that would have been too easy, too convenient, but she wanted to have, if not proof exactly, at least something to show she was who she said she was and the file on the laptop would do that. Even if she did discover his existence today, how she dealt with it would depend on the circumstances – how approachable he appeared to be, what kind of health he was in, whether he had a wife hovering anxiously at his side.

Vivienne caught her breath. That was something she hadn't considered before. Another person to be thought about in all this. No point in worrying until she had uncovered some definite evidence of a connection.

There was a knock on the door. 'Hi, I'm just about ready,' Vivienne said, smiling at Olivia.

Olivia shook her head. 'I just wanted to say sorry I can't come today after all and to wish you the best of luck. I've messaged Maxine to apologise. Full report when you get back?'

'Thank you. Such a shame you can't come, but yes, definitely tell you everything later.'

After locking the apartment door, Vivienne followed Olivia downstairs and set off to meet Maxine at the cafe. After a quick coffee, they set off for Puget Theniers.

'I look at the map and think we take the scenic route – Vence, Gilette, Roquesteron and then make our way across country to Sigale before heading up to La Penne and then Puget. *D'accord*? Coming back, we'll come straight down the N202.'

'The names mean nothing to me, I'm afraid,' Vivienne said. 'But the scenic route sounds great if you're happy to drive.'

As they drove out through Antibes and made for Vence, Vivienne looked across at Maxine.

'I can't thank you enough for offering to take me today. I really appreciate it, especially as I think you don't really approve of me doing this.'

Maxine sighed. 'You need to do what you feel is the right thing for you. But sometimes a lost little pebble being kicked up can cause a huge landslide in other people's lives. I worry about the consequences for you because knowing the truth about the past isn't always a good thing.' Maxine gave a small shrug. 'We enjoy a day out in the countryside whatever happens when we reach Puget and I...' She hesitated and didn't finish the sentence. 'A change of scenery is good,' she added after several seconds.

Vivienne nodded in agreement, but wondering if Maxine had been about to say something else, she said, 'Are you okay? You've seemed a bit tense the last few times I've seen you. I'm a good listener if you need to talk.'

'*Merci*. You are right, I do have something on my mind, but I prefer not to talk about it today. *Peut-être* another time.'

'I'm going to have a complete change of scenery soon,' Vivienne said, deciding to respond to Maxine's earlier remark. 'And I have no idea where to start looking.' Vivienne explained about signing the authorisation forms for the house to be sold. 'So when I get back to the UK, I have that to deal with. Deciding where and what – house or apartment? Countryside or the coast? Ironically, I did suggest to Jeremy that we could move house this year, but I didn't think for a moment that I'd be doing it as a divorced woman.'

'You stay in England?'

'Yes, of course. I've lived there all my life. Where else would I go?'

'You like it down here. *Peut-être* you think about moving to the South of France?'

'No, I don't think so. My life is in England.' Even as she spoke the words, though, Vivienne found another question forming in her own mind. What life would she have left in England after the divorce? And that question was closely followed by an unexpected one. What was there to stop her from making a completely new life for herself in France? As a writer she could live and work anywhere. Nice airport was one of the largest in France – she could be in London in a couple of hours if she needed to be.

Natalie and Tim were her only family now and she was sure they'd love to visit frequently. She was certainly enjoying the climate down here and the happy, relaxed Mediterranean lifestyle.

'I help you house hunt while you're here if you like?' Maxine said as she stopped at a T-junction and took the road signposted Gilette. 'I have a few villas on my books I can show you. Then, when you leave, you can have things to think about.'

Vivienne laughed. 'I already feel I'm going round and round in circles. There is so much to think about.'

'*Peut-être* you discover a whole new family today and that help you decide.'

Vivienne lapsed into silence as Maxine's words sank in. Did she want a whole new family? Was she being selfishly foolish like Maxine had insinuated earlier? In finding her own roots, did she have the right to invade someone else's privacy, even tear their family apart by her unexpected presence in their lives? Jacqueline and Oscar had given her a secure life – they were her roots. Would it spoil the memory of the life they had so generously given her if she did meet her birth father and started indulging in a game of 'what if'. Vivienne sighed and shifted in her seat, trying to settle her tense shoulders against the upholstery, uncertain now as to whether she was doing the right thing or not.

'You are okay?' Maxine's voice broke into her thoughts. 'The road it is very twisty and soon there will be tunnels and horseshoe bends.'

'I'm fine. The countryside is very beautiful,' Vivienne said, gazing out of the window.

'I think it will be another hour or so before we reach Puget,' Maxine remarked. 'Maybe I stop when we reach Roquesteron. A stop there would break the journey.'

'Sounds like a plan.' Vivienne smiled, remembering the promise to herself to have 'a cunning plan' for her future. Between now and reaching Puget, she'd try to come up with a second plan regarding the French connection.

* * *

They reached Puget Théniers an hour and a half later, having had a quick break in Roquesteron to watch the Estéron river, a tributary of the Var, flowing through the village. A restaurant overlooking the river tempted them to stay for lunch, but they decided it was too early and they'd wait until they reached Puget Théniers.

Maxine parked in the car park and they wandered around the old town before finally settling on a restaurant in one of the main streets. Looking at the menu, Vivienne said, 'Lots of lovely Italian pasta dishes.'

'The border with Italy is only just over there somewhere,' Maxine said, waving her hand in the air. 'There has always been a strong Italian connection up here. In fact, during World War Two, there was a huge resistance movement based up here.'

Vivienne, now she was actually in the village, felt a shiver of excitement run through her body.

'You okay?' Maxine asked, raising her eyes from the menu and looking at her anxiously.

Vivienne nodded. 'Just wondering where to begin asking questions after lunch. I think perhaps the Tourist Office? See if they know of a family called Rocher who lived in the village over fifty years ago, or possibly their descendants?'

* * *

When they left the restaurant an hour later, they discovered the Tourist Office was closed until three o'clock and Vivienne sighed.

'I think my search is doomed. Shall we just forget about it for today?'

'Nonsense. We're here now. The sky is blue, the sun is shining and Puget is a lovely old town. We explore a little more and three o'clock will soon arrive.'

Their steps took them around a different part of the old town this time and whilst she walked the narrow streets with their ancient arches, looking at medieval buildings that in some cases were truly showing their age, admiring an ancient fountain in a tiny square, Vivienne's thoughts strayed. What had she hoped to gain by coming here today, dragging Maxine with her on what really amounted to nothing more than a wild goose chase? When they left here later, no doubt without having discovered anything, she'd forget about tracing her roots. Natalie and Tim were the only family she needed. Best to forget the whole family tree ancestry thing, but at least she could tell Natalie she'd tried.

At the bottom of some well-worn steps, she saw a shop with the word '*Quincaillerie*' written on a board across the top of the doorway. In the shop window amongst the manly tools were lots of cookery pots, cake tins, mixing bowls and electric kitchen aids.

'This is like an old-fashioned yet modern hardware store,' Vivienne said. 'Natalie would love this shop. And they are open. Shall we go in?' Without waiting for Maxine to answer, she pushed the door open and stepped inside.

It was a cornucopia of household goods, DIY equipment and kitchen utensils. Vivienne wandered around trying to take it all in, knowing she was in the perfect place to buy Natalie a present.

The man behind the counter smiled at them as he said, '*Bonjour mesdames.*' Vivienne picked up a cake tray for madeleines and a dozen moulds for some small cakes called canelés complete with a recipe leaflet and took them to the counter. Natalie was going to love experimenting with these.

Glancing at the receipt she was handed after she'd paid, the name on the top of the receipt jumped out at her – '*Quincaillerie du Rocher.*' She looked at the man behind the counter, questions wanting to tumble out of her mouth.

Wordlessly, she pointed out the name to Maxine. 'Can you ask him? I doubt he'd understand my poor French.'

Maxine smiled and moved closer to the counter. '*S'il vous plaît, monsieur.*'

Vivienne heard the words Rocher, *un ami de la famille*, saw the man shake his head and answer Maxine in rapid-fire French, that she couldn't make head nor tail of.

'Merci, monsieur,' Maxine said eventually and the two of them left the shop.

'What did he say?' Vivienne asked impatiently.

'He tell me the Rochers sold the business about twelve years ago. A family from Nice buy it and he works for them in their similar shop in Nice. He's just helping out here today. They keep the name because it is an old business since 1921 and it made business sense. He personally knows nothing about any Rochers.'

Vivienne sighed. 'I was truly hopeful for several moments. D'you think it's worth asking in the Tourist Office?'

Maxine shook her head. 'I think the *Mairie* would be better now we know a little about the family. Come on. It's this way. We passed it earlier.' She pointed to the *Hôtel de Ville* with its French flag fluttering in the breeze.

The middle-aged receptionist in the office at the *Mairie* could speak a little English and nodded vigorously when Vivienne asked if a man called Pascal Rocher lived, or had lived, in the village.

'*Mais oui*, he was the *Maire* several years ago. He lives in the rue near the church. Why you ask?'

'He is a friend of my family from years ago, but they lost

touch,' Vivienne said, not wanting to say bluntly that he knew her mother in case the receptionist jumped to conclusions.

'And you try to reconnect? *Mais*, sadly it is not possible today. He is not here. He is on holiday with his daughter. They go to Corsé. They return in a week. You come back then?'

'I will try. Is it possible to leave a contact number for you to give him?' Vivienne asked, scrabbling in her bag for one of her business cards that had both her telephone and email address, as the woman said, 'Yes, *bien sûr*.' 'Thank you. I will try to come again before I leave, but if you can make sure he receives the card, I'd be grateful. Perhaps you could tell him Deidre's daughter was asking after him. *Merci*.'

* * *

Maxine dropped Vivienne off at the apartment before locking the car in the garage and walking home. She'd enjoyed driving Vivienne around the countryside today, grateful to have her mind occupied with something else other than Leonie Toussaint. When Vivienne had quietly said she was a good listener if she ever wanted to talk, she'd been so close to confiding in her, but really the less people who knew about her past until she'd finally sorted things with the solicitors, the better. She couldn't bear the thought of being judged, of being pitied. Once it was sorted, she could give everyone a sanitised version of things.

Reaching L'Abri, Maxine unlocked the letter box at the side of the front door and took out the weekly offering of publicity mail from local businesses, before locking the box again. Once indoors, she began thinking about supper. Something light after that lovely pasta at lunch time. There was no sign of Thierry being home, so she guessed she'd be eating alone, in which case a salad with a couple of slices of baguette washed down with a glass of red wine would do her.

As Maxine dropped the promo post on the kitchen table to look at later, she realised a white envelope had somehow got tucked in amongst the leaflets and she caught her breath. The London solicitor. She'd expected them to reply direct to her email, not with a formal written letter. She'd read it as she ate some food.

Quickly, she placed a slice of ham alongside some baguette slices, poured herself a glass of wine and, picking everything up, including the letter, went out into the garden.

Sitting at the table under the loggia, Maxine took a deep breath, hesitating before she opened the envelope, knowing that once she did, there would be a decision to make. A decision that could change her life once again. A change that she'd wished and wished for down through the years, but now it was finally a possibility, she couldn't help but think that it was too late. Any attempts on her part to right the past and explain away the lies and accusations that were sure to be thrown at her were likely to be dismissed. And once again she would be left reeling and alone – just like thirty years ago, when her life had fallen apart.

* * *

That day had started normally enough. She'd woken early, left Daiva sleeping and crept down the hallway to have a shower. Leonie's bedroom door was open and Maxine caught a glimpse of her beloved daughter, a thumb in her mouth and her arm clutching close the knitted soft toy mouse 'Anatole' that Maxine had bought her for her recent third birthday.

As she'd showered, Maxine had thought about her day. Daiva would usually leave for work at about seven thirty, she would get Leonie dressed and the two of them would have breakfast. Their walk, through the park to the *l'école maternelle* just a street away, was the highlight of her day. It had become their special time. After leaving Leonie at school, she would do a small shop for tonight's dinner, drop her purchases off at the apartment, before going to work in the *agent immobilier* where she was a general assistant while she studied for her exams.

That particular day, Daiva hadn't left for work as usual while she and Leonie had breakfast, which was strange. When she returned to place the dinner ingredients for that evening in the fridge, he was still there. Scowling at her as she came in. Maxine quickly put the shopping away before turning to leave. She knew better than to antagonise him when he was in a mood.

'I'm off to work now. I'll see you later.'

And she left quickly before he could stop her on some pretence or other. Stopping to ask what time he would be home that evening wasn't worth the risk. Not for the first time, she inwardly berated herself for the situation she found herself in. How could she not have seen the real man behind the facade Daiva presented to the world? But the bigger question was – how the hell was she going to get herself and, more importantly, Leonie away from him?

It was mid-afternoon when she arrived at the gates of *l'école maternelle* to collect Leonie.

A puzzled teacher looked at her. '*Mais*, Monsieur Toussaint collected your daughter early. His maman is ill and he's taken Leonie to see her.'

Maxine had reeled in shock, barely managing to stay upright, and ran frantically back to the apartment. His mother had died a year ago. Daiva had finally done what he'd threatened to do so many times when, according to him, she was being 'difficult'. He'd taken Leonie and disappeared.

* * *

Maxine's hand was shaking as she picked up her glass and took a sip, staring at the envelope. Since that fateful day, she'd had no contact with either Daiva or her daughter. She'd gone straight to the gendarmes, saying her daughter had been kidnapped, but they basically told her, he was the child's father so there was nothing they could do about it. Six anxious, despairing months later, Maxine had received a letter from the London solicitors, telling her that in future they would be her only way of contacting Daiva Toussaint. They also told her that their client did not reside in London and that the child was safe and living happily with her father. Maxine, heartbroken and desperate to find Leonie, tried every avenue she could find to trace her daughter, all to no avail. Daiva had covered their traces well. In the end she had no choice but give up looking – but she never gave up hope.

Were the contents of this envelope about to give her the means of contacting her daughter – bringing her back into her life after thirty years? Or would it all be a waste of time, ending in a rebuff with Leonie deciding not to meet her after all these years? Because there was no doubting the fact that Daiva would have filled Leonie's mind with poisonous thoughts about her absent mother.

23

As she prepared for the day out with Thierry, Olivia couldn't help but wonder what sort of business he was investigating in Tourrettes-sur-Loup. He'd refused to tell her, teasingly saying 'wait and see'. She'd visited the perched village several times and knew that it had fabulous views overlooking the gorge it was positioned above, with glimpses of the Mediterranean Sea in the distance. She also knew that it was home to lots of artists, sculptors and was known for its violets that grew all year round and were used for conserves, perfume and the crystallised fruits the village was famous for.

Thierry arrived promptly at nine thirty and they set off, with Thierry driving her car as she'd promised. It wasn't long before they were on the mountain road that would take them up to the village. Thierry's rendez-vous wasn't until eleven o'clock, so there was plenty of time for a wander around. Still early in the day, there were relatively few people about as they parked in the car park outside the village and walked into the centre of the medieval stronghold.

Olivia sighed contentedly as they wandered around, getting lost in narrow streets, discovering little squares – one with a lovely circular fountain – passing through vaulted passageways and climbing stepped streets with blowsy red geraniums lined up on individual steps. Together, they strolled in and out of artists' workshops and galleries, admiring the work and discovering they had similar 'arty' tastes. They sampled various violet jams and crystallised flowers and sniffed violet perfume. 'It's truly the Village of Violets,' she said to Thierry.

Stepping to one side to allow a couple with a toddling little girl to pass on one of the narrow streets, Olivia smiled as she glanced from the laughing child to the happy parents. They looked about her own age and for a split second she wondered whether she would ever scoop a small child up and cuddle it, like the mother was doing now. She watched them, deep in thought for several seconds, before they disappeared from her sight and Thierry broke the silence.

'Do you hope for a family like that one day?' he asked quietly.

'Do you know, I've never been really sure about having children, as much as my mother longs for grandchildren, but I realised recently, yes, I do want a family. Not sure what kind of mother I'll make, though,' she said, laughing.

'Nobody knows what kind of parent they're going to be until it happens, I don't think,' Thierry said. 'But most people I know muddle along and the children turn out okay.'

'How about you? Do you want a family someday?'

Thierry nodded. 'I would like the full works – a wife, two or three children and a dog or two, even a paddock with a horse in it.' He laughed. 'But someday is the operative word – when I've got myself sorted out. Talking of which, we'd better make tracks and meet up with Madame Jackman. We should get back to the car if we go down this way.'

'Where are we meeting her?'

'She lives about half a kilometre outside the village. The details are in the satnav. Shouldn't be difficult to find,' Thierry said.

Ten minutes later, he turned the car onto a tarmacked lane with neatly tended verges and a stone built mas covered in purple bougainvillea at the end.

'What a lovely house,' Olivia said.

Madame Jackman had clearly heard the car arriving and was waiting to greet them at the front of the mas.

'*Bonjour*, Thierry. Please call me Marie-France. How lovely, you've brought your wife.'

Before Olivia could deny it and say they were just friends, Thierry had shaken his head and smiled. 'Olivia is my business partner. She owns the pink flowers and champagne taxi in Antibes. You may have seen it.'

Olivia, rendered speechless by the idea that she was Thierry's business partner, could only smile weakly at Marie-France.

'That would certainly fit in well with my side of the business,' Marie-France said. 'Let me show you around.'

Following Marie-France to the back of the house, Olivia wondered what she'd meant by her side of the business. Exactly what sort of business was Thierry looking at here? Stepping around the corner of the house, she got her answer. It was a violet farm. A large greenhouse filled with violets and an open field with row after row of the earth-hugging plants greeted them.

'Two different varieties,' Marie-France said. 'The outdoor one is hardier than the one in the greenhouse. It helps to stagger production.'

During the next quarter of an hour, Marie-France showed them the barn with its small but immaculate kitchen where the spring flowers were taken to be turned into the jams and confectionary they'd seen in the village.

'In summer, the leaves are picked and sent down to the Grasse perfumery, and in winter, the flowers are picked for bouquets. There is something to do every season,' Marie-France said. 'We have two permanent employees and several seasonal workers. And, of course, Charles and I work with them. Well, it's just me now since he died.'

'I'm sorry for your loss,' Olivia said. 'Is that why you're selling the business? It's too much for you on your own?'

Marie-France nodded. She glanced at Thierry. 'This side of the business was my responsibility and the other, the one I think you're really interested in, was Charles's domain.'

Olivia looked from one to the other. 'What sort of business is that?'

'Outdoor activity centre,' Thierry said. 'And yes, that's of more interest to me. The house would be included if both were sold together?'

'That would be the ideal for me. My daughter wants me to join her in Sardinia. But the two businesses are such different propositions, I'm struggling to find a buyer who would like the two,' Marie-France shrugged. 'I think I'm going to have sell the house with whichever one of the businesses sells first.' She turned to Olivia. 'Would you like to view the house?'

'Yes please,' Olivia said. 'It looks an amazing property from the outside.'

The door of a large barn was open as they walked past and Olivia caught a glimpse of canoes in racks, a six-seater inflatable RIB, and shelves of wetsuits and life jackets. A Land Rover and trailer took up some of the free floor space. Thierry stopped to have a longer look before catching the women up as they reached the iron-framed conservatory at the side of the house, with its breathtaking view down over a gorge.

'Why don't the two of you have a wander while I organise some coffee and set the laptop up ready to show you the other side of the business,' Marie-France suggested.

Olivia was deep in thought as she and Thierry wandered around the sitting room, a dining room, a family-sized kitchen and a cloakroom, before climbing the stairs to look at the three bedrooms, one with an en suite, a family bathroom and a study/office.

'Are you seriously thinking about buying an outdoor activity centre and the rest of it?' She gestured with her hand.

Thierry nodded. 'It definitely appeals, but depends on a lot of things working out that I have no control over.'

'Like?'

'We'll talk later. Right now, Marie-France is waiting for us and I need to hear what she has to say.'

Sitting around the table in the kitchen with coffee and biscuits in front of them, Olivia and Thierry listened as Marie-France explained how she and her husband had run the businesses.

'I was in charge of the violet farm and Charles organised the activity centre. Mind you, I also did all the paperwork for both.' She pushed the laptop towards Thierry and Olivia. 'Activities are booked on a daily basis either by individuals or groups and depend on various things – weather, number of visitors, their experience and the particular activity they want to do. Activities take place either in Bar-sur-Loup or in the Gorges du Verdon – both, as you know, are quite close. We would transport the equipment and meet everyone there.'

'Did you ever think about offering the complete package?' Olivia asked. 'Accommodation and food?'

'We did think about it in the beginning, but the house isn't big enough. There is a barn that could be converted into dormitory-style accommodation if you or whoever buys the business wants to go down that road.'

Marie-France pressed a key on the laptop and a slide show started up showing scenes from past seasons. As it finished, she looked at them hopefully. 'I know it's impossible for you to make a decision just like that, but do you think you could possibly be interested in buying the business? It would be wonderful if you were. You both feel like you could be the right people for me to sell to.'

* * *

It was gone one thirty before they left Marie-France, with Thierry promising her he'd be in touch one way or the other very soon.

'Lunch in Tourrettes?' he suggested as they did their seatbelts up.

'We can be home in about three quarters of an hour, less if there's not much traffic,' Olivia said. 'Back to my place for an omelette and salad? You have a lot to think about and you can use me as a sounding board without anyone overhearing.'

'Your place it is,' Thierry agreed as he turned onto the main road.

'Bit naughty of you to tell Marie-France that we were business partners,' Olivia said quietly. 'Gave her the wrong impression of us, I think.'

'She already had the wrong impression of our relationship,' Thierry said. 'I was just correcting her tactfully. But I have to ask does the thought of us being business partners for real appeal to you? The violet farm and the activity centre clearly worked as a business for her and her husband.'

'Probably because they were married and spent more time

together than we would as just business partners. Would you live in the house?'

'Definitely. We could both live there if you wanted to leave Antibes. It's not got enough accommodation for paying guests, but for the two of us there's plenty of space to live separate lives. We could share the office, although as partner you'd have to agree to doing the paperwork for both businesses, okay?' Thierry gave her a cheeky grin. 'I hate paperwork.'

'There's the deal-breaker right there then,' Olivia said, shaking her head and striving not to think about living with Thierry. 'Because I hate paperwork too.'

'No problem. We'll employ someone in that case.'

There was silence for a few moments as Thierry concentrated on his driving and Olivia lost herself in thoughts about what it would be like to be Thierry's partner in business, or even in life. She pushed that thought away quickly. They were friends and that was the way it was going to remain.

'There's still a little bit of a problem, though,' Olivia said. 'I can see you as a macho all-action man, white-water rafting your clients down the Gorges de Verdon and I'm sure that side of the business would work well for you. On the other hand, I know nothing about violets and I'm no horticulturist, or even that good a gardener. Cut flowers I can deal with, but growing them, I'd probably kill the lot off within the year.'

'Do you know that English ditty about violets. Is ditty the right word?' Thierry looked across at her.

'Depends, tell it to me.'

'Roses are red, violets are blue, my dog is my favourite, but you're okay too.'

There was a stunned silence, before Olivia burst out laughing. 'That's definitely a terrible ditty. How about this one. Roses are red, violets are blue, these jokes are getting old, and so are you.'

'That's a cruel ditty. I'm not old. I'm in my prime.'

By the time Thierry drove into the garage at the villa, they were both aching from laughing so much.

Once indoors, Olivia quickly threw a salad together, grated some cantal cheese, whipped four eggs up, and made them both an omelette. Thierry opened a bottle of rosé before taking cutlery and glasses out to the small wrought-iron table in the tiny back-yard. Olivia had done her best to brighten it up and make it an inviting place to eat during the summer months. White geraniums in two old terracotta tall pots livened up the two corners of the far wall and a lemon tree in another terracotta pot stood between them.

'This is really nice,' Thierry said. 'Just the right size for two people.'

Olivia placed the salad bowl on the table.

'Maman is always on at me to move upstairs and rent this apartment out, but...' Olivia shrugged. 'But this one was Auntie Daphne's home, the flower room is handy and I like it. I feel close to her, if that isn't silly.' She returned to the kitchen and finished cooking the omelette, dished it up and carried the two plates out, placing them on the table. '*Bon appétit.*'

'So, seriously, what do you think about the two businesses?' Thierry asked, as they started to eat.

'It's such a funny combination when you think about it,' Olivia said slowly. 'Ideal for a married couple, especially if one is into the horticulture side of things. But I'm not sure about the viability of the violet farm – especially with climate change happening – but buying the activity side of the business with the house is definitely worth thinking about. Marie-France did say she'd thought about splitting it like that. How do you feel?'

'I'm definitely interested in looking further into the activity business and buying the house.' Thierry sighed. 'But then I would feel bad to be responsible for breaking the businesses into separate bits. I think everything should be kept together like Marie-France and her husband set it up.'

Olivia nodded thoughtfully. 'Breaking it up would probably mean one of the last violet farms in the Alpes-Maritimes would be lost and just become a three-hectare field, because surely nobody will want it without the adjacent sorting room and kitchen, both of which are too close to the house to be sold on.'

'And I wouldn't want that on my conscience,' Thierry said. 'So, if you're not tempted to become my business partner and at least help me run the violet farm, paperwork aside, do I make Marie-France an offer for the outdoor activity business and the house? Or do I tell her sorry but it's not for us? I did like the thought of living in Tourrettes, I have to admit.'

Olivia nodded. 'The house was rather lovely.' She could definitely see them both living there, sharing the house as business partners. Maybe even becoming 'friends with benefits'. She pushed that thought away swiftly. 'Of course, you could try to find another business partner just for the violet farm. Maybe there's a local violet farmer who would like to expand and already has premises close by? They could just harvest each crop and deal with it on their own premises.'

'That's an idea,' Thierry said thoughtfully.

The two of them spent the rest of the afternoon talking about both the violet farm and the activity centre, how much they both loved the house and what kind of deal would make it feasible for Thierry to buy the business. It was nearly six o'clock when Thierry said he had to go back to L'Abri.

'I'll think about it for forty-eight hours. I don't think Marie-France has buyers clamouring at her door. And who knows in those forty-eight hours you might come round to what I think is the best and right decision for both of us.'

'Which is?' Olivia stared at him.

'For us to become business partners, move in to the house and run things together. *A bientôt*.'

And he was gone, leaving Olivia dumbstruck at the seriousness of his voice.

24

Maxine was still sitting in the garden, the uneaten food on her plate dried and discoloured from the sun, a wine glass and a half-empty bottle of red wine were all pushed to one side on the table, when Thierry arrived home. The opened envelope with its letter was in front of her.

'How long have you been sitting here?' Thierry asked gently, looking at her. 'Are you all right?'

'Since I got back from Puget. A couple of hours maybe.' Maxine shrugged and tried to pull herself together, not wanting Thierry to be concerned. 'Have a glass of wine with me and tell me about your day before I go and organise some supper for us.'

Thierry fetched a glass and poured himself a splash of wine and sat down. 'My day can wait. And I'll organise supper after we've talked.' He glanced at the letter. 'May I?'

Maxine nodded and he picked up the solicitor's letter, quickly reading it before looking up at her.

'She lives in Paris?'

Maxine nodded. 'The 7th arrondissement. Just two or three

streets away from our apartment. How ironic is that? We could have passed each other in the street unknowingly. Sat in the same restaurants having a meal. Did you ever meet anyone called Leonie when you and Pierre lived there?'

'Not that I remember,' Thierry said. 'Now you have the address, will you contact her?'

'So much of me wants to dash up to Paris, knock on the door of her apartment and say, hi it's me. But the other part of me knows that is not a good idea. If she closed the door in my face and rejected me...' Maxine paused. 'I couldn't cope with that, it would truly break me.' She took a sip of her drink. 'Rejection by letter or email would be easier to handle than face to face.'

'You are assuming that she will reject you,' Thierry said. 'She might be as desperate to meet you as you are to reconnect with her.'

'*Peut-être*, but I know Daiva will have filled her head with lies and hate about me for over thirty years. I need to ask her to listen to my side of the story. After which she can decide.' Maxine wiped away a tear that somehow had escaped while she was talking. 'I want so much to hug her close again. I can only pray that she will let me.'

Thierry caught hold of her hand. 'Maxie, just write to her. You need the chance to tell her the truth.'

Maxine sniffed. 'Sorry. I cried myself dry over Leonie years ago, I didn't think I had any tears left. Every birthday, every Christmas, is clouded by thoughts of her. Is she well? Happy? Perhaps she is even married? The thought of seeing her again is wonderful, but terrifying at the same time.'

'I can understand that,' Thierry said, standing up. 'Fancy a takeaway pizza for supper? I'll go and ring for one while you fetch your laptop and start to think about what you're going to put in your email to Leonie.'

* * *

Half an hour later, the two of them were tucking into the pizza.

'So, tell me about your day,' Maxine said.

'Today was interesting. We both love Tourrettes-sur-Loup, we both like the house, the activity business appeals to me, but – and it's a big but – Olivia isn't keen on the violet farm for various reasons.'

'It sounds like you were hoping she would be?'

Thierry gave a rueful nod. 'I was. And if you breathe a word of this conversation to Felicity, I shall have to kill you,' he said, pulling a mock-threatening face.

'Thierry, you know me better than that,' Maxine said. 'You're very fond of Olivia, aren't you?'

Thierry nodded. 'Today I suggested we became business partners. I thought having an excuse to see more of each other officially would help us get closer. She didn't exactly jump at the offer, so I don't think it will happen,' he shrugged.

'But I think you want more than a business partnership with Olivia, *n'est pas?*' Maxine said.

Thierry nodded. 'Much more. Meanwhile, she insists we're friends.'

'Then forget suggesting a business arrangement and go for what you truly want. Tell her how you feel.'

Ruefully, Thierry shook his head. 'It's not that easy with Felicity hovering in the background intent on pushing us together, and Olivia determined to keep her mother away from her love life.'

'I'm sure between us we can do something about that,' Maxine said, as Thierry gave her a look. 'Do not look at me like that. Trust me. I would not dream of interfering like Felicity.'

'Good. Now, have you thought about what to say to Leonie?'

Maxine nodded. 'I drafted the email while we waited for the pizza.' She pulled her laptop towards her and opened her mail programme. 'I'll read it to you and you can tell me what you think.'

Dear Leonie,

Your father's solicitors, on his instructions, have been in touch with me with your contact details after your father's untimely death. I would very much like us to meet as there is so much I want to explain to you face to face, rather than put it in this email. Perhaps you would consider coming to Antibes for a few days and we could talk and get to know each other. Or I would be happy to come to Paris if you would prefer? My home address is at the bottom. I look forward so much to hearing from you and to finally seeing you again after so many years. Your father disappearing with you all those years ago left me heartbroken and there hasn't been a day since when I haven't longed to hold you in my arms and tell you how much I have always loved you.

Your loving mother,
Maxine.

As she finished reading the letter out loud, Maxine looked at Thierry, her eyes glistening. 'Is that all right? I did think about calling it a sad death, but that would have been hypocritical of me because I'm not sad about it and I'm determined to be honest with Leonie from the beginning about everything.'

'I don't think you could have put it any better,' Thierry said. 'Now you just need to send it.'

Maxine moved the letter out of the drafts folder, read it through again and pressed send. There, it was done. She'd reached out and could only hope and pray that Leonie would at least answer and want to meet her. And give her the chance to tell her that she'd thought about and missed her every single day since Daiva had so cruelly snatched her away.

25

The morning after spending the day with Thierry, Olivia was up early to drive to the flower market for some stock. As she drove along the A8 in the early-morning sunshine, her thoughts were all about Thierry. It was his birthday soon and she wanted to get him something really special. Having her old friend back in her life was wonderful. She was only now beginning to realise just how much he meant to her.

After spending most of yesterday with him, she'd actually missed him when he'd left to get back to Maxine. Had even been tempted to ask him to stay, but she knew he was worried about Maxine. Thinking about how comfortable she felt with him, how she loved his sense of humour, the way he protected her, Olivia realised something with a shock. Yes, he was a boy – a man these days – who was a friend, but he wasn't her boyfriend in the way people interpreted the word, and never had been. But, albeit unconsciously, she'd measured all her boyfriends – not that there had been that many – against him – and found them all lacking. Thierry, it turned out, was the reason why none of her relationships had lasted. He'd spoilt her. Which gave her a major problem

– one that she had no idea how to deal with. Was there any chance he felt the same way? He'd said asking her to be his business partner was the best and the right solution for both of them. Did he realise how complicated their lives could become if they grew too close – was it too much to hope that that was what he wanted to happen?

Becoming his business partner and running the violet farm with him and seeing what happened between them was so tempting. After all, she'd learnt and passed exams in floristry – she could do the same in horticulture surely? And she'd get to live in that lovely house.

No. She wouldn't move in with him. That would be tempting providence. She could already see it fulfilling his dream of a family home, meals in the kitchen, children running around, numerous cats and dogs, a pony in the paddock.

As she pulled into the car park of the flower market, a smile crept across her face. Suddenly she knew exactly the present she was going to give him. Hopefully, there would be time to organise things before his birthday.

Parking the car and pulling the handbrake on, Olivia took her phone out of her pocket. Her mother would be able to point in her in the right direction for what she wanted. And if she asked who the present was for, she'd be vague and simply say 'a friend' and ignore any probing questions. Her mother would discover the truth eventually, of course, but not until after Thierry's birthday.

* * *

After the failed excursion to Puget Theniers, Vivienne concentrated on her book for several days. Losing herself in writing was the only way to push all thoughts of Pascal Rocher out of her mind. But when she wasn't writing, the thought of him was there, instantly disrupting everything she did, knocking Jeremy off the number one worry spot that he'd been hogging. Thinking about Jeremy and all the problems she had to face in the near future had been depressing, whereas thoughts of Pascal Rocher were full of hope and unknown possibilities.

Was he back from holiday yet? Had the receptionist remembered to give him her card? Mentioned the name Deidre? Had he glanced at the card and thrown it away? Deciding it wasn't important and, besides, he didn't remember anyone called Deidre, which in itself would be horrible. She could only pray that that wouldn't happen.

She wished she'd asked for a contact email for him, but the woman probably wouldn't have given it to her. No, she'd done the right thing, leaving it to him to get in touch. Hopefully, once Pascal Rocher had her card he would email – or even phone her. She still had a couple of weeks go before she returned to England. If she didn't hear from him soon, she'd go back to Puget and track him down somehow. In the meantime, she'd try to concentrate on finishing her book so she'd be in a with a chance of being free for Natalie's promised holiday.

When her thoughts weren't occupied with Pascal Rocher, it was Maxine's words about moving to France that niggled away at her mind. She even looked at some estate agents websites. A lot of property was well outside her price range, but there was also lots that she could afford. It would be a huge life change, a new beginning like no other and totally her own decision. She picked up her phone. It wouldn't hurt to ask Maxine if she'd been serious about helping her house hunt and to arrange some viewings for maybe next week.

* * *

Maxine was weeding an already immaculate border in the garden in an effort to take her mind off of Leonie, when Vivienne rang.

'You want to go look at property? Okay. We go now if you like. I collect you in ten minutes.' She registered the surprised tone of Vivienne's 'Thank you.'

Vivienne was waiting for her outside the villa, and as she got in the car and put her seat belt on, she said, 'I didn't expect you to drop everything and drive me around this afternoon. I'm sure you're very busy.'

Maxine shrugged. 'No, I wasn't. I'm glad to have something to do, if I'm honest.' She sensed Vivienne's look. 'I have a little problem at the moment. One that I'm not sure how – if – it will work out.'

'Would it help to talk about it?' Vivienne asked.

'*Non*, but *merci* for the offer. I'd rather forget it for an hour or so.'

'Well, if you ever change your mind.'

'Have you heard from Pascal Rocher?' Maxine asked, changing the subject.

'No. Not yet. I'm hoping it's because he's still on holiday. Where are the properties situated that you're going to show me?'

'They're both in Juan-les-Pins. One is on the far end near the beach and the other is nearer the centre. I have the keys for the two. The owners are both absent. They are holiday lets at the moment, and a bit run-down, but either of them would make a good permanent base without too much work. Next week, I arrange viewings for some more.' She glanced at Vivienne. 'You seriously think about living down here?'

'Thank you, I really appreciate it,' Vivienne said. 'And yes, I am. I've discovered that Brexit has made it difficult to have a holiday home here, but full-time residents are welcome. Anyway, I've looked at several properties on the internet, but viewing some in person with you will give me a better idea as to what I need and what to look for.'

Maxine pulled into a parking space in front of a large apartment block. As the two of them rode the lift to the top floor, Maxine explained, 'This apartment has been rented out for about six years now and is really in need of refreshing.'

The rooms were a nice size, there was a storage cave and a parking space in the underground garage. Vivienne loved the view out over the sea and along the coast towards the Esterel mountains which was spectacular, but she shook her head when Maxine asked if she liked it.

'I can't see myself living here, although it does have potential.'

'Come on, let's go see the next one,' Maxine said.

The second property – a detached villa in a small cul-de-sac on the outskirts of Juan-les-Pins – appealed to Vivienne more. Electric gates opened on to a small front garden and a garage. The rooms were a good size, the kitchen was modern, but the main bathroom was sadly dilapidated. Vivienne wandered around the three bedrooms upstairs, one with an en suite, and a smaller room that would make a nice book-lined study. Back downstairs, Maxine opened the shutters on the French doors and they stepped out into the garden with its large swimming pool.

When Maxine looked at her, Vivienne shook her head. 'I don't dislike this one, but it's not really calling *buy me*.'

'Let's go back to L'Abri and I'll show you everything I have on my list at the moment,' Maxine said.

* * *

Having made the decision about Thierry's birthday present, Olivia lost no time in organising things. Her mother was surprisingly helpful when she rang and said yes, she was sure her friend who lived in Antibes would be able to point her in the right direction, even if she herself couldn't help, and for once Felicity didn't ask too many questions. Olivia had decided if her mother did ask the important one, 'which friend are you buying for?' she'd cross her fingers and say she was buying it for herself. She'd apologise to her mother for the little white lie afterwards. It was just that she wanted it to be a big surprise for Thierry. A surprise that he was sure to love.

Within days, everything was settled. Olivia had contacted Jilly, her mother's friend, driven to the outskirts of Antibes, talked it through, seen everything and finally, after a lot of deliberation and input from Jilly, made a decision. All that was left to do was to get everything else organised before returning to collect the present twenty-four hours before Thierry's birthday. Now she was ready to invite the man himself to lunch on the day. Text or phone? They hadn't spoken or seen each other for days and Olivia wanted to hear his voice. Phone it was.

'Hi Thierry,' she said. 'How's things?'

'Still mulling things over. I'm sorry I haven't been in touch since our day in Tourrettes, but I've been asking questions of various people and doing a lot of thinking. How are you?'

'I'm fine. I'm not sure if you have any plans for your birthday next week, but I thought you and I could celebrate at lunchtime here at the villa. I'll even cook for you. Only if you'd like me to, of course,' she added.

'I'd love for you to cook me a birthday lunch. Thank you. Can we talk about the violet farm and your thoughts then?'

'Perfect time to do it,' Olivia said. 'See you about twelve then on the day. Ciao.' And she ended the call with a smile on her face. Next week couldn't come quickly enough now. She just knew it was going to be an extra special day.

26

Natalie rang Vivienne early one evening to finalise her holiday details and to tell her how much she was looking forward to seeing her.

'I'm booked to fly home on the same flight as you, so I can drive you home and spend the night with you. And head back to my flat the next day.'

Before they hung up, Vivienne tentatively broached the possibility of her moving to the Riviera.

'Maxine asked me if I'd thought about moving down here. To be honest, until she mentioned it, I hadn't. But I do like it down here. I've looked at a few houses online and Maxine has already taken me to see two that weren't right for me, but I must admit I'm seriously tempted. Would it bother you if I moved so far away?'

'Gosh, no. I'd be a regular visitor,' Natalie replied instantly. 'Especially if you buy a villa with a swimming pool. I know Tim would visit often too.'

'It's just that after the divorce I can't bear the thought of staying in the neighbourhood and bumping into them unexpectedly, especially in a few months when they're pushing a pram,' she explained.

'They're having a baby?' Natalie sounded stunned down the phone and Vivienne caught her breath. Damn. Jeremy obviously hadn't told the children about the baby yet.

'Yes. Dad hadn't told you?'

'No, and he hasn't even told us her name yet, but she's clearly younger than him. It sounds like a classic case of a male midlife crisis and I hate them both for what they're doing to you. Is she somebody he met through work? Do we know her?'

'We do know her yes.'

'I know you said Dad had to tell us himself, but come on, Mum, now I know about the baby, there is no point in you not telling me the woman's name.'

Vivienne took a deep breath, knowing that Natalie would be upset by what she was about to tell her. 'It's Sadie,' Vivienne said and waited for the explosion that was sure to come.

Instead, there was a short silence before Natalie said, 'Your agent, Sadie Murphy?'

'Yes.'

'That's great. Your so-called friend is stabbing you in the back. Twice. Once by having an affair with Dad, breaking up your marriage and making you give up your home, and secondly, by forcing you to change agents because there is no way she can continue to represent you now, is there?'

'The problem is that even when I get a new agent, Sadie will still be dealing with, and taking her percentage from the books she has already been involved with,' Vivienne said quietly. She knew that Jeremy's affair with Sadie had broken more than their marriage. It was also going to have a huge impact on her professional life.

'So that's a third stab in the back – you'll partly be financing her and Dad's new life together. Mum, I don't know what to say. Have you tackled her about it? Has she contacted you?'

'No, I haven't spoken to her and I have no intention of ever speaking to her again. I blocked her the day I arrived down here and I've tried to put her out of my mind until I'm home and then I know I've got to deal with it. But it's certainly going to make life complicated.' Vivienne sighed, knowing and dreading the fallout from Jeremy's affair that would start landing in her lap the moment she arrived home.

'Well, I just hope neither she nor Dad expect me to play happy families with them when the baby arrives.'

'It's not the baby's fault,' Vivienne said gently. 'Your dad was never a hands-on father and this time round at his age, it's going to be even harder.'

'Good. A bit of karma being dished out then.'

The call ended shortly afterwards, a subdued Natalie leaving Vivienne feeling cross with herself for being the one to tell her the name of Jeremy's new woman. He should have told the children himself, both about Sadie and the baby.

She and Sadie had first met at a publishers party about eight years ago. Sadie, in her late twenties at the time, had recently joined a prestigious agency and was being hailed as a rising star. She'd bounded over to Vivienne, all shiny hair and trendy clothes, congratulating her on her latest bestseller before saying that she'd heard Vivienne was looking for an agent and that they should talk. 'I'll phone you tomorrow and we'll talk.'

Forty-eight hours later, Vivienne had signed with the agency, delighted to have Sadie as her new agent. For eight years as Sadie's star had indeed risen and she became a well-respected agent, Vivienne's own life had changed alongside Sadie's as her books became increasingly popular.

Never for one moment had Vivienne ever thought it would all end like this.

When Thierry told Maxine he would be out for the evening so not to worry about supper for him, she rang Olivia and Vivienne and invited them both over. Leonie had not yet replied to her email and Maxine knew that if she was alone for the evening, she'd drink too much wine and upset herself with depressing thoughts and worry about what the future would hold.

It was a typical balmy summer evening on the French Riviera as Olivia and Vivienne walked to Maxine's together.

'I'm going to miss this weather when I return home,' Vivienne said. 'The evenings are rarely as balmy at home as they are here. Sitting out on your roof terrace at eleven o'clock at night has been so lovely.'

'Has Maxine showed you any interesting properties yet? She did mention that you were thinking of relocating down here and she was looking around for something suitable for you.'

'No, nothing yet, but it's not been long. I'll keep looking on the internet too. Something will turn up if it's meant to be.'

'Just hypothetically, would you buy my villa if it ever came on the market – just for the roof terrace of course?'

Vivienne laughed. 'I might. I do like the apartment almost as much as the terrace, but I'm not sure I'd want the fuss of renting out the bottom one. I suppose I could always turn it back into a single villa. Anyway, you're not thinking of moving, are you?'

Olivia shook her head. 'You never know what's around the next corner as they say, but no, the question really was hypothetical.' Unless... She pushed the thought away.

Maxine had some antipasti and wine on the terrace table

when they arrived and the three of them were soon sat sipping wine, eating crisps and olives and listening to the music Maxine had set up. Tonight it was piano jazz, courtesy of Jamie Cullum.

'Where's Thierry tonight?' Olivia asked as casually as she could.

'He's gone to Tourrettes-sur-Loup for another informal chat with Marie-France,' Maxine said. 'It seems he's going ahead with this activity centre business.'

'These activity centres are all the rage these days, aren't they? Here and in the UK,' Vivienne said. 'I think tennis and sailing were the only things on offer when I was younger, not that I have ever had the desire to go white-water rafting or anything like that.'

'I was wondering what to do about Thierry's birthday,' Olivia said. 'It will be his first without his father.' She gave Maxine an apologetic look before continuing. 'I'm making him lunch on the day, but I was wondering about giving him a small party in the evening? What d'you think? I know if I mention it to Maman she'll throw him a dinner party, but I'm not sure that he'd enjoy that.'

'I'll give him a party here,' Maxine said instantly. 'Just an informal get-together of his friends. We'd have to ask Trent and Felicity, though,' she added, looking at Olivia.

'No worries,' Olivia said. 'If you're sure, thank you, Maxie.'

'Before I forget,' Maxine said to Vivienne. 'I think I may have found your perfect home. It belongs to some friends of mine.'

'Really? Where? Pictures?'

'No pictures yet and I can't take you to see it either for a little while. I can tell you a bit about it because I've been to parties there in the past. It's in a gated domain of about eight houses in the countryside close to Valbonne, the village you loved. Four bedrooms, a large kitchen, sitting room with a view out over the Alpes-Maritimes, a study and it has a large swimming pool.'

'When can I see it?' Vivienne asked.

'Not sure. It's been rented out for the past few years, but now the owners have decided to sell. The tenants leave soon and the owners have promised me first look and first refusal.'

'Can't wait to see it. Maybe Natalie will get to see it too when she's here.'

'Any news from Puget?' Maxine asked.

'Not a word,' Vivienne said. 'I'd have thought Pascal Rocher must be back from holiday by now? I guess either the receptionist forgot to give him my message and card or he doesn't want to know anything about the past.' She paused. 'Natalie's hiring a car when she arrives so we can explore a bit, we'll drive out that way and see if we can locate him. If not, well, I've come to the conclusion in the scheme of things, it's not that important really.'

'*Peut-être* for the best,' Maxine said. 'Stirring up muddy water is not always the wise thing to do.'

27

Vivienne was working up on the terrace the next day when her mobile rang. Snatching it up hoping it was Pascal Rocher making contact, her heart sank seeing the caller ID. She took a deep breath before pressing the button.

'Good morning, Jeremy.'

'We've had an offer on the house,' he said without preamble. 'Not as high as I would have liked, but I'm happy to accept it.'

'I thought the agent said there was a lot of interest? That it was a good house in a sought-after area. Surely we don't have to accept the first offer we get?' Vivienne protested.

'I can see you're being difficult again,' Jeremy said. 'Because I want to accept it.'

'What is the offer?'

'Fifteen thousand below the asking price.'

'No way. Tell the agent to negotiate it up another ten and then we'll consider it. Let me know when it happens. Bye.'

'Hang on. There's something else I need to talk to you about.'

Vivienne smothered a sigh. 'What now?'

'Sadie says she can't get through to you.'

'That would be because I've blocked her.'

'But she's desperate to talk to you.'

'Does she really expect me to talk to her after what she's done?'

'But this is business. She's had a film company contact her. There could be quite a large sum involved, which would be good for both of you. She wants to provisionally accept on your behalf.'

Silently, Vivienne absorbed his words and thought about her reply for several seconds. There was no way she was going to be responsible for putting any extra money into Sadie Murphy's bank account even if it meant none going into her own.

'You still there?' Jeremy demanded.

'Yes, I'm still here. I'll discuss it with Sadie when I get back,' Vivienne said.

'But that could be too late.'

'I'll take that chance. Now I'm busy, I have to go,' and she ended the call.

* * *

The next week flew by for Vivienne. The writing was going well and she'd soon have a first draft finished, ready to show to her agent. That thought brought her up short. She certainly wasn't going to show it to Sadie, but, in truth, she didn't quite know what to do with it. When she got home, she'd ask the Society of Authors for advice and try somehow to sever all professional contact with her. Surely sleeping with one of your clients' husbands and having his baby was a severe case of professional misconduct? On the other hand, maybe not in this day and age.

Maxine rang one morning to say she had the keys for the house she'd mentioned the other week and when would she like to view it? 'Now' was Vivienne's instant response.

Maxine laughed. '*D'accord*. I'll pick you up in fifteen minutes.'

On the drive out to Valbonne, Maxine explained that the villa was basically in good condition – 'It's got a good roof and everything structural is fine' – but after being rented out for ten years, certain things needed modernising and it would need decorating throughout.

When Maxine buzzed open the electric gates of the community with a remote from the villa key ring, they drove slowly in and along the road, past immaculate terracotta red-roofed villas with weed-free front gardens and beautiful roses that wouldn't dare drop a petal. Maxine pulled up in front of a sprawling villa built on three different levels, with windows of different shapes and sizes peering through the rampant orange bougainvillea covering the honey-coloured stones.

'It's one of the older villas in the community,' Maxine said. 'But I honestly think it's one of the prettiest, don't you?'

Vivienne nodded. She couldn't speak as she gazed at the villa. If anyone had asked her to describe her idea of a perfect house, this would be it. And she hadn't even been inside yet. She pulled out her phone and took a photo.

'Are you sure this is within the price range I gave you?' she said quietly. 'I couldn't bear not to be able to afford this. It's wonderful.'

'It's definitely within your price range,' Maxine said. 'Come on, let's go inside.'

Inside, as Maxine had warned her, was showing signs of wear and tear, but as Vivienne wandered through the empty rooms, she could visualise the walls repainted, the floor tiles cleaned and polished, shiny windows letting the sunshine in and the rooms filled with rugs and furniture. There was even a bookshelf-lined room that would make a perfect study. A conservatory at the back opened onto a terrace and a swimming pool filled with inviting blue water. A summer kitchen was in one corner and a wicker chaise longue was under a vine-covered pergola in another corner.

Vivienne imagined the parties she could have here, the family visits that would happen, the morning swims she'd take in the pool.

Maxine nudged her. 'I think you have what we French call the *coup de foudre*. You've fallen in love with this house.'

'Yes I have. I'm definitely going to buy it.' Vivienne turned to Maxine. 'Even if I have to mortgage myself up to the hilt.'

'Come on. I'm going to treat you to lunch in the village as a thank you.'

A couple of hours later when Maxine dropped her off back in Antibes, Vivienne ran up the stairs and into the apartment, feeling happier than she had for years. On the way home, she'd asked Maxine to contact the owners of the villa and begin the negotiating process, although Vivienne had also told her she would happily pay the asking price. When her phone rang, she automatically glanced at caller ID. Jeremy. She hesitated before answering it, but not even Jeremy could dispel her happiness this afternoon, so she answered.

'Hi, Jeremy.'

Vivienne's happy mood vanished in a flash as Sadie's voice purred in her ear, 'Hello, Viv. We really need to talk. It's important.'

Without saying a word, Vivienne pressed the off button.

28

'Who's this then?' Thierry asked as Olivia opened the door to him when he arrived for his birthday lunch and a collie dog cautiously edged forward to greet him as well. 'You looking after her for a friend?'

'Sort of. She's called Topsy,' Olivia said.

'You're a lovely girl, Topsy,' Thierry said, bending down stroke her. 'She's gorgeous. I've always fancied having a collie.'

'I'm glad you like her because she's my birthday present to you,' Olivia said in a rush. 'Happy Birthday.'

The silence that greeted her words was loud, before Thierry straightened up and looked at her. 'You're not serious?'

'Yes. I've made sure she comes with everything you need – a month's supply of food, a new bed, a harness for the car, a lead, poo bags and a cage with a blanket for her safe place, which Jilly told me is really an essential requirement for every dog, especially at the beginning.'

'Who's Jilly?'

'She's a friend of my maman's who runs a babysitting service for dogs when their owners go away. She takes them in, they live in the villa with her like her family dog would, no kennels.'

'So how come she sold you Topsy?'

'Would you believe her owners went away for Easter, paid a fortnight's babysitting fees and never returned. When Jilly tried to contact them, their French number no longer worked. She went to the address they'd given her and the neighbour told her they'd sold up and moved away. Jilly was happy to find a good forever home for her because she needs to babysit six paying dogs at a time for her income and Topsy has basically had a free holiday for the last few weeks.'

Absently, Thierry stroked Topsy's head and the dog edged closer to him until her head was leaning against his leg.

'Look, she likes you,' Olivia said. 'I collected her yesterday and she's been really good. I needn't have bothered with a new bed for her, she much prefers the settee – and she slept on my bed last night.'

'But...'

'But what?' Olivia asked anxiously, Thierry's reaction was not what she'd been expecting.

'I've got so much going on at present, I won't be able to give her the attention she needs for a start. And I'm not sure how Maxine will feel about me having a dog at L'Abri.'

'I know you're busy, so any time you can't take her with you, I can have her. If Maxine doesn't want her at L'Abri, she can stay here. She'll be your dog, but we can look after her together if you like until you've bought the farm. She'll love it up there when you move in.'

Thierry looked at her, a grin slowly spreading across his face. 'So she's my dog, but if Maxine would rather not have her at L'Abri, she's going to live with you full time and we're going to look after her together.'

'Yes,' Olivia said, not sure that having Topsy full-time had been quite her plan, but she was happy to agree. It would at least mean she would see Thierry on a regular basis.

'It sounds very much to me, Ms Olivia Murray, that you wanted to buy her for yourself.'

'No. It was you who gave me the idea when you said you eventually wanted a family home with pets around. I've just helped you set that plan in motion. I'll get you a pony for Christmas if you like.'

'You have indeed set the plan in motion,' Thierry agreed, a glint in his eye, and he leant forward and kissed her on the cheek. 'Thank you. But please, no ponies.'

Over lunch, he told her he'd made an official offer for the complete business in Tourrettes-sur-Loup. 'It's mainly the activity centre I want but...' he shrugged. 'Something or someone will turn up to help with the violet farm eventually.'

Olivia took a deep breath. 'I've been thinking about that. I would quite like to be your business partner.'

Thierry looked at her and waited.

'If I'm going to be involved though, I'll need to do a horticultural course to make sure I have some idea of what I'm doing. I can keep the flower taxi business going, do all my deliveries on one, maybe two days a week, and the rest of the time I can spend at the farm. What do you think?'

'I think it's brilliant news,' Thierry said.

'You and Topsy can live in the farmhouse and I'll stay down here, so you'll have the complete run of the place,' Olivia said, smiling at him. But the moment those words had left her lips, contrarily she found herself wishing she was going to live with them both as soon as Thierry moved in.

After lunch, Thierry suggested they took Topsy for a walk out to Cap d'Antibes woods. As they walked, Thierry talked about his plans for the business and Olivia told him about the courses she'd started to research for learning about violets. Topsy behaved impeccably on the lead and was friendly with the other dogs they met, including a large mastiff that Olivia was secretly terrified of, but who, the owner assured them, was as gentle as a lamb. Topsy certainly wasn't intimidated by his size either.

The afternoon flew by and it was nearly six o'clock when they returned to Olivia's. Thierry, under Olivia's instruction, fed Topsy before it was time for him to leave and return to L'Abri and get ready for the party.

He turned at the door. 'Thanks for today, Olivia. It's been a lovely birthday and thanks for Topsy too. I'm sorry I was mean about her at first. I adore her, thank you.' And once again he leant in and brushed Olivia's cheek with a kiss before the door closed behind him.

Topsy whined after he'd left and turned to look at Olivia as much as to say, 'He's gone without me.'

Olivia laughed and sat on the floor to cuddle her. 'We'll see him later,' she promised, hoping that Thierry would have squared it with Maxine. It was too soon to leave Topsy on her own.

Two hours later, she clipped Topsy's lead on and the two of them walked to L'Abri, with Olivia secretly looking forward to her maman's reaction when she met Topsy and realised that she'd bought the dog for Thierry.

* * *

Maxine and Thierry hung the fairy lights around the garden again ready for the party.

'Why don't you leave them up all year?' Thierry said.

'I think I will, such a nuisance taking them down all the time.' Maxine smiled. 'They certainly add a festive touch to the garden.

Do you want party balloons? If you do, you'll have to blow them up.'

Thierry shook his head. 'I think I'm far too old for balloons. Besides, with Topsy coming, I'd hate for one to burst and frighten her. She's a lovely dog.'

'You sound delighted to have had a pet thrust on you without notice,' Maxine said.

'I've wanted a dog for a long time and sharing her with Olivia, although she doesn't know it yet, is the perfect arrangement for me.'

Maxine gave him a look. 'Maybe she knew exactly what she was doing.'

'In that case, I'm even happier,' Thierry said as the front door-bell buzzed.

'That will be Felicity and Trent with your cake. I'll let them in, you stay here. You're not allowed to see your cake before we light the candles.'

Thierry groaned. 'That will be a fire hazard. *D'accord.* I'll start the music.'

Vivienne and Olivia arrived together soon afterwards and Topsy was immediately the centre of attention.

'You bought the dog for yourself?' Felicity said, looking at Olivia. 'Why didn't you say that's what you were doing?'

'I bought it for Thierry, not me,' Olivia said. 'But we've decided to share her until Thierry has a place of his own.'

From the look that Felicity gave her, Olivia knew her maman would be silently digesting that piece of information. She was glad that she and Thierry had decided to keep the news of their business partnership quiet, until it was a signed deal.

A quieter piece of music was streaming from Thierry's laptop as Felicity carefully carried out the cake with its burning candles and placed it on the table. Just as everyone drew breath ready to sing 'Happy Birthday', the doorbell buzzed.

Thierry quickly blew out the candles before turning to Maxine.

'I'll go. You stay here. Hope it's not the neighbours complaining about the noise,' he joked.

A young woman was standing in front of the doorway when he opened the door and Thierry's heart hammered. Tonight was not a good night for this to happen. He knew without asking who this woman was, the likeness was there in her eyes. He also knew Maxine was not keen on surprises. Before she spoke, Thierry was already wondering how to handle this unexpected guest situation.

'Is this the house of Maxine Zonszain?' the woman asked in French.

'Yes,' Thierry answered. 'Am I right in thinking you are Leonie Toussaint, Maxine's daughter?'

The woman gave a surprised nod. 'She's told you about me?'

Thierry nodded and smiled. 'Yes. Do come in and I will take you to Maxine.'

Leonie stepped into the cottage, but hesitated as she heard the sound of music and chatter. 'You are having a party? Perhaps tonight is not a good time. I come back tomorrow.'

'No, not lots of people, just a few friends,' Thierry said, doing a quick head-count. 'Six people including me – I'm Thierry Zonszain by the way.'

Leonie stepped back, staring at him. 'I did not know she had a son.'

'Stepson. Maxine married my father eight years ago. Now...' Thierry paused, coming to a decision. 'I think it better for me to fetch Maxine and the two of you meet privately, yes?'

Leonie gave him a grateful look. 'Please.'

'Two minutes.' And Thierry went to fetch Maxine, who was talking to Vivienne and glanced at him questioningly.

'Maxie, you have a visitor,' he said gently.

'How lovely, who is it? Why haven't you brought them out to join the party?'

'She'd rather see you on your own.'

'Why? Who on earth is it?' Her voice faltered as she looked at him. 'It's not...?'

'Leonie, yes.'

Maxine clutched his arm. 'I'm not ready for this tonight.'

'Yes, you are. Take a deep breath, smile and think how much you've longed for this moment.' Thierry pulled her arm through his before turning to speak to everyone. 'Excuse us for a moment or two. Help yourself to everything. I'll be back soon to cut the cake.'

Four pairs of astonished eyes followed their progress up the garden. Even Felicity was silent, as they all wondered what was going on.

Thierry could feel Maxine shaking as they walked back into the cottage and squeezed her hand reassuringly.

Leonie had moved to look at the photos on the small table and had her back towards them as they entered the sitting room. She turned as she sensed their presence and for several seconds she and Maxine stood staring mutely at each other.

It was Maxine who broke the silence, her voice breaking as she spoke. 'I don't know what to say, Leonie, except it's wonderful to see you.'

'It's been a long time,' Leonie said flatly but didn't echo Maxine's happy words.

'Leonie, can I get you a coffee, or a glass of wine maybe?' Thierry said.

Leonie shook her head. 'No, thank you. I shouldn't have come tonight. You're busy with a party. I'll come back tomorrow.'

'Please stay now you're here. Meet my friends,' Maxine said.

'No. Meeting you tonight is enough. I promised myself I'd make myself come and find you as soon as I arrived in Antibes and I've done that. It is enough for one day.'

'Where are you staying?' Thierry asked.

'A hotel in Antibes.'

'You are welcome to stay here,' Maxine said. 'We'd be able to talk properly then.'

'I'm not sure.' Leonie regarded her with a thoughtful expression. 'But I have a lot of questions I'd like to ask.'

'We certainly have a lot of catching up to do,' Maxine said. 'Come and stay tomorrow for as long as you like. How long are you here in Antibes for?'

'I have some days off work. Whether I decide to stay for them all, I don't know,' Leonie shrugged. '*D'accord*. I'll come back tomorrow morning. Now I'll return to my hotel.' And before either Thierry or Maxine could stop her, she'd slipped out of the sitting room into the hall and was gone.

Maxine exhaled a deep breath as she heard the door close. 'Was that really my daughter? Or did I imagine it?'

'It was definitely your daughter. She has your eyes,' Thierry said. He kept the thought that they were the only things about Leonie that had reassured him that she was related to Maxine. Her uptight, introvert manner was so far removed from her mother's outgoing personality, it was hard to put them together as mother and daughter. Hopefully that would change as they got to know each other. 'I'll move out of the guest room in the morning,' Thierry said. 'It's not a problem,' he added as Maxine went to protest. 'Me not being around will give you both some privacy to get to know each other.'

'Thank you. We'd better rejoin the others. And you need to cut that cake,' Maxine said.

'Are you going to tell them about your visitor?' Thierry asked.

'Yes.' Maxine nodded. 'I've hidden the truth for too long. If Leonie is to be back in my life, my friends need to know about what happened. Your birthday champagne is still in the fridge. I think it's time to open it.'

Back out in the garden, the birthday atmosphere had faded somewhat, but Thierry quickly cut his cake while Maxine poured the glasses of bubbly.

Everyone raised their glasses and wished Thierry a happy birthday before Maxine said, 'I have to tell you about my unexpected visitor. I have a daughter, Leonie, whom I haven't seen for over thirty years.' She gave a self-depreciating shrug. 'And I definitely wasn't expecting to see her this evening.'

'Is she still here?' Felicity asked, looking towards the cottage.

'No. She's returned to her hotel. Tomorrow she is coming back to stay with me and we're going to talk.'

'Bring her to lunch next week,' Felicity said. 'I'd like to meet her.'

Maxine smiled gently at her friend and shook her head. Far too soon to introduce Leonie to Felicity. 'We'll see. I'm not sure how long she will actually be staying,' she said diplomatically.

Olivia wandered over to stand by Thierry. 'Sounds like the guest bedroom here could get a bit crowded tomorrow?' she said quietly.

Thierry smiled ruefully. 'I've told Maxine I'll move out in the morning, give them some privacy.' He bent down and stroked Topsy, who was sitting at his feet gazing up at him adoringly. 'I'll find a hotel room for a few nights.'

'My guest room is empty,' Olivia said. 'You're more than welcome to stay with me and Topsy.'

Thierry looked at her, a smile hovering on his lips. 'That would be great, thanks.'

It was not long before everyone drifted off, Felicity and Trent to drive back to Monaco and Olivia and Vivienne to walk Topsy back to their villa.

Together, Maxine and Thierry cleared the remains of the party away and sat with the last of the champagne under the loggia.

'I can't believe Leonie's here in town. That she and I are going to sit down together tomorrow and talk about everything,' Maxine said. 'I'm not sure I'm going to get much sleep tonight.' She took a sip of her drink. 'Seeing the grown-up version of Leonie for the first time, actually standing in my house after all these years, was amazing. I just wanted to throw my arms around her, but I didn't dare. I know we're a long way from the kind of mother-daughter relationship that does that kind of thing. But I'm going to do my upmost to make sure we get there.'

29

Thierry was up early the next morning, packing his things away and changing the sheets on the bed. He refused breakfast but had a coffee with Maxine, saying he'd buy croissants on the way to Olivia's. He gave Maxine a hug and wished her good luck.

'Everything will work out, you'll see.'

'Please – won't you stay? I'm a nervous wreck. I'm worried I'll do or say something that will send her away again. She seemed so diffident last evening.'

'That's because she as nervous as you are,' Thierry said gently. 'It's best if the two of you are alone and can get to know each other without anyone else around. You can both talk honestly to each without fear of interruption.'

'I'm so scared.'

'If things get heated between the two of you and you'd like me to come back and referee, just text and I'll be here. But I'm sure it won't be necessary.'

'*Merci*, Thierry. I'm sorry your birthday party was interrupted and ruined.'

'It wasn't ruined. I'm happy for you that you now have a chance to reconnect with your daughter. Right, I'm off to Olivia's.'

'Make the best of the opportunity,' Maxine called out, laughing, with something of the old Maxine creeping into her voice. 'And, by the way, I love your new dog.'

After Thierry had left, a thoughtful Maxine went to the cupboard under the stairs, where, right at the back, she found the plastic container on wheels that she wanted and pulled it out. She lifted the lid and stared at the contents, remnants of a long-ago life. Slowly, she picked up Anatole the knitted mouse and held it tight.

'Come on, Anatole, let's see if you can help heal the breach between Leonie and me.' She pushed the container back into the cupboard and climbed the stairs to the bedroom that Thierry had vacated. Carefully she placed the soft toy on the pillow and left the room.

* * *

Sitting out in the yard with Topsy under the table waiting patiently for crumbs, Olivia and Thierry ate a late breakfast of coffee and almond croissants that Thierry had bought on his way from L'Abri.

'How was Maxine this morning? A long-lost daughter turning up like that must have been one hell of a shock for her last night.'

'It was. She's nervous about Leonie returning today.'

'Did you know she had a daughter?'

'Yes. Papa told me before he died. It's a complicated story and not mine to tell, but he wanted me to know so I could help if necessary, in case Maxine ever needed someone on her side and he was no longer around. She's got no other family. I hope it all works out between her and Leonie, but if not, I'll be there to pick up the pieces like Papa would want me to be.'

'I can be there with you too,' Olivia said. 'I don't need to know the full story. Maxine and I have a lovely relationship, I can talk to her about anything – she's easier than my maman in that respect.'

'Do you have any plans for this morning?' Thierry asked.

'No, other than walking the dog.' There was a short bark as Topsy appeared from under the table and stood looking at them expectantly. 'I deliberately didn't say her name, but she obviously knows the w word,' Olivia laughed, giving her a stroke. 'Later.'

'How about you?'

'I want to stay fairly local in case Maxine rings, so I'll unpack my things, come with you on the w-a-l-k and then come back here and work on my laptop.'

'I've got a small arrangement to do for a restaurant near the ramparts, so I'll do that while you unpack and we can go that way and drop it off,' Olivia said. 'Give me half an hour.'

In Olivia's guest bedroom, Thierry unpacked the few possessions he'd brought with him, wondering whether he was doing the right thing moving in with Olivia, even though it was on a temporary basis. It would be a sort of practice run of living together, which might persuade her to move to the farm when it was finally his. Something that he sincerely hoped would happen sooner rather than later. On the other hand, the next few days and nights might prove to be a total disaster.

Trent had phoned him last night offering him a room in the Monaco apartment for as long as he needed. Thierry had thanked him and said he was all sorted for a few nights, but had guiltily held back from telling him he was moving into his daughter's guest bedroom.

But now everything was going ahead for him to buy the violet farm and outdoor centre, it made sense to stay local. Besides, staying here would also give him a great opportunity to bond with Topsy, as well as the chance to grow closer to Olivia. He wasn't about to say no to either of those opportunities.

30

It was mid-morning before Leonie arrived at L'Abri. Maxine was so sure that she'd run away and wasn't going to turn up that she was about to ring Thierry and ask him to come back when the doorbell buzzed. Taking a deep breath, willing herself not to say the wrong things, Maxine opened the door and smiled. 'Good morning, Leonie. You're here. I'm so relieved. I thought you might have changed your mind.'

Leonie shook her head. 'No. I have questions that need answering, so I have to stay until we have talked.'

Maxine stifled a sigh as she heard the forceful tone in Leonie's voice. Hopefully there would be some understanding absolution when they had talked and she'd heard Maxine's side of their family story. 'Come into the kitchen. I will make us a coffee and we can sit in the garden and talk. Leave your suitcase in the hall. We'll take it up later to your room.'

'Your stepson, I forget his name... he is not here?'

'Thierry. No, he's gone to stay with a friend. He wanted to give us space to get to know one another.' As she made the coffee,

Maxine said. 'I wish you'd told me you were coming. I would have been better prepared.'

'I didn't want to tell you in case I changed my mind. Also, I wanted it to be a surprise for you. To catch you unexpectedly.'

'You certainly did that,' Maxine said. 'Just so you know, for the future, I'm not a fan of surprises,' she smiled at Leonie as she added, 'However welcome they may turn out to be.'

Leonie gave an indifferent shrug. 'Your husband, Thierry's father, he was not here last night?'

'*Non*. He died last year.'

'Before my father then.' There was a short silence before Leonie said, 'Thierry lives with you?'

'At the moment yes, but not all the time,' Maxine said, trying not to let Leonie's lack of a sympathetic response to her loss of Pierre bother her.

Taking their coffees out to the garden, they sat under the loggia in silence for a moment or two, Leonie looking around the garden and Maxine deep in her own thoughts. This daughter of hers was a strange mixture of confidence and uncertainty. It was hard to work out how best to respond to her. How best to draw her close again, push away the distance of the missing years?

'I've never lived in a house with a garden,' Leonie said. 'This is beautiful. So peaceful.'

'Thank you. I find spending an hour out here weeding or just sitting down by the pond very therapeutic at times. Tell me where you have lived?' Maxine said.

'India – although we were only there for six months when we first left, so I don't remember much of that time, just that I cried a lot for a long time. Papa would get so cross with me. Then London for a little while. All over France for years and for the last six years, Paris.'

'Pierre and I lived in the 7th Arrondissement until last year,' Maxine said quietly.

'You did? We could have passed each other any time.'

'I thought that when I received your contact details.'

'Would you have instinctively known me if we had?' Leonie demanded.

'*Non*, I have to say I don't think I would. Maybe if we'd met and spoken, something would have aroused my maternal suspicions.' Maxine glanced at her. 'I never forgot you. There's never been a day when I didn't think of you. I have missed having you in my life so much.'

'Papa always told me you didn't have any maternal instincts,' Leonie said, matter-of-factly.

'He was very wrong. But then I don't suppose you'd have recognised me as your mother either,' Maxine said. 'Excuse me for a moment. I need to fetch something.'

A moment later, she handed Leonie the photograph from the sitting room.

'I saw this last night. Who is it?'

'You and me, shortly before your father took you away.'

Leonie studied the photograph for a moment. 'We both look happy here and yet for years Papa always told me you couldn't cope with me. That you didn't love me enough. You weren't a natural mother, that's why he had to rescue and look after me alone.'

'That is not true. I loved you from the moment you were placed in my arms – and I've never stopped. I extended my maternity leave to be with you, would have stopped working altogether, but Daiva insisted I returned to work when you went to *l'ecole maternelle*. Possibly because we depended on my money to pay the rent.' Maxine tried, but failed, to keep the anger out of her voice. Leonie had obviously, as she had expected, accepted the lies Daiva had fed her down the years. She shook her head. What was it going to take to get Leonie to accept the true version of events?

'You are telling me a different story to the one he told me,' Leonie said, staring at her.

Maxine looked at her. 'Are you really surprised about that?'

Leonie sighed and shook her head. 'No. I've known forever that my father had a way of bending the truth to suit his purpose.'

Maxine nodded. 'He did.' She stood up. 'Come on. I'll show you your room.'

As Maxine opened the bedroom door, Leonie stared across at the toy on the pillow and burst into tears before running across the room and clutching him tightly.

'It's Anatole! You kept him. I've never forgotten him, I missed him so much in the beginning. Papa told me I was being a baby.'

Maxine went to give her a hug her but stopped. Leonie might not be a hugger. The days were long gone when she used to run to her for a cuddle four or five times a day.

'My friend Olivia and I have a phrase we use when we'd like a comfort hug, we say I'm needy. Are you needy at this moment?'

Leonie gulped and sniffed. 'I... I think I am.'

Maxine's arms went round her in an instant and she held her tight, not caring that she too was crying as she held her daughter in her arms for the first time in thirty years.

31

Vivienne was waiting for Natalie to ring to say she'd landed at Nice airport and was about to pick up her hire car so when her phone rang, she snatched it up without looking to see who it was.

'I have to tell you we've had another offer for the house, just five thousand short of the asking price.'

'Hello, Jeremy,' Vivienne said, needled by the fact that once again Jeremy hadn't even said hello before straightaway hitting her with the details in an ego-led conversation. 'That's good. We can accept it,' she said brightly. 'Get things moving.'

'Talking of moving, Sadie doesn't want me to move out. She wants us to live here. Has got lots of ideas for modernising the place.'

'I bet she has,' Vivienne muttered.

'The thing is, Viv, I don't really want to move either and we were wondering about me staying put and buying your share.'

'I'm sure your solicitor will have pointed out that legally I'm entitled to half the value of the marital home. So that translates to you needing to pay me roughly half of the current offer on the asking price,' Vivienne said crisply. 'If you want to do that, you can keep the house.'

'Oh come on, Viv, you know I don't have that kind of money stashed away. Besides, house prices have increased massively in the last few years.'

'Exactly, so if you buy me out for less than I'm entitled to, how do you expect me to be able to buy another house? And Jeremy? Hasn't it occurred to either of you I'm the loser in this situation? I'm having to move out whether I want to or not because of your affair. How can the two of you be so selfish and inconsiderate of my feelings?' Vivienne took a deep breath and tried to calm down before she really lost it with her soon-to-be ex-husband. 'I'll email the agents and tell them we accept the current offer.'

'I can do that,' Jeremy blustered. 'No need for you to.'

'Okay. Anything else? Only I'm waiting for Natalie to phone to say that she's landed in Nice and will be here soon.'

'She's coming all that way to see you? I haven't seen her since... well, since I told her my news.'

'You only told her half the news as well. How did you expect her to react when she heard Sadie was your new partner? Not to mention the fact that she is pregnant? Goodbye.'

Ending the call, Vivienne opened her laptop and pulled up the estate agent's email. She'd write and make sure they knew the offer was acceptable. She wouldn't put it past this new Jeremy to delay things in the hope she'd be forced to accept less than her due. As she sent the email, Vivienne gave a sigh. The thought of returning to England, to home, to all the problems that she would be faced with, not least divorce papers, was becoming less and less appealing. She looked at the photo of the Valbonne villa she'd taken on her phone. She'd transferred it to her laptop as soon as she'd got back to use as the wallpaper for her screen. She had to keep the thought that the villa in Valbonne was waiting for her uppermost in her mind, and that would make everything so much easier to deal with.

* * *

Three quarters of an hour later, Natalie arrived. 'Sorry I couldn't get through to tell you I was on my way, the line was busy and then I was driving. Which, I have to say, was an experience! I thought the Italian drivers were bad enough, but the French appear to be as bad.'

'It was your dad on the phone. He's had a higher offer on the house, which I've told him to accept, but there's a new problem. Sadie wants to live there. Anyway, let's forget all that,' and she pulled Natalie in for a hug. 'It's so good to see you.'

'Tim sends his love,' Natalie said. 'He said he'd spoken to you?'

Vivienne nodded, remembering their conversation. 'He, like you, is so cross with your dad – and cross with himself that he didn't tell me his suspicions.'

For the next hour, they sat up on the terrace with a bottle of rosé, a basket of baguette chunks and a plate of charcuterie, catching up with everything and planning a few excursions.

'I'd love you to meet Maxine and Olivia, so I thought I'd invite them for aperitifs one evening.'

'Have you discovered anything about our French connection yet?' Natalie asked eagerly.

'Sadly no. Maxine took me out to Puget Theniers a couple of weeks ago and we think we've found a Pascal Rocher, but he was away on holiday.' Vivienne jumped up. 'I bought you some things while we were there. I'll just run down and get them. They're in my room.'

She handed Natalie the baking trays she'd bought a few minutes later.

'There's this wonderful old-fashioned hardware shop in the village that you're going to love when we go. It's about an hour and a half by car. I can always ask Maxine if she's free, if you'd rather not drive.'

'No, I'm happy to drive, as long it's not along that bord de mer road,' Natalie said. 'I love these tins, thank you.'

'Good. But whether we find Pascal Rocher or not, I intend to stop looking after this next visit. There's too much else going on that I need to concentrate on. Oh, I nearly forgot,' and she opened her phone to show Natalie the picture of the villa. 'There's a bigger one on the laptop, and some of the interior too. What do you think? I'm waiting to hear if my offer has been accepted.'

'You're buying this villa?' Natalie looked at her mother. 'I think I might have to move over here with you permanently. It looks out of this world.'

'It needs a little TLC inside, but it's picture-book perfect, isn't it? I can't wait to live there,' Vivienne confessed.

32

After Maxine had hugged Leonie and handed her a tissue to help dry her tears, she'd left her to compose herself and to unpack the small suitcase she'd brought. 'See you downstairs when you're ready and we decide how we are to spend the day,' she said.

Downstairs, she poured herself a glass of water and drank it standing in the kitchen doorway looking out over the garden. How on earth was she going to help this strangely mixed-up and vulnerable daughter of hers? There were lots of things they both had to learn about each other, but Leonie's attitude was so matter-of-fact as she asked the questions, that it was rather upsetting.

Maxine would bet money on the fact that Leonie had never talked to anyone about her life, the problems she faced at home. And Maxine was convinced there had been problems, she knew how Daiva operated after all. Getting her to open up about them to her would be the first step to giving Leonie the help she needed and then Maxine could hopefully start to deal with it. Somehow she had to get her to tell her exactly how her life for the past thirty years had been. She knew so little about her. They both had ghosts to lay. Maybe if she started to talk about her own life with Daiva, Leonie would open up about hers?

'Your garden is beautiful,' Leonie said, making Maxine jump. She'd been so deep in thought, she hadn't heard her coming down the stairs.

'Thank you. Pierre, my husband, did the hard work. It's easy to maintain now.' Maxine glanced at Leonie. 'Shall we have another coffee – or tea – and decide how to spend the day?'

'Tea please. Can we sit down by the pond? I like watching the fish.'

'Why don't you take a couple of chairs down there while I organise tea,' Maxine said.

Leonie was sat looking at the fish gobbling up the food she'd thrown them from the tin Maxine kept nearby when Maxine took the teas down. 'I hope you don't mind me feeding them?'

'I usually feed them in the evening, so we must be careful not to overfeed them tonight.' Maxine handed Leonie her tea and sat down alongside her. 'Do you remember anything of your early childhood apart from missing Anatole?' She noticed Leonie's body tense before she shook her head.

'No.'

'That's a shame. Will you talk to me about your childhood with Daiva?'

'Why? My childhood was over years ago, there's little point in discussing it. The past is past, nothing will change what happened.'

'True. But talking about things helps to rid the system of any lingering negativity,' Maxine said quietly, realising that the conversation was going nowhere. 'Have you been to Antibes before? Lots to explore then,' she said when Leonie shook her head. 'Shall I be your tour guide and show you around? We can have lunch in my favourite restaurant. And when we get back I have some things to show you.'

'Thank you,' Leonie said. 'I'd like that.'

* * *

It was mid-afternoon when they returned to L'Abri from seeing the sights of Antibes and having lunch in the covered garden of The Auberge restaurant there. The temperature was in the high twenties by the time they settled themselves in the garden with glasses and a pitcher of iced water with slices from a lemon Maxine had cut from the tree in the garden, floating in it.

Maxine had taken the first refreshing gulp of her drink when Leonie asked, 'There is nothing of my father here in the house, is there?'

'Did you expect there to be?'

'No not really. The house has a good vibe about it.' Leonie studied the water in her glass. 'Which it wouldn't have if there was a trace of him here.' She paused. 'Where are the things you were going to show me?'

'In a box under the stairs. We can get it out later. It's nothing much, but they meant the world to me after you'd been taken away. Toys, books with stories I used to read to you, clothes and, of course, Anatole was in there.'

'Why didn't you come after us in the beginning? Papa always told me you didn't care enough.'

Maxine stilled and put her glass down. 'You'll never know how much I longed to do that, how much I tried to do it. But I literally didn't have a clue as to where he'd taken you. And nobody would help me. It was a dreadful time for me. The solicitors every time I asked – which was often daily – repeated like a mantra, "the child is well and being cared for by her father." I doubt they even knew where you were living most of the time. As for the gendarmes in Paris, they didn't want to know. He was your father so he had every right to take you on holiday, they said. I screamed at them once that you'd been kidnapped, not taken on a jolly holiday.'

Leonie was silent for a moment. 'Did Papa have a drink problem when he was with you?'

'He was an alcoholic long before me,' Maxine said quietly. 'As what they call a high-functioning alcoholic, he was adept at keeping it hidden from me until we were married. It was mere weeks before he stopped hiding it from me and showed his true self. He knew if I'd realised about it before I would never have married him.' Maxine bit her lip as she looked at Leonie. 'Other people always found him charming. They'd see him as a happy social drinker. If I – or you, I suspect – had told anyone what he was like behind closed doors, they would have called us liars before they believed it.' Maxine picked up her water but put it down again without taking even a sip. The moment she had been dreading had finally arrived. The moment when she had to voice the concerns that had plagued her every day. 'There is something I dread asking but I need to know – was Daiva ever abusive in any way towards you?'

Leonie gave an unexpected shiver, and Maxine looked at her anxiously.

'He controlled every aspect of my life, but he never touched me or hit me,' Leonie said. She gave Maxine a sharp glance as she heard her sigh of relief. 'He abused and hit you?'

'Frequently. It got so bad, the local hospital would ask me what I'd tripped over this time or which door had walked into me? They guessed the truth and did try to get me to tell someone, get some help, but...' Maxine sighed. 'I wouldn't. I was terrified he'd take it out on you, I couldn't take that risk. Even when he started threatening to take you away from me if I didn't do what he told me to do.'

'I'm sorry he did what he did to you,' Leonie said quietly, looking at her for the first time with empathy.

Maxine nodded. 'I need you to know that although our estrangement was not my fault, I do feel I was partly responsible. That sounds like a contradiction, but it's not really. I think Daiva had guessed that I was secretly trying to find a way of leaving and taking you with me. So he decided he'd go before I did, and then cut contact completely. If I'd managed to escape with you, I'd probably have done the same to him for a different reason. Not merely to punish him, but also because I was terrified of what he might do to you. My big regret is that I left it too late to leave him. But to cut me out of your life so totally was more than cruel to both of us. It was the action of a barbaric man.' Maxine wiped the tears away from her cheeks with her hand. 'Leonie, however you feel about me, however much you blame me for things, I am so happy that you and I are back in touch.'

Leonie, at her side, caught hold of her nearest hand and squeezed it tightly. 'I can give you a hug if you are needy,' she whispered.

33

After a couple of days sightseeing with Natalie, Vivienne felt like a tourist intent on ticking off places and experiences. They'd walked around Antibes looking at the sights until their feet hurt, tick; they'd caught the train to Nice on another day and walked along the Promenade des Anglais, tick; they'd been on a boat trip to the Îles de Lérins, tick (that was somewhere Vivienne was determined to revisit) when she suggested that a nice quiet drive out into the back country up to Puget Theniers would be a good idea before they ran out of time.

Vivienne and Natalie had a leisurely breakfast out on the terrace the next day before setting out for Puget. Vivienne suggested they drove straight up the main 202 road and as they left Nice behind, Natalie was intrigued by all the steel nets hanging across the face of the mountainous sheer rock sides of the road. 'What are they for?'

'In bad weather, there are often rockfalls and landslides in this area, roads are closed for days, weeks sometimes. Maxine told me there was a devastating landslide over there in the mountain village of Saint-Martin-Vésubie after a big storm only a couple of years ago,' Vivienne said, gesturing to the hills and mountains on their right-hand side. 'Hard to believe now, isn't it?'

An hour later as they drove past the village sign, Puget Theniers and saw the modern bridge over the river, Natalie asked, 'Do you know where this Pascal Rocher actually lives?'

'The lady in the *Mairie* we spoke to said he lives by the church.'

'Let's hope there aren't too many houses around the church, but presumably we can ask a neighbour.'

'It shouldn't be a problem finding the right house,' Vivienne said. '*La Poste* always delivers letters to a box outside houses with the owner's name on it. We just have to look at the postboxes.' She hesitated and glanced at Natalie. 'D'you think we're doing the right thing? I mean, I did leave my contact details and he hasn't used them. Maybe we...' Her voice died away as she gave Natalie an anxious look.

'Mum, we're here now. Maybe your message wasn't passed on. If we find him, you can talk to him face to face and if he doesn't want to know,' Natalie shrugged. 'It won't matter – we can forget all about him.'

They parked in the main car park and began to walk through the village towards the church. Vivienne pointed out the Quincaillerie du Rocher to Natalie as they passed. 'There's the shop where I bought your catering tins. Want to pop in and have a look around now?'

Natalie shook her head. 'Maybe afterwards. Let's get this French connection sorted.'

They walked along the street peering as discreetly as they could at names on the house postboxes.

'Mum, I think I've found it,' Natalie called, standing by the front door of one of a row of terraced cottages.

Vivienne joined her and together they read the name on the box 'Rocher et family'.

'Maybe it's a relative of Pascal and not the man we want,' Vivienne said.

'May I ask why two English ladies are standing at my front door hoping to find a man?' an amused voice behind asked in accented but perfect English.

They both turned in surprise to find a tall man, with piercing blue eyes and sun-bleached grey hair, regarding them with a smile. The thought 'now he's a real silver fox' was the first thing that went through Vivienne's mind before she collected herself.

'We're looking for a man called Pascal Rocher. Are you a relative?' When he nodded, Vivienne asked, 'Could you tell me where we can find him? I'd like to talk to him.'

'I'm Gilles Rocher and Pascal is my father,' Gilles said. 'And you'll find him indoors in the family house he was born and raised in and where he has lived the majority of his life.'

Vivienne registered Pascal had a son as well as a daughter. She had siblings about her own age then.

'Would it be possible for us to meet him?' Natalie asked.

'Of course. Papa likes meeting new people.' Gilles opened the front door and gestured for them to enter. 'Papa, you have visitors from England,' he called out.

The likeness between Gilles and the elderly man who appeared was striking and there was no denying they were father and son. Vivienne felt a shiver of excitement as she saw Pascal Rocher for the first time. Was she finally meeting her birth father?

'For our English visitors, I will make the tea,' Gilles said.

'*Bonjour*, Monsieur Rocher,' Vivienne said holding out her hand towards Pascal, which he took and shook. 'I am Vivienne Wilson.'

'*Bonjour, Madame*, it is a pleasure to meet you. And this is?' He turned, holding out his hand towards Natalie.

'My daughter Natalie.'

'Again, it is my pleasure to meet you, Mademoiselle Natalie,' Pascal said, shaking her hand too.

'I'm afraid neither of us speak very much French,' Vivienne said apologetically.

'Speak *Anglaise*. I will understand. A long time ago, I live in England for a short time. Please come into the salon and sit down. Gilles will bring the tea. You are on holiday in Puget?'

'Thank you,' Vivienne said as she and Natalie sat on the settee. 'We're staying in Antibes. I left my card at the *Mairie* here several weeks ago and I was hoping you'd ring me. Did the receptionist not pass on my message about Deidre's daughter when you returned from holiday?'

'She did. The name Deidre meant nothing to me, so I decided there was no point in contacting you. I owe you an apology for that, but it didn't seem important to me at the time.'

'I see.' Vivienne took a deep breath. 'It's just that I believe you may have known my mother a long time ago,' she said, looking him straight in the eye, and leaving an unspoken and unacknowledged suggestion hanging in the air.

'And why do you believe that?' Pascal asked quietly.

'I found your name, address and a photograph with my birth certificate when I was clearing out my mother's house after she died. Your name and address is actually on a sealed envelope.'

'I do not understand. You did not know your mother had these things?'

'Not until after she died. They'd been hidden away in a drawer forever. She was my adoptive mother, not my birth mother. It was my birth mother who was called Deidre.'

Pascal looked at her and shook his head. 'I am sorry, but I have to tell you again, I never know an English woman with that name.'

'Are you sure? I mean, I realise it's a long time ago. Could you have forgotten her name?'

'My memory is still good, and I am a Frenchman,' Pascal gave her a smile. 'I haven't known so many English women to forget one. I am sorry.'

Vivienne sighed. No relatives after all. 'I had hoped the name would lead me to learn about my birth father, but it seems I've been heading down the wrong road. Thank you for your time.' And she and Natalie stood up to leave at the same moment as Gilles appeared with tea for them all.

'Please stay and have tea with us,' Gilles said. 'Sweeten the disappointment of not having the result you would like. I make the canelés today. We share with you.'

'Mum has bought me some of the special tins for me to make them. She bought them in the shop here with your name on,' Natalie said. 'I'm looking forward to making them when I get home. Are you a chef?' she asked.

Gilles shook his head. '*Non.* I like cooking. You do too, I think?'

'I am a trained chef, but I specialise in cakes and desserts. These are good,' she added after taking a bite of the small fluted pastries with their soft centres and caramelised sides. 'I hope the ones I make turn out as well.'

Pascal looked at Vivienne. 'You have the envelope and the photograph with you?'

Vivienne nodded.

'I know I don't know of the lady in question, but please may I see the photograph out of interest?'

'Of course,' and Vivienne reached into her bag and handed it to him.

Vivienne watched him as he stared at the photograph and the expression on his face froze.

'*Papa. Ça va?*' Gilles said concern written over his face.

Pascal nodded. '*Oui, oui, ça va.*' He took another look at the photograph. 'I recognise the place where this was taken.' His voice was trembling as he asked her, 'This envelope you have. It is definitely addressed to me?'

'It's addressed to a Pascal Rocher who lives in Puget.'

'Please may I have it in that case?' Pascal looked back at the photograph, shaking his head in wonder. 'She kept it all this time.'

'What do you mean?' Vivienne asked as she reached in her bag for the envelope and handed it to him.

Pascal took the envelope and regarded her intently for several seconds. 'May I ask you a question or two?'

'Yes,' Vivienne said, wondering where on earth the conversation was going.

'Your adoptive mother – she was English?'

'Yes.'

'And where in England did she live?'

'London and after she was married, near Bristol.' She watched as Pascal took a deep breath.

'This photograph is of your mother and me and was taken at one of the happiest times of my life. Your adoptive mother's name...' he closed his eyes and paused. 'Was Jacqueline, was it not?'

Vivienne gasped. 'Yes. You knew her?'

'More than that. I wanted to marry her.'

34

_____

A stunned silence followed Pascal's words as Gilles, Vivienne and Natalie all stared at him in shock.

'_Je suis désolé_. Forgive me, _s'il vous plaît_,' a clearly emotional Pascal said. 'I think I would like to be alone to read the letter, so I go to my room. Gilles, _peut-être_ you could entertain Vivienne and Natalie for an hour and then we could all have lunch together in town and I will attempt to explain how I knew Jacqueline.'

Pascal stood up and left the room, leaving the others sitting in stunned silence. As they sat there, they could hear his slow foot-steps mounting the stairs and then walking across the floor of the room above them.

It was a clearly shaken Gilles who finally spoke. 'To say I am speechless is the understatement of the century I think,' he said slowly. 'Papa has never ever mentioned having another woman in his life. I thought my mother had been the only one for him. They were married for nearly fifty years and revelled in their family life.' Agitated, he ran his fingers through his hair. 'I don't understand how he could have kept this secret to himself for so long.'

'I'm so sorry,' Vivienne said. 'I've been so fixated on trying to find my birth father that I didn't really think of the consequences for other people. But really, nothing has changed for you and your family, has it? Pascal and your mother were happy and you clearly had a lovely childhood. I think this love affair with Jacqueline happened when he was a young man and before he married your mother.'

Gilles nodded. '*Oui*, you are right of course,' he said slowly. 'It was the shock of Papa saying he'd wanted to marry someone else.' He took a deep breath. 'You will stay for lunch and hear what he has to say?'

Vivienne gave a soft laugh. 'I just hope it isn't too upsetting for your father, but wild horses wouldn't drag me away without hearing the whole of his story.'

'Me neither,' Natalie said. 'We're definitely staying for lunch.'

'*Bon*. How about we go and book a table in the hotel – Papa eats there a lot, he'll know to find us there – and then have a wander around and I can tell you a little history about the town. Or we can have a drink in the bar.'

'Sounds good. If there's time, can we also show Natalie the Quincaillerie du Rocher please,' Vivienne said.

'I'll book the table and we can go there first, it's not far away,' Gilles said.

* * *

An hour later when they arrived at the hotel, they found Pascal already sitting at a table in the garden waiting for them and he stood up to greet them with a smile on his face.

'*Ça va*, Papa?' Gilles asked for the second time that morning.

'*Oui, ça va*. Ladies, I have taken the liberty of ordering a bottle of Prosecco to toast our new friendship and to remember my old friend.'

Waiters appeared as soon as they were seated, one with the Prosecco, the other with a bread basket and a plate of charcuterie. Once the sparkling wine had been poured, Pascal raised his glass in a toast. 'Jacqueline,' and they all followed suit. 'Now a toast to our new friendship,' Pascal said. 'To us.'

As they sipped and then placed their glasses on the table to help themselves to bread and meat, Pascal began to tell them about his and Jacqueline's love story.

'Because it was a love story,' he said sadly. 'And it's only today that have I finally learnt the reason why it ended. I was nineteen and I went to London on an exchange visit with my college for three months. I met Jacqueline the first week I was there.' He smiled at the memory. 'She worked in a cafe part-time earning extra money and there was a spark between us immediately. We spent every moment available to us together. She showed me parts of London that visitors rarely see. We made plans for the future when we'd both finished our studies. She was going to come to France to live and we were going to be together here. I was hoping to qualify as a *vétérinaire* eventually, and Jacqueline, well, she'd hoped to become a nurse.' He turned to Vivienne. 'Did she fulfil that ambition?'

'She did for a while before she and Oscar adopted me.'

'Oscar?'

'Her husband.'

Pascal gave an accepting nod of his head. 'The last week of my time in England arrived. The day before I left, we talked about the house we would live in, how happy we would be and I told her how beautiful the children we would make together would be. The photograph of us standing by Eros was taken on that last day. The day I plucked up the courage to ask her to marry me. She squealed with joy and threw her arms round me. It was only later that I realised she'd not said yes. The next day, poof, like that it was over. She'd disappeared out of my life. And I never knew the true reason why until today.'

'Had you met her parents? Couldn't you have gone to her home and asked?' Vivienne said.

Pascal nodded. 'I did, just hours before I had to leave. Her father answered the door. He was visibly upset as he spoke to me. Said he was sorry to be the one to tell me, but she didn't want to see me, that she'd had a change of heart and that I was to have a happy life without her. When I asked him if he knew why she'd changed so suddenly, he looked at me and shook his head, and closed the door.'

'Papa, I'm so sorry,' Gilles said.

Pascal bit his lip. 'I had to catch the boat train back that evening. I wrote a letter, telling her I loved her and asked her to write and tell me why she had finished with me?'

'The letter you gave me this morning was the reply that never got posted for some reason.'

Silence fell around the table.

'I hope you forgive me, but I'm not going to share all the contents of that letter with you, they are very personal and private. But that day we discussed having a family, which I always dearly wanted, was the day she decided she had no choice but to end things with me. She'd known for some time that she would never be able to have children and me talking about the beautiful children we would have made her realise how much I wanted them and she knew she couldn't be responsible for depriving me of them. She set me free to meet someone else who could give me those beautiful children I wanted.' He glanced at Gilles. 'Your maman was that person and I did love her with all my heart. You and your sister are the two beautiful children I wanted.'

'I truly don't know what to say,' Vivienne said quietly. 'I'm sorry for the way things turned out between you and Jacqueline and I'm truly sorry for bringing all the pain back.'

Pascal shook his head, giving her a sad smile. '*Non*. Some pain brings happy memories too and your arrival has done that. I thank you for coming and giving me the letter. I have closure finally over something I've wondered about for over fifty years.'

Lunch itself began quietly with everyone somewhat lost in their own thoughts, but gradually normal conversation returned and by the end of the meal the four of them found themselves laughing at some ridiculous joke Pascal regaled them with.

Vivienne tried to pay for everyone, but neither Pascal nor Gilles would hear of it. Leaving the restaurant and standing in the main street to say their goodbyes, Pascal turned to Vivienne. 'Thank you for tracking me down. I am so happy to have met you and hope we can meet again. You might not be Jacqueline's natural daughter, but she certainly passed on her values and compassion for others to you.'

'Oh Pascal, that's a lovely thing to say,' and Vivienne reached up and kissed his cheek. 'I'm sure we will meet again. I'm planning on moving to Valbonne soon and I'd love to visit you again – and of course for you visit me in my new home.'

'That is something I look forward to,' Pascal smiled. 'Let us know when you're here and we'll be there.' He left them then to return home, while Gilles insisted on walking them to the car park.

'My father is happy to have met you,' he said as Natalie beeped the car and opened the driver's door. 'And so am I. Perhaps you and I could have lunch together? Or even dinner? I come to Antibes quite often. If you give me your number, I'll give you a ring you in a few days.'

'I'd love to have lunch or dinner with you, but I'm returning to the UK soon. It may have to be when I've moved to Valbonne, which will be a few months yet,' Vivienne said, pulling a card out of her bag and handing it to him. 'There you are. It's been lovely meeting you and your father.'

Natalie started the engine and Vivienne slipped into the passenger seat.

'*A bientôt*,' Gilles said.

'*A bientôt*,' she replied before Natalie drove them out of the car park.

'No French connection for us, then,' said Natalie, indicating to turn right as she pulled out. 'Shame. But I think you've made a new friend.'

Vivienne smiled. 'Pascal you mean? He's lovely, isn't he? He would have been perfect as my birth father.'

'No, I didn't mean Pascal, although you are right – I'd have loved him as a grandfather. No, I was thinking of Gilles.' Natalie glanced at her mother mischievously. 'I saw you give him your card.'

Vivienne smiled to herself. Gilles Rocher, like his father, certainly had charisma in spades and she hoped that he would ring her when she'd settled in at Valbonne. Today had proved to be the end of her dream of finding her real father but the day had brought two new men as friends into her life and that couldn't be bad.

* * *

As they arrived back at the apartment, Vivienne and Natalie bumped into Olivia and Thierry, who were taking Topsy for a walk. After introducing Natalie to them, Vivienne impulsively invited them to supper that evening. 'Topsy is more than welcome too.'

Pleased when they accepted, she rang Maxine when she got upstairs and invited her too.

'If your daughter is still staying, please bring her. Olivia and Thierry are coming, so she'll have younger company. And I've got lots to tell you about Puget.'

Maxine happily accepted and hoped that Leonie would agree to come.

35

Maxine put the phone down and turned to Leonie. 'My friend Vivienne and her daughter Natalie have invited us both for supper tonight. You will come with me, won't you?'

'I'm not sure. I'm not good with lots of unknown people,' Leonie said.

'There won't be lots, the apartment isn't big enough. Six at the most and you've met Thierry, so that's somebody you know already, and Olivia is lovely. Please come.' Maxine hesitated. 'I like the thought of introducing my daughter to my friends.'

Leonie bit her lip. 'This evening I was going to ask if we could look at the box of things you mentioned.'

'We can do that now,' Maxine said instantly. 'I'll fetch it.' She stopped and looked at Leonie. 'Promise me, though, you'll come with me this evening if we do this now.' Leonie gave her a reluctant nod accompanied by a smile. 'Good.'

Maxine dragged the plastic container out from under the stairs and Leonie helped her to lift it onto the table. Maxine sensed that although Leonie wanted to see the contents she was nervous.

'Please don't be disappointed at the contents,' Maxine said.

'They're special to me because they were all I had to keep you close, but they're mostly everyday things.' She lifted the lid off as she spoke and Leonie leant forward in anticipation.

It was mainly small clothes on top. A pink dress Maxine remembered wrapping in the tissue paper that Leonie carefully pulled back to take a closer look at before placing it on the table. Maxine lifted out small T-shirts, socks, a vest and a pair of trousers in a summery flower print. 'It's mostly what Daiva didn't have room for in the two suitcases he took.'

Leonie gave an acknowledging nod, as she picked out a pair of red wellington boots with white daisy flowers stamped over them and looked up at Maxine. 'Did we play puddle jumping? I vaguely remember a flooded park and standing in the middle of the biggest puddle ever splashing up and down wearing these.' She looked at Maxine, who was smiling.

'It was one of your favourite games to play. You loved a rainy day.'

'Still do if I'm honest, but not too many, one after the other.'

At the bottom of the container were several picture books all about the adventures of the mouse called Anatole by Eve Titus. Maxine picked *Anatole et Le Chat* out of the pile. 'This was your favourite. I read it to you so many times.'

'I wanted a cat for my eighth or ninth birthday, could have been my tenth, but Papa said no. Wouldn't even talk about it. He bought me a china cat for my bedroom. Which was not the same. I've promised myself I will have a real cat one day.'

The last item in the bottom of the box was a childish hand-drawn card. Lots of colourful crayoned squiggles and circles and crosses. Leonie glanced at Maxine.

'It was the first Mother's Day card you made for me when you went to *l'ecole maternalle*. I had to stop Daiva from tearing it up and throwing it away.'

'Why would he do that?'

'He was furious and jealous that you hadn't made him a card for Father's Day. Refused to acknowledge the fact that you hadn't been at school then.' Maxine paused. 'I received a black eye for that particular error.'

Leonie gave her a thoughtful look. 'I made him a card one year when I was thirteen. He hated it and said it was about time I grew up and realised people preferred shop-bought cards, not amateur childishly made ones.'

'Not everyone,' Maxine said quietly. 'I put this card out every Mother's Day for, oh, at least fifteen years, after he'd taken you. And every time, I'd say a little prayer that the next year I would have a new one. It took that long for me to finally accept that I'd lost you and there was very little point in the exercise, which was when I put it safely at the bottom of the container. It was such a precious memento of a life I'd lost.' She carefully placed the card back in the container and started to replace the other things.

'Thank you for sharing that with me,' Leonie said. 'I am truly beginning to realise how badly Papa treated both of us and accept that a lot of the things he did were criminal. Nothing was done out of love for me, despite him telling me that was the sole reason he took me away. I realise now it was all about his addiction, controlling me and causing you pain.' She wiped a tear away as she looked at Maxine. 'I'm so sorry I believed the lies he force-fed me about you. I should have challenged him more.'

'*Non, ma cherie.*' Maxine opened her arms. 'He wouldn't have liked that and it could have been even more disastrous for you. Come here. It's my turn to give you a hug.' And Maxine pulled Leonie into her arms and held her tight.

36

After a flying visit to the *supermarché* to buy food and wine for the evening, Vivienne and Natalie made sure the apartment was visitor friendly – 'Especially Olivia friendly,' Vivienne laughed. 'As she's my landlady.' Afterwards, they both had a refreshing shower and sat out on the terrace sipping a glass of rosé, watching the Mediterranean and waiting for people to arrive.

A short bark from Topsy and a 'Cooee' from Maxine told them that everybody was arriving at once. Leonie, at Maxine's side, was looking apprehensive and Maxine quickly introduced her to Olivia and Natalie, as well as Vivienne.

'How do you like Antibes?' Vivienne said. 'And your mother's cottage is wonderful, don't you think?'

There was silence for a second or two before Leonie smiled briefly. 'I like Antibes very much and, yes, the cottage is lovely.'

'How's Topsy settling in?' Vivienne asked, turning to Olivia. 'I find it hard to believe that anyone could just abandon her. She's beautiful.'

'She has us well trained already,' Thierry said. 'The words "not on the bed, Topsy" have no meaning for her.'

Topsy, hearing her name, ambled over to Thierry and sat at his side.

'Especially you,' Olivia laughed. 'You're such a softie where she's concerned. Do not feed her bits and pieces tonight.'

Thierry gave her a wounded look. 'As if I would.'

Vivienne and Natalie passed around plates of food and made sure everyone had the drink they wanted.

'Before I forget to tell you the news, your offer for the villa has been accepted,' Maxine said.

Vivienne exhaled a big breath. 'Brilliant news. What happens now?'

'I'll bring the intent to buy paper up tomorrow for you to sign, then the owners will sign it, and after that I'll start organising diagnostics and surveys that are now required – for energy and efficiency – and after all that you'll need to pay a deposit. I'll put you in touch with the notaire I use.'

'Can I appoint him – or you – to act for me? Seeing as how I won't be here in a few days' time.'

'Yes, I can organise that for you too.'

Maxine glanced across at Leonie, who had moved to stand by the balcony with Natalie, looking out at the view.

'How was Puget today?'

'Amazing. We found our man. Very briefly – he'd never met a woman called Deidre so he's not my birth father, but it turns out he was in love with Jacqueline, my adoptive mum, when he was nineteen. The photograph I found was of them both. Keeping my original birth certificate in the same drawer was just a misleading coincidence that sent me off in the wrong direction – something that actually turned out to be good.'

'*Mon dieu*, what a story,' Maxine said. 'I'm glad you're happy with the outcome.'

'How are things with you and your daughter?' Vivienne asked quietly as Olivia went to join Natalie and Leonie.

'I had to persuade her to come this evening. She's shy, but there is more to it than that, I think. We progress, but my ex-husband has a lot to answer for.'

Vivienne looked at her.

'Alcoholic control freak,' Maxine said quietly. 'Who filled her mind with lies about me.'

'That must be hard to deal with. At least she's back in your life now,' Vivienne said. 'And as she gets to know you, she will realise the truth.'

'But I not know how long she stay,' Maxine replied. 'It is going to take a lot of talking and loving. And if she leaves, I cannot help her.'

Natalie wandered across from the balcony. 'Mum, Olivia has asked Leonie and I if we'd like to go to Monaco with her the day after tomorrow when she has a flower delivery to make. We haven't got anything planned, have we?'

'No. Go, you'll enjoy Monaco, especially with a local to show you the sights. And I can have a day catching up with a few bits of writing that I need to do before we go home.'

'Has Leonie agreed to go?' Maxine asked quietly.

'Almost. We are both working on her. She says she's never had a girly day out. That can't be allowed. Olivia and I are aiming to change that,' and Natalie picked up a plate of biscuits and cheese and went back to rejoin the other two on the balcony.

Vivienne raised her eyebrows at Maxine, who was staring after Natalie in shock. 'Sounds promising.'

Maxine took a gulp of her drink. 'I must ask Olivia not to introduce her to Felicity if she does decide to go. Trent maybe, but definitely not Felicity. Poor Leonie would fall at the onslaught of questions.'

37

With Natalie out for the day with Olivia and Leonie, Vivienne was determined to take the opportunity to edit the last chapter she'd written. Today was probably the last day she'd get to do any work. They were leaving in forty-eight hours. She'd barely settled herself on the terrace with her laptop when her mobile rang. The caller ID read unknown caller and she hesitated before picking it up. If it was Sadie again with a different phone, she'd hang up.

'Hello?' she said cautiously.

'Vivienne, it's Gilles Rocher.'

She smiled as she let out a sigh of relief.

'I'm down in Antibes unexpectedly and I was wondering whether you, and possibly Natalie, would like to have lunch with me.'

'Natalie has gone to Monaco with friends,' Vivienne said.

'How about you? Would you like to have lunch? Or are you busy?'

'I'm editing, but I do stop for lunch and...' Vivienne hesitated. 'It would be lovely to see you again,' she said, surprised at how pleased she was to hear his voice and to accept the surprise invitation.

'*Bon*. Would twelve o'clock suit? Or is that too early?'

'No, it's fine. Where shall I meet you?'

'How about by the bandstand in Square Nationale?'

'I'll see you there at twelve.' Which gave her precisely an hour to get ready.

Vivienne closed her laptop and went downstairs to have a shower and to think about what to wear. It was a lovely day and at midday it would be warm, if not downright hot. She'd not yet worn the wrap dress she'd bought at Giselle's all those weeks ago. It would be cool and smart, but was it too much for a lunchtime date?

She stopped as she went to put the dress on. Was this a date? She was still a married woman, so no, it couldn't in any way be regarded as that. It was simply two new friends having lunch together and hoping to get to know each other better. Was she hoping to get to know Gilles better? She couldn't deny that she'd liked him from the moment he'd spoken to them outside his family home. She slipped the wrap dress on. Gilles had said he often came to Antibes; the fact that he had rung her so soon after meeting didn't mean anything. Right, sunglasses and sunhat and she was ready.

Gilles was waiting for her as Vivienne crossed the square and smiled his welcome. 'Will you accept the usual French greeting of a kiss on the cheek?' he asked.

'Just the one,' she laughed as she caught the whiff of his after-shave – spicy with a hint of sandalwood – as he kissed her fleetingly.

'You look lovely.'

'Thank you.'

'I've booked a table at a restaurant near the marina, I thought we could have a look at the boats on our way.'

'Are you a sailor?'

'Not a sailor who longs for his own boat but a sailor who likes the occasional day sail and is quite happy to spend time on the water crewing for someone else,' Gilles said. 'I preferred to be up in the sky. I was a pilot until recently,' he explained. 'I was made redundant in the last round of cutbacks at the airline I worked for after the various lockdowns of Covid which hit the travel business badly.'

'I'm sorry.'

'Don't be. At my age, I was lucky to be employed for so long. I'm enjoying life right now and I got a generous redundancy package. We go this way,' and they walked under an archway and there in front of them was the marina. 'The restaurant is on that side of the marina,' and he pointed past the boats to the left, where Vivienne could see a cluster of tables with open parasols in the far distance.

'So many boats,' Vivienne said. 'I wonder what would happen if they all decided to put to sea at once.'

'Chaos is the answer, I think,' Gilles said. 'May I ask you a question? Your name is Vivienne, but the card you gave me had a different name on it.'

'Ah, yes,' Vivienne said. 'My secret alter ego. I gave you the wrong card by mistake.'

Gilles nodded thoughtfully. 'You do not like people knowing you are a successful author?'

'It's not that exactly. When I meet people as that person, it's fine and I'm happy to talk about and sign books, but it gives me and the family a degree of privacy if people don't always know about my day job.' Vivienne smiled at him.

'I looked you up and bought one of your books.'

'You did,' Vivienne said nervously. 'Are you enjoying it?'

'Very much. I read it in one sitting.'

'Phew, that's a relief,' Vivienne remarked. And it was. Jeremy had only ever read one of her books, and when she'd asked if he'd enjoyed it, he'd shrugged and told her it wasn't his kind of book. She'd have hated it if Gilles had said something belittling about the one he'd read. They reached the restaurant at that moment and were shown to a table near the back of the outdoor seating area and in the shade.

'What would you like to drink? I'm driving, so I'll just have some Perrier water.'

'I'd like a gin and tonic with lots of ice and lemon please and then I'll join you with water. I'm planning on doing some work later,' Vivienne smiled.

Once the waiter had brought their drinks and the menus for them to look at, Gilles said, 'I have to thank you for tracking my father down. Meeting you and learning why the woman he loved rejected him all those years go has given him peace of mind over something none of us knew he'd suffered.'

'Your father is a lovely man,' Vivienne said gently. 'I'm sorry he didn't turn out to be my father.'

'I think he is too – he didn't stop talking about you and Natalie after you left.'

'I know more about your father than I do you,' Vivienne said.

Gilles smiled. 'That's easily changed. I'm fifty-four, divorced for three years. I have a grown son a little older than Natalie, I think. He's currently in the US with my ex-wife and her new husband. Your turn, because apart from being a writer I know very little about you.'

'I'm married, but not for much longer. Jeremy, my husband, has been having an affair with my agent and is now leaving me for her and starting a new family. You've met my daughter, I also have a son, Tim, who is a paramedic. And in about six months I shall be living down here. Which if you, or anyone, had suggested to me a month ago I would be moving permanently to the South of France, I'd have said you were mad. But I honestly can't wait,' she said and took a sip of her gin and tonic. 'Would you like to see the house I'm buying. I'm so excited.' She took the phone out of her bag and held it for him to see.

'That's one beautiful villa,' Gilles said.

'I've already promised Pascal a visit to see it when I've moved, you must come with him.'

'I'll be sure to do that,' Gilles said. 'But I hope to see you again before then.'

The waiter returned at that moment to talk them through the menu and to take their order. After much discussion, they both opted to skip an entrée and share the freshly roasted leg of lamb for two, served with roasted Mediterranean vegetables.

Sitting there nibbling the breadsticks placed on the table, drinking a second gin and tonic, listening to Gilles telling her tales of his pilot days, Vivienne felt her cares drift away for an hour or two. The meal when it arrived was delicious, as was the tiramisu she enjoyed whilst Gilles had cheese and biscuits.

Noticing other diners starting to drift away, Vivienne glanced at her watch, and gasped. 'It's nearly three o'clock. Don't you have people to see this afternoon?'

'Ah, about that. I have a confession to make,' Gilles said.

Vivienne gave him an intense look and waited.

'I didn't unexpectedly find myself in Antibes today. I wanted to see you again before you left, so I drove down to specifically ask you to join me for lunch. If you'd been busy, I'd have gone straight home.' He paused and gave her a serious look. 'But on this occasion I wanted to confirm the overwhelming attraction I felt for you was real. I'm not normally this impatient to get to know someone when I meet them, but I really wanted to have a memory of time spent with you before you disappear. I really like you and think – hope – we could be more than good friends.'

'Oh Gilles. If I'm honest, I have to admit to feeling the same, but the facts are I'm still married – I haven't even contacted a divorce lawyer yet. I'd love for us to be friends, but it's too soon for me to think any further.'

'We will stay in touch whilst you are away. I'm a patient man,' Gilles said. 'I'll wait until you're ready.'

After paying the bill, Gilles offered to walk her back to the apartment. Vivienne agreed, purely to have his company for longer.

When they reached the villa, Gilles caught hold of her hand. 'Thank you joining me for lunch,' he said. 'The first of many, I hope.'

'Thank you for the lovely lunch. Drive carefully and give my regards to Pascal when you get home.'

Gilles squeezed the hand he was still holding. 'I'm sorry you didn't get the result you hoped for yesterday but...' he looked at her, with eyes that had a sudden mischievous twinkle in them. 'I have to say I'm glad we're not related.'

'That thought had occurred to me too,' Vivienne said, smiling at him.

Gilles leant in and lightly kissed her cheek. 'I'll see you when you return. Take care of yourself.' And he was gone.

'You too,' Vivienne said quietly as she watched him go, wondering what on earth had happened to the sensible middle-aged woman she used to be.

38

Olivia lay in bed the morning after she and the girls had been to Monaco, absently stroking Topsy, who was snuggled under her arm on top of the duvet, listening to Thierry in the kitchen. Thierry not only did the croissant run every morning before making the breakfast coffee they shared sitting outside at the small table, he was thoughtful and caring. Living together but not living together in one sense had worked out without any real effort on their parts. They fitted together so well. They respected each other's space, but it was wonderful to come home to someone whose face lit up when you walked in the door.

Yesterday, because he was home all day working on his laptop, he'd taken Topsy for a long walk, prepared supper for the evening and insisted on giving her shoulders a wonderful massage when she said they were aching from the driving. And then he'd run a bath for her.

If she were to be honest, she was beginning to dread the day Leonie returned to Paris when Thierry would have no reason to stay with her any longer. His room at Maxine's would be free once again and he would be able to return. If it wasn't Leonie's departure that triggered his moving out, it would be his purchase of the farm and activity centre being completed. Olivia sighed. So, really, it was just a case of which one of those two things happened first.

Topsy fidgeted in her arms and moved up a little so that she could nudge Olivia's cheek with her cold nose. 'Cheeky girl,' Olivia said. 'I shall miss you too when you have a permanent home up on the farm. I don't say this to everyone, but I love you both to bits, d'you know that?' she whispered into the dog's ear. And it was true. She did love them both.

Topsy gave her a serious look and nudged Olivia's cheek again.

A knock on the door, and Thierry calling out, 'Come on, lazy-bones, breakfast is ready', had Topsy jumping off the bed and streaking to the door.

'Five minutes,' Olivia called, throwing off the duvet before standing up and stretching, the answer to her problem blindingly obvious. She'd move to the farm with him and life could continue like it had for the last few weeks, living together but not living together, and maybe, just maybe, things would develop of their own accord. Thierry had seemed disappointed when she'd told him her plan about staying and running the flower taxi from Antibes, so he was sure to be happy when she said she'd changed her mind. They were going up to Tourrettes-sur-Loup later for a meeting with Marie-France and planned to walk Topsy around the farm afterwards. She'd tell him then.

Marie-France was pleased to see Olivia again and promised to give her all the help she could with learning about the violet farm. 'I knew nothing when we took it over and I've still got the books I read and all my notebooks. More than happy to pass them on to you if you'd find them useful.'

'Thank you, that would be brilliant and give me a head start,' Olivia said.

The three of them, with Topsy on the lead walking obediently to heel, walked out to the field, where a couple of women were bent over among the rows picking the leaves for the perfumery in Grasse.

'It's still a manual task. I have to say my knees won't miss the squatting. It was fine when I was young like you two, but now...' Marie-France smiled.

After Marie-France had answered some of Thierry's questions about the activity centre, she left them to wander around by themselves, saying she was expecting a call from her daughter.

'I'll see you before you go,' she said. 'If you walk to the far end of the land in that direction, you'll have a wonderful view of Tourrettes.' And she left them to it.

They did as she suggested, leaving the neat rows of violet plants behind them and walking towards the uncultivated part of the field at the far end.

'I really love it up here,' Olivia said, holding her arms up in the air and twirling around, making Topsy bark excitedly. 'It's so beautiful. I'm glad I'm going to be your business partner. Talking of which, we haven't spoken about money. I sort of feel that to be a proper partner I should invest some money and I've still got some of Aunt Daphne's inheritance tucked away.'

Thierry shook his head. 'No. It's all organised. The bank have approved my business plan. You just have to invest yourself – and from the sound of it, your knees – in the farm.'

'I can do that happily. And I've changed my mind about staying in Antibes. I will move up here with you and Topsy.'

Thierry stopped in front of her and gave her a serious look. 'You want to move in with me and Topsy?'

'Yes,' Olivia said, giving him a worried look. 'I thought you wanted me to? You said there was room.'

Thierry sighed. 'I did, but that was before.'

'Before what?'

'Before we lived together but not together.'

'But it's worked out well,' Olivia said, a catch in her voice.

'That's the problem.'

'How?'

'I'm glad we're partners in the farm, but I'm not sure about living in the same house on that "not living together" basis would work for me up here.'

'Why not?' Olivia whispered.

'Because I love you and want to live with you properly, even get married and have the family we talked about before.'

Speechless, Olivia stared at Thierry for several seconds as a feeling of happiness flooded through her body, before she found her voice again. 'You love me?'

Thierry gave a slow nod as he looked at her. 'Yes, Tuppence, I do. When you were little, I used to pretend that you were my little sister and that it was my brotherly duty to look after and protect you. But that all changed as you grew up and my feelings became less brotherly and more sensual towards you. I still want to protect you, look after you, but my feelings are not at all brotherly anymore. I'm definitely in love with you, Tuppence.'

Olivia's heartbeat quickened as a smile spread across her face and she shook her head in wonder at Thierry's declaration. 'That's good because I was talking to Topsy this morning, telling her I loved her and I realised I loved you too.' Olivia reached up and gave him a quick kiss.

Thierry pulled her into his arms. 'Hey, we can do better than that.' And he proceeded to do so.

When the kissing stopped, a breathless Olivia laughed. 'You do realise my maman is going to be delirious with happiness when she hears about us.'

'That would make three delirious people then,' Thierry said, pulling her close again.

Marie-France, who happened to glance out of the conservatory window at the right moment, smiled to herself in satisfaction as she saw the two figures in the distance become one. Her violet farm was going to be safe with those two.

39

Leonie was unusually quiet at breakfast the day after she'd experienced her very first girly day out with Olivia and Natalie. Maxine, anxiously asking her if she'd had a good time, was relieved to receive a beaming smile.

'I had the best time. I've never had friends like that before. If you will excuse me, I have something I need to do in my room.'

Maxine took her second cup of coffee out to the garden and sat down by the pool to drink it, deep in thought. Thierry had come round yesterday to see how things were and to tell her the news about Olivia moving in with him – on a proper basis.

'I'm so pleased for you both,' she'd said, hugging him. 'Does your prospective mother-in-law know yet?'

'We're going to try to keep it quiet for a little while, so you're sworn to secrecy.'

Maxine had made a zipper movement across her mouth. 'I promise Felicity will hear nothing from me.'

'How are things with Leonie?'

Maxine had sighed. 'I don't know. We've talked a bit about her life with Daiva, but I still don't know much about her. She clams up like a fish if I ask the wrong question, so I've been waiting for her to talk. She hasn't mentioned the future. Whether she's got any plans. I don't know if she has a job to return to in Paris. I don't know whether she has enough money – whether Daiva left her anything. I'd love her to stay down here and be near – she can live with me if she wants or get her own place. But, again, I don't know if that's what she wants to do.'

'I'll ask Olivia how she was with them when she gets back. Maybe she answered their questions and they'll have some information to pass on.'

'That would be good,' Maxine had said with feeling, hoping the girls had managed to make friends with Leonie yesterday.

When Leonie came down from her room an hour later, she was clutching a large envelope. 'This is for you,' she said, holding it out to Maxine. 'It's the best I can do at the moment. I hope you like it.'

Carefully, Maxine opened the envelope and pulled out a beautiful card with 'Thank You Maman' written in flowing golden script across it. Maxine promptly burst into tears. 'Thank you. It's beautiful.'

'There was an art shop in Monaco selling the most beautiful crayons and pastels and sketch books. I was naughty and bought lots.'

'I didn't know you could draw like this,' Maxine said. 'You have such a talent.' She looked at the scene on the card again. Barn owls, deer, rabbits, a mouse, all in a fantasy forest of trees lit by a full moon in a dark sky.

'Papa, he always said I would never earn any money with my crazy drawings.'

'Something else he was wrong about,' Maxine said firmly. 'I know there is a market out there for pictures like this.' She took a deep breath. 'Leonie, there is so much we don't know about each other and some of it will take years for us to learn, but we do have to talk about the immediate future. Like what you are going to do now you are free? Do you have a job in Paris? Do you have any money to live on? Oh, the list of things I don't know, and need to know, is endless. You have to talk to me, tell me how I can help you.'

'I'm sorry. I lied about having a job. I thought I might need an excuse to leave. He didn't like me to work,' Leonie said quietly. 'After I gained my Baccalaureate, he wanted me to stay at home and look after him. Said it was my duty as a good daughter to do that for him. He did stop himself from saying it was his due after all he'd done for me.' She sighed. 'I did have a part-time job in an art gallery for three years which I really enjoyed, but he didn't like me talking about it and stopped me meeting up with the friends I made there. In the end, it was easier not to work.'

'This gets worse and worse,' Maxine said, covering her face with her hands.

'I have some money, but I would like to earn my own living. Do you really think my drawings would sell?'

'I do. There are many artists down here. I can introduce you to several who will help you with contacts and suggest places where you can sell your work.'

'I have a few things in Paris I need to collect and then...' Leonie looked at Maxine. 'Could I come back down and live with you for a while?'

'I would be upset if you didn't. You can stay for as long as you like. There will always be a room here for you. I hope you will think of L'Abri as your home now.'

* * *

Vivienne and Natalie spent the next day packing their things, tidying the apartment and having a last wander around Antibes. Natalie treated herself to a lovely, soft, cream-coloured leather tote bag, which she said would remind her of the holiday every time she used it. Vivienne treated them both to a last lunch in one of the pavement cafes down by the market, before stopping off at L'Abri on the way back to return the jazz books Maxine had lent her and to say goodbye to both Maxine and Leonie.

Natalie was pleased to hear that Leonie would be there when she came down to visit her mum and promised they would have another day out. Maxine hugged Vivienne and said she'd keep in touch with the notaire and push him for a quick completion. 'You'll be back before you know it. A new life ahead of you.'

Back at the villa, they said goodbye to Olivia and Thierry, wishing them good luck with the farm and they both gave Topsy a cuddle before making their way up to the terrace and a last glass of rosé.

Sitting there talking through her plans for the Valbonne villa and her future, Vivienne felt full of optimism and enthusiasm. 'I'm so sorry Maxine was too busy with Leonie's unexpected arrival to take us out to show you the Valbonne villa,' Vivienne said.

'No worries, I've seen the photographs and it looks wonderful. I can see why you've fallen in love with it and I'll see it for real as soon as you move in,' Natalie said. 'Mum, I've had a lovely holiday, thank you. I'm so sorry for the way Dad has treated you. I'm going to find it very hard to forgive him. As for Sadie...' Natalie shook her head. 'There are no words.'

Vivienne nodded ruefully. 'I know. Who'd have guessed even four months ago that my life – our lives – were going to change so radically. But...' she took a deep breath. 'I'll get through this. I know it will be hard saying goodbye to everything I believed to be entwined in, and fundamental to, my existence, but I'm looking forward to a new life in the South of France in a few months' time. It will be a challenge because it's a life that I'd never ever considered before, but I shall do my utmost to make it a good one.'

Their flight wasn't until four o'clock the next day, but Vivienne had suggested they spend the morning in Nice, see the famous Cours Saleya market and have a quick walk along the Promenade des Anglais. They'd drive out to the airport after that and have lunch in the restaurant there once Natalie had handed the hire car back.

As the time got closer for them to board their flight, Vivienne could feel herself getting more and more depressed at the thought of returning to the house that had been her home for so long. Even though she knew she was coming back to France soon, all the optimism she'd started to feel about her new life was slowly dissipating as the problems facing her at home gathered pace in her mind. Could she really do it? Leave everything behind in England and return to make a new life for herself in the South of France?

40

The evening they arrived back in the UK, Vivienne and Natalie, both tired from the journey, walked into a silent, empty house. Vivienne was profoundly relieved when she realised that Jeremy was not home, even if Natalie thought he should be there. Vivienne wanted a night's sleep before she faced him. There was a brief note written on a scrap of paper and placed on top of a large envelope on the kitchen table.

> *Thought it better if I wasn't here when you arrived back so I've moved out to Sadie's. I'll contact you tomorrow. Jeremy.*

Wearily, Vivienne moved across the kitchen and filled the kettle. 'Cup of tea? I suppose it's too much to hope there is anything to eat in the fridge.' A fridge that she had left stocked with food so that Jeremy wouldn't have to worry about shopping for at least a week. Tonight it contained half a dozen eggs, a couple of tomatoes, a few dried-up mushrooms and half a bottle of long-life milk. The bread bin on the work surface held a few slices of a white loaf. 'Scrambled eggs for supper okay?' Vivienne said. 'I'll have to do a supermarket shop tomorrow.'

The food and a glass of wine revived them both somewhat, and afterwards, while Natalie loaded the dishwasher, Vivienne took her suitcase upstairs into the main bedroom. Thankfully, there was no sign that Sadie had stayed here during her absence. No feminine products in the bathroom, no lingering perfume smell in the bedroom. But Vivienne stripped the bed and remade it with fresh linen just in case. Natalie's bedroom along the hall, when she checked it, didn't look as if it had been disturbed since Natalie's last visit a couple of months ago.

Vivienne took the bed linen downstairs and put it in the washing machine, setting the timer for early morning, before going into the sitting room, which was curiously tidy. No books or papers on the coffee table. Cushions neat on the settee. TV remote on the book shelf. The house felt strange. Like it already belonged to someone else, her tenure of it over. Vivienne suppressed a sigh. Feeling like a stranger in what had been her home for so many years was horrible.

Natalie, sitting at the kitchen table scrolling through her phone and checking emails, glanced up as Vivienne walked in.

'Does the house feel different to you?' Vivienne asked. 'Not like home anymore? Or is it just me?'

'It has a sort of empty feel to it, if that's what you mean, even though it's full of furniture,' Natalie said thoughtfully.

Vivienne nodded. 'Yes, that's it.' She reached out and picked up the large envelope from the table. 'I'll put this up in the study and then I think I'll go to bed. I'm shattered.'

'Me too,' Natalie said, jumping up and giving her a hug. 'It's all going to work out, Mum. You're going to live in the South of France and have a wonderful new life. Hang on to that thought for the next few weeks.'

Vivienne returned the hug. 'Thank you.'

Before placing the envelope on her desk in the study, Vivienne finally opened it. Divorce papers from Jeremy's solicitors. She took a piece of paper out of the desk drawer and began to make a to-do list: contact her own solicitor; telephone the literary agency; pack up her personal stuff and the study; check with Jeremy about the contents of the house; sell her car. The list was sure to grow as the weeks went by. She blew out a breath. Vivienne had no doubt the next few weeks were going to be difficult ones.

She was in bed when her phone pinged with a text from Gilles.

Just wanted to make sure you were home safely.

Quickly she typed a reply.

Thanks. Yes, home safely. Hope all is well with you.

She pressed send, placed the phone on the bedside table and snuggled under the duvet. Within minutes she was asleep, her dreams filled with thoughts of Gilles and the South of France and the future that awaited her down there.

* * *

The next morning after a breakfast consisting of the last of the sliced bread toasted and a mug of coffee, Natalie left to drive home to her flat. 'I'm happy to stay for a day or two, Mum, if you want me to.'

'Don't be silly, you've got your business and your own life to live,' Vivienne said. 'Dad and I are grown-ups, I'm sure we can behave civilly around each other.'

After Natalie had left, Vivienne unpacked her case, emptied

the washing machine of the clean bed linen and reloaded it with her clothes. After making another mug of coffee, she carried it upstairs to her study and, sitting at her desk, she looked at the list she'd written last night. Time to start dealing with things that would end her old life but kickstart a new one. Which to do first? Engaging a divorce solicitor, preferably a woman, would be a good start. Half an hour later, she had an appointment with a Michele Roberts for eleven o'clock Friday morning.

Two hours later, she regretted not asking Natalie to stay when a belligerent Jeremy slammed his car door and marched into the house. Slowly, Vivienne went downstairs to meet the husband who to all intents and purposes was now a stranger to her. She'd half expected him to look different but no, he still had the careworn look of a stressed middle-aged man. And thankfully, she felt no lingering affection for him, just a stab of resentment for the way he'd treated her.

'Hello, Jeremy.'

'You're back then. How was your holiday?'

'I was working a lot of the time, but the whole of the Côte d'Azur is beautiful. I'm really looking forward to moving down there.'

Jeremy gave her a stunned look. 'You're moving to the Riviera?'

'Yes. I think I'll have a better life there. The weather alone will make a difference.'

'But you've lived here all of your life. Your roots are here. Your children are here.'

'They will visit. Natalie had a lovely time and made friends down there. She can't wait for me to move so she can visit again. I know Tim too will enjoy the lifestyle.'

'Have you thought anymore about me buying you out of this house?' Jeremy asked, ignoring her comments about the children.

'No. I assumed you didn't want to pay the price. Have you told the agents we accept the offer?'

'You did – which made me sound like a fool,' Jeremy said, glaring at her.

Vivienne stayed silent at that remark.

'Sadie is going to ring you later.'

'She needn't bother. I'm not talking to her.'

'You're being childish. These things happen; you have to learn to live with it.'

Vivienne was too angry to even hit back on that remark. 'Are you staying at Sadie's until the house sells?'

'I'll probably come and go. I'm not moving my stuff out. I know what the law says about that.'

'Well, if you intend to stay here overnight you'll need to make up the bed in the spare room,' Vivienne said. 'And find your own food. Are you staying here this morning? Only I've got work to do.'

'I've got to get back to the office. I'll be back later. I need some clothes and I haven't got time to get them now.'

Vivienne closed her eyes and let out an exasperated sigh as he left. She hadn't been back twenty-four hours and she was already wishing she'd stayed in Antibes. The thought of being here for another month or two was almost unbearable.

41

The day after Vivienne and Natalie left, Maxine drove Leonie to Nice airport to catch a flight to Paris. Leonie was quieter than she had been in recent days and Maxine gave her a quick glance as they got out of the car and made their way to the departures hall. Leonie had booked in online already, so within minutes they were approaching the departure lounge doors.

'Are you okay? You're very quiet. Not worried about returning, are you?' Maxine said.

Leonie shook her head. '*Non*. There is nothing to be afraid of anymore. It's just...' she hesitated. 'My life has been so different since I found you in Antibes, it is like I've been living someone else's life and now I am having to leave it.'

'*Mais* you are coming back at the weekend to stay forever,' Maxine said forcibly.

'But I cannot help worrying that whilst I am away you might realise how big a burden it will be to have me in your life full time.' Leonie looked at her, her eyes shiny with tears that were threatening to fall.

Maxine stopped and, regardless of the throng of passengers

around them, pulled Leonie to a stop in front of her. '*Maintenant* you listen to me. You will never, *ever* be a burden to me, *d'accord*? All those years we were forced apart, they were a burden to carry and get through – having you in my life now is pure joy, understand? I'm going to miss you while you are up in Paris and be counting the days until I come back here to pick you up.' She pulled Leonie into her arms and gave her a tight hug. 'Don't you dare think ever again that you are an unwanted burden to me. I love you.'

Leonie closed her eyes and took a big sniff. 'I love you too, Maman. I can't wait to come back.' And she kissed Maxine on the cheek. 'Thank you. See you in a few days.' And she walked into the departure lounge, turning at the door to give Maxine a wave before she disappeared.

Back outside, Maxine automatically fed the parking ticket machine with the required amount before making for her car and driving home. It wasn't until she was back in the safety of the garden at L'Abri that the tears started to flow as she sat by the fishpond and let her pent-up feelings and emotions escape. If Daiva Toussaint wasn't already dead, she was angry enough to kill him with her bare hands for the mental damage he'd inflicted on their daughter.

It was some time before she was calm enough to go indoors to make herself a cup of tea. Waiting for the kettle to boil, she stood in the open doorway of Leonie's bedroom. There were a few of her personal things on show in the room, something which gave Maxine a definite happy feeling. The paint crayons Leonie had bought on her day out in Monaco with Olivia and Natalie were lined up neatly on the small table that served as a desk. Maxine made a mental note to find Leonie a desk, create a proper working space for her art.

She crossed over to the wardrobe and saw the old-fashioned

clothes that Leonie had been wearing that first evening she'd knocked on the door hanging there. She'd suggest to Leonie when she returned that they could be donated to the Monaco Kermesse later in the year. Today, Leonie had returned to Paris wearing white jeans, a summery top and a denim jacket. It was going to be fun helping her to find her style and to buy clothes for her new life.

Pulling the door closed, Maxine smiled seeing Anatole the mouse on the pillow. Leonie had only been gone a couple of hours and already she couldn't wait for her to return at the weekend.

Maxine had just made herself a cup of tea when Thierry arrived. 'Would you like a cup of tea or coffee?'

'Tea would be good. Are you okay?' Thierry asked. 'You look as if you have been crying?'

Maxine nodded. 'I have. Tears of outrage at Daiva for his behaviour after something Leonie said when I took her to the airport. But I also shed a few tears of happiness knowing that Leonie is back in my life.' She made him a cup of tea and handed it to him. 'I wasn't expecting to see you today?'

'I wanted to check you were all right after seeing Leonie off.'

'Thank you.' Maxine looked at him. 'You are so like Pierre, such a kind man. You know your papa was very proud of the man you have become? And I think he had every reason to be. I wish he was here to hear the news about you and Olivia. He adored Olivia and would be so happy to know that the two of you are planning to marry.'

'I wish he was still here too,' Thierry said quietly. 'But it is good you and I – and Olivia too – can talk about him.'

* * *

Vivienne spent the first eight or nine days back in England in a flurry of sorting things out. Being busy helped to stop the ache in her heart of longing to be back in France.

After organising the divorce lawyer, the next thing to do was to ring the literary agency and speak to Rupert, the owner and senior agent. When she told him she wanted to leave the agency because of Sadie's behaviour, he was gratifyingly horrified on her behalf and asked if she would reconsider if he personally handled her account.

'I don't want to lose you as a client,' he said. Vivienne had hesitated, but in the end agreed, simply because it made sense for her not to change. The agency in the past had always been so supportive of her work.

'I'd like to stay with the agency on the condition that I don't have to deal with, or see Sadie, ever,' Vivienne said.

'I will personally make sure of that,' Rupert agreed. 'I will also look into this film offer and see if it's still on the table.'

Gilles rang a couple of times to see how she was and one morning he rang minutes after Jeremy had left, following one of his unwanted and infuriating visits, which invariably left Vivienne feeling uptight. The divorce was in the hands of the solicitors now, but Jeremy was furious every time her solicitor not only challenged his demands but laid out Vivienne's own legal rights.

Gilles clearly sensed her tension over the phone. 'Are you okay?'

Vivienne sighed and tried to shrug her annoyance away. 'Jeremy has just left after another moan at me for using a woman solicitor who is obviously a feminist and out to deprive him of his rights. Honestly, if the words coming out of his mouth weren't so blatantly sexist, it would be funny.'

'How's everything else going? You told me you were ticking things off your to-do list every day, so do you have a date for returning yet? Maybe you could return sooner rather than later? I'd like that.'

'Oh, if only that were possible. Anyway, enough of that. How are you and Pascal?' Vivienne said, changing the conversation.

Afterwards, she found herself wondering about her return date to France. Could she go back sooner than she'd planned? She'd far rather be in Antibes. She didn't have to wait for the Valbonne villa to be hers officially. She could rent somewhere whilst all the official stuff was happening. Why couldn't she go down now rather than wait another six or eight weeks? She could deal with everything back here from down there – it was the age of the internet after all. Jeremy and the solicitors could deal with selling this house and she'd be on hand for anything the notaire needed for her new villa purchase. She'd already paid the deposit by bank transfer and the ten-day cooling-off period required under French law would finish in a couple of days. Neither she nor the seller could pull out of the transaction after that without paying a penalty. Her divorce solicitor was sorted, surely from now on they could correspond by email or Zoom.

Vivienne picked up the phone, found the number she wanted and pressed. There was no harm in finding out.

'Hi Olivia, it's Vivienne. How are you? I was wondering...'

Ten minutes later, she had a plan in place. She'd stay for one more week to give her time to sort things in the house and then she was going to return to Antibes. Olivia's top apartment wasn't available until the end of September, but Olivia was moving out to the farm with Thierry very soon and was more than happy to rent the bottom apartment to Vivienne while she waited for her house purchase to go through. So long as she didn't mind Olivia popping in to use the flower room a couple of times a week. Vivienne had assured her that wouldn't be a problem at all. Suddenly, her optimism about the future bounced back.

She bought a book of red stickers and went through the house sticking them on the few things she wanted to take – mainly things she'd inherited from Jacqueline. She emptied her wardrobe, taking most of it to the local charity shop, packing the things she was taking into a suitcase. Different clothes were going to be needed for her new life in the sun.

For the next few days, she either avoided Jeremy whenever he came to the house or refused to engage in one of his rants. She didn't intend to tell him she was leaving until the last possible moment, knowing he would probably react selfishly to the news.

Natalie and Tim both came for supper on her last evening in the house, with Natalie staying overnight to drive her to the airport in the morning. Both were fully supportive of her moving to Antibes early.

'I think you will find it easier to deal with things here when you're away from them and getting on with your new life down there. And having Gilles around will help as well,' Natalie said, smiling.

'We'll both miss you, Mum,' Tim said. 'And as soon as you own your new home, we'll organise getting your bits and pieces down to you. Must say I'm looking forward to visiting. How's Dad reacted to you leaving early?'

Vivienne looked at the two of them. 'I haven't actually told him. I thought I'd leave a goodbye note on the kitchen table in the morning!'

42

The next day, an exhausted but happy Vivienne found herself boarding the midday flight to Nice. Natalie had driven her to the airport and after she'd handed over a fortune for her excess luggage, the two of them had had lunch. Outside the entrance to the departure lounge, Vivienne hugged Natalie tight as the reality of what she was doing suddenly hit her. 'I'm going to miss you so much. You will visit soon, won't you? There's a spare room in the apartment.'

'I'll be down for the weekend at the end of the month, and Tim's going to try to come with me,' Natalie said. 'Too late to get cold feet, Mum – you're going to have a wonderful new life in France.'

As the plane taxied down the runway and she settled into her seat, Vivienne took a deep breath. Just two more hours and she would be in the place where she would begin her new life. She knew she'd miss Natalie and Tim, but they had their lives to lead and now she had a new one of her own to get to grips with, and despite that little wobble with Natalie in the airport, she couldn't wait to call Valbonne home. Sitting there, literally flying above the clouds, Vivienne thought about the things she wanted to do in the weeks to come: a visit to Cannes to finally meet up with Céline; start to visit *brocantes* and *vide-greniers* for furniture and other things for the villa; think of a name for the villa; get to know Gilles properly.

Ah, Gilles. He'd wanted to meet her when she arrived, but Vivienne had protested, saying Maxine had already promised and it wasn't fair to drag him all the way down from Puget. She'd suggested instead he came down and spent the day with her tomorrow, something she was looking forward to.

The plane landed on time in Nice, but by the time Vivienne had fought the conveyor belt for all three of her cases and loaded them onto the trolley, most of her fellow passengers had disappeared. Approaching customs, she waited to see if anyone wanted to inspect her luggage, but nobody approached her and she walked confidently through the Nothing to Declare aisle and out into the arrivals hall, looking for Maxine, who was nowhere to be seen. But holding a large bouquet of flowers was Gilles.

'I had to come,' he said, placing the flowers on top of one of the cases. 'I couldn't not be here to welcome you to your new life. I've missed you so much,' and as he enveloped her in a tight hug before kissing her, Vivienne felt a huge surge of happiness.

'Thank you for coming, I've missed you too,' she said.

'Come on, let's get out of here,' Gilles said, taking charge of the laden trolley.

As she walked alongside him towards his car, Vivienne had a sudden mental picture of Jacqueline looking at them both and smiling. Whoever would have thought that her adoptive daughter would be starting a new life in France that would include Gilles, the son of the man Jacqueline herself had once loved.

EPILOGUE

MIDSUMMER'S DAY – A YEAR LATER

Vivienne is hosting an evening garden party in her newly named 'Villa Sérénité' home in Valbonne, where she has been living her new serene life for the past six months. Tonight's party is a celebration of several things: her divorce, her new life in France, meeting Gilles, as well as a way of saying thank you to all her family and friends who have helped her to make the transition to this new life. All the people who are important to her are here on this balmy summer's evening in the South of France as the sun goes down and the cicadas slowly quieten.

Natalie and Tim drove a transit van down with the few possessions Vivienne had taken from her old home just before last Christmas and helped her to move in. The three of them were joined by Gilles and Pascal to celebrate Vivienne's first Christmas Day in the villa. Natalie stayed for New Year before going home, but Tim had to leave on 28 December. Both are delighted to be back down for tonight's party. Vivienne has told both Natalie and Tim that due to the lack of any clues she has given up on the idea of searching for her birth father.

Vivienne's new home is still sparsely furnished as she is having fun visiting auction houses and *vide-greniers* and taking her time to buy only things she really likes. Her book, written in Antibes, is set to be a major bestseller – Rupert, her agent, is currently discussing another film deal with Netflix. Gilles has become an important part of her life and they've grown close over the last few months and she's realising how much she is in love with him. She has no idea that tonight, once all the guests have left and they are alone, Gilles is going to propose and slip an emerald engagement ring on her finger. He had wondered about asking her in front of her family and friends but decided Vivienne would prefer it to be a private moment between the two of them. Pascal, also here this evening, knows about Gilles's plan. He couldn't be happier for the two of them. He already regards Vivienne as though she really was his daughter with Jacqueline – to have her officially as his daughter-in-law will be wonderful.

Thierry and Olivia have just finished their first season of violet picking and jam making. It was definitely a steep learning curve, but Olivia feels a glow of pride whenever she goes into Tourrettes-sur-Loup and sees her crystallised violets and pots of jam on sale in the shops. Olivia also feels a glow of happiness when she looks at the platinum ruby and diamond three-stone ring Thierry placed on her finger the day they moved to the farmhouse. A vintage ring, it had been handed down from his grandparents, to his parents, and now it is her turn to wear it with love.

Thierry is preparing for a busy season with the activity business and all indications so far are that it is going to be a successful one. They are both loving living in the farmhouse together as a couple and Topsy has settled in well too. Olivia is a little apprehensive about how Topsy will cope with a certain new arrival later this year but is sure it will all work out.

Maxine is the happiest she's been since Pierre died and gives thanks every day for having her daughter back in her life. She knows there is nothing she can do to erase the memories Leonie has of her difficult life with Daiva, but she fully intends to make sure the rest of her life will be different and as happy as she, Maxine, can make it. She is learning to control the emotional tears when Leonie, more often than not these days, calls her maman.

Leonie is a different, happier, woman these days. Now living in L'Abri with Maxine, there are times when she is overcome with memories of the past and struggles not to show it. She's been accepted at a local art college and will start there in September. A beautiful fluffy grey cat seems to be permanently asleep at the side of the pond at L'Abri, with one eye open watching the fish while he waits for Leonie, his mistress, to come home, when he greets her with a loud miaow as he weaves in and out of her legs.

Felicity and Trent are at the party and both thoroughly approve of Olivia being with Thierry, and even if Felicity secretly regrets that he is no longer a high-flying financier but a rugged action man, she hasn't voiced that opinion. When Thierry and Olivia finally told her that they were a couple as well as business partners, Felicity took great delight in telling them, as well as anybody else who would listen, she'd always known the two of them were perfect for each other and knew they'd realise it eventually. She is currently counting down the days until she will become the grandmother she longs to be.

P.S. Jeremy and Sadie, who were definitely not invited to the party this evening, are the fraught parents of a lusty baby boy who has yet to learn the art of sleeping through the night. Vivienne refused to give way over her rightful share of the marital home when it was sold and Jeremy eventually found a run-down three-bedroom house for him and Sadie in town. He is starting to wonder what on earth he's done and is hesitating about marrying Sadie, and has stopped asking her where and when she'd like to get married. Sadie herself, currently on maternity leave from the literary agency, is now stuck at home all day with a demanding baby, in a house that needs some major renovations, and she, too, is starting to wonder what on earth she's done.

ACKNOWLEDGMENTS

As always, everyone in the Boldwood team has my unreserved gratitude for everything they do. After four years of being my editor, Caroline is still as patient as ever with my haphazard methods of writing a novel and quite frankly deserves a medal. Grateful thanks to Jade my copy editor and Rachel my proof reader and to Debbie Clement for the lovely cover.

Thanks to all the bloggers out there who do so much for all writers – we really do appreciate it.

And, of course, huge thanks to my readers, the people who enable me to carry on doing the job I love.

Love Jennie

xxx

ABOUT THE AUTHOR

Jennifer Bohnet is the bestselling author of over 14 women's fiction novels, including *Villa of Sun and Secrets* and *The Little Kiosk By The Sea*. She is originally from the West Country but now lives in the wilds of rural Brittany, France.

Sign up to Jennifer Bohnet's mailing list here for news, competitions and updates on future books.

Visit Jennifer's website: http://www.jenniferbohnet.com/

Follow Jennifer on social media:

facebook.com/Jennifer-Bohnet-170217789709356

x.com/jenniewriter

instagram.com/jenniewriter

bookbub.com/authors/jennifer-bohnet

ALSO BY JENNIFER BOHNET

Villa of Sun and Secrets

A Riviera Retreat

Rendez-Vous in Cannes

A French Affair

One Summer in Monte Carlo

Summer at the Château

Falling for a French Dream

Villa of Second Chances

Christmas on the Riviera

Making Waves at River View Cottage

Summer on the French Riviera

High Tides and Summer Skies

A French Adventure

Boldwood

Printed in Great Britain
by Amazon

38410571R00155